BEFORE YOU GO

BEFORE YOU GO

A Novel

TOMMY BUTLER

HARPER

An Imprint of HarperCollins*Publishers*

HarperCollins books may be purchased for educational, business, or sales promotional use. For information, please email the Special Markets Department at SPsales @harpercollins.com.

FIRST EDITION

Art by nasidastudio/Shutterstock, Inc.

Library of Congress Cataloging-in-Publication Data has been applied for.

ISBN 978-0-06-293496-3

20 21 22 23 24   LSC   10 9 8 7 6 5 4 3 2 1

PART I

Let them think what they liked, but I didn't mean to drown myself. I meant to swim till I sank—but that's not the same thing.

—Joseph Conrad, *The Secret Sharer*

Before

In a room that is not a room, with walls that are not walls and a window that is not a window, Merriam considers her handiwork. The finished form lies on a table (that is not a table), illuminated by a divine light that Merriam dialed to peak radiance so that she could tend to the last, delicate touches. The brass call it the "vessel," because it is both the container into which the travelers will pour themselves and the ship that will bear them on their journey. Merriam prefers a different name, one she believes the travelers themselves will use. *Humana corpus.* The human body.

It's good, she thinks. Right? Anyone can see that it's good. Everything the brass asked for and more. The blueprints were detailed, and Merriam followed them precisely, adding her own flourishes where the brass had allowed her some creative leeway. She is particularly fond of the splash of color in the irises, and—for some unknown reason—the spleen. Yes, she decides, it is good.

"*Very* good," she says aloud, though her voice is no more than a whisper. The words seem hesitant to emerge, as if the lingering doubt within her were a pair of human hands tugging them back, imploring them to wait until they are sure.

Her internal dialogue is interrupted by Jollis, who appears in the doorway with a hopeful, eager air. He looks around the room, noting the stray bits of cloud in the corners, the row of brightly colored bottles on the shelf. When he sees the body, his typically discriminating aspect slips into one of guileless wonder. "Merriam, wow." A laugh escapes him. "It's magnificent."

"Do you think so?"

"Absolutely." He moves in for a closer look. "Have the brass seen it?"

"Not the final," says Merriam. "But naturally they had a hand in it, so to speak. Everyone contributed—the brass most of all."

Jollis circles the table, continuing his appraisal. "Good bones," he says. "And I love what you did with the spleen." Slowly, reverently, he leans in toward the face and gently pushes back the eyelids. He gasps. The eyes glisten, collecting the room's divine light and amplifying it, before sending it back in a chromatic gleam. "Exquisite," says Jollis. "They're going to love it, Merry."

"Really?"

"Oh, definitely. We're talking major promotion."

Merriam tries to hide her excitement. "This is just the prototype, of course."

"Oh?"

"I mean, it's finished, and fundamentally they'll all be the same, but there will be all kinds of variations—different shapes, colors, idiosyncrasies—because obviously the travelers will want that. It's not like they'd ever declare just *one* type to be beautiful and then desperately try to imitate it."

"No, of course not," agrees Jollis. "That would be ridiculous." He moves toward the window. "Do you want to see where they're going?"

Merriam freezes, her insides suddenly aflutter. She does want to see, doesn't she? The others have been working so hard, and with such secrecy. Finally she nods, and Jollis pulls back the curtain. "Merriam," he says, "allow me to present . . . Earth."

There in the window is a shining, distant orb so lovely it is almost painful to behold. Crimson fires warm it from within, while a yellow sun bathes it in light. Argent clouds swirl over an intricate mosaic of tawny sands and emerald wilds. And everywhere the sparkling blue of water—gathered in vast oceans, rushing madly in rivers, falling from an ethereal sky.

Though she should be elated, Merriam feels oddly cold, almost numb. She can't seem to find her voice, but Jollis's expectant gaze is on her. "It's magical," she says.

"Pretty sweet, right? They say it can accommodate up to two billion people. Any more than that would be a disaster."

"So, it's ready to go?"

Jollis nods happily. "Just waiting on the vessel."

The vessel. Merriam turns back to look at the body on the table. The lingering doubt within her finally crystallizes into a clear danger, a peril against which she might still be able to offer some defense. She begins to shoo Jollis out of the room. "Right," she says. "The vessel. Almost there! Just one last thing."

"But you said it was done."

"Just about," she says. "You can't rush these things, after all." Once Jollis has been successfully ushered out, Merriam returns to the body. She takes one last look at the wondrous new world shining in the window. Then she gets to work.

By the time Jollis returns, Merriam is slumped beside the table, exhausted. She rises to greet him. He gives her a nervous nod and turns his attention to the body, immediately discerning her latest and final edit—a small cavity inside the chest, shaped vaguely like a crescent, nestled beside the heart.

Jollis pales. When he finally speaks, his voice is brittle. "There's a hole in it."

"No," says Merriam. "It's—"

"What did you take out?"

"Nothing."

"But what's supposed to go there?" Jollis gestures urgently. "What's missing?"

"Nothing's missing," says Merriam. "It's complete."

Jollis gapes at her as if she just proclaimed she was a jelly bean. "But there's a hole in it!"

"It's not a hole," she insists. Jollis's distress jangles her nerves, threatening her newfound certainty. "It's . . . an empty space."

He doesn't seem to hear her. "You need to fix it," he says. "Change it back."

"It's too late," says Merriam. "Look." She points to the eyes of the body. Though they remain closed, the skin of the eyelids undulates as the eyes dart and roll beneath the surface.

"What's it doing?" asks Jollis.

"Dreaming," she says. "First comes the dreaming, then everything else."

Jollis begins to shake until Merriam fears he will shatter. Instead he begins to move around the room, searching. "Okay, don't panic," he says. "We'll just fill the hole before it wakes up." He gathers up fragments of cloud from the corners of the room and packs them together, then stuffs them into the crescent-shaped cavity, careful not to disturb the adjacent heart. He draws back and watches as the white mist expands to fill the space. But clouds are restless things, and this one dissipates, dissolving like fog in the morning sun, leaving the emptiness behind.

Jollis grimaces. He begins to gather the divine light of the room itself, sweeping it up in great heaps until his visage is ablaze and the corners of the room retract into shadow. He squeezes the light down, pressing it into the cavity. Illuminated now from both within and without, the crescent space is striking in its beauty. Yet, light being what it is, it cannot fill the void.

"No," moans Jollis. He turns to the shelf full of colored bottles. "What are these?"

"Emotions," says Merriam. "The full spectrum, but I've already included the prescribed amounts."

Jollis grabs a bright red bottle and tilts it over the body's chest. A shimmering substance pours forth, filling the cavity. Jollis sighs with relief and puts the empty bottle back on the shelf. "There," he says. "That'll do it. Which emotion is that?"

"Love."

"Perfect," says Jollis. "That should work out just—" As he speaks, the shimmering substance drains from the cavity, leaving it empty again. "What happened?"

"It got absorbed," says Merriam. "By the heart."

"Dammit!" Jollis grabs more bottles from the shelf. He pours them in one after another. Each time, the emotion is absorbed by the heart. As Jollis gets to the darker ones, Merriam tries to stop him, but he surges on, frantically emptying bottles until only one is left—a small, twisted vial the color of ash and flame. He begins to pour it, too, into the cavity, but Merriam pushes him away before he can finish.

"Jollis, that's enough. It won't work."

Jollis drops the vial. He slumps, his countenance dimming. "We're doomed."

"But why?" asks Merriam. She is scared now. She has never seen him so distraught.

"Because it's got a hole in it!" he cries. "And they'll know it, Merry. They'll feel it, and they're going to constantly be looking for things to fill it with. They'll eat too much. They'll fall in love with the wrong people. They'll hoard money, and watch too much television, and buy useless crap from holiday catalogs, like potato scrubbing gloves or a spoonula."

"What's a spoonula?"

"Never mind." Jollis softens. He is more despondent than angry. "Don't you see? Nothing will work. There will always be this void. No matter how they try to fill it, they will always want the one thing we can never give them enough of."

"What's that?" asks Merriam.

"More."

Merriam feels hot tears gathering inside her, wanting out. She realizes she hadn't thought it through. Not completely. "I didn't mean for that to happen," she says quietly.

Jollis sighs. "But why did you do it?"

Merriam glances out the window. "Because of that world," she says. "I saw that beautiful world we made for them, and I was afraid they'd love it so much they'd never want to leave. So I gave them a little empty space, to make sure they'd come home."

Elliot

(1981)

The leaves fall in a mad rush—an unruly circus of yellow, orange, and red—hurled down from the trees by a mutinous wind. It's easy to get lost in it. I stand at the center of our little front yard, staring up at the long-limbed giants and the roiling cauldron of sky. My eyes fill with color, my ears with the sweep of air through the branches. The sharp scent of ozone heralds distant lightning. Nothing else exists, and a long moment passes before I remember who I am or what I'm doing out here beneath the front edge of an autumn storm. I am Elliot Chance. I am nine years old. I am catching leaves with my brother.

Action gets the glory, but most great endeavors begin in stillness. Leaf-catching is no exception. After the opening of the front screen door and the rush to the middle of the lawn, your first move is *not* to move. You stand frozen, gauging the speed and direction of the wind, feeling instinctively for any pattern in the bend and sway of the trees. Once all the data is collected, once it has run through you and blended with whatever else is inside you until the distinction between you and the storm begins to blur—and providing you do not forget yourself in the process—you do what every good adventurer does at the outset of a good adventure. You follow your gut. In this case, you pick that particular spot in the yard where you believe the leaves are most likely to fall. Once there, you bend your knees, keep your hands up, and wait.

Falling leaves do not, of course, drop in straight and steady lines. They are unpredictable, feisty, weird. They hitch and pause their descent at random, which makes them difficult to catch, but which also provides the best opportunity for catching them, because among those sharp turns and changes of speed and other machinations there is often a midair hesitation, a momentary hovering, when the little scrap of color checks its fall but doesn't immediately replace it with anything. For a split second, it simply stops, and—if you're close enough—a split second is all you need. Your knees uncoil. Your hand fires out. Your fingers widen to cast the largest possible net, and—

"Ha!" yells my brother, knocking down my outstretched arm with an impish glee. The leaf slips to the ground, uncaught. My brother laughs and rushes past me. "That's a miss!" he shouts. "Doesn't count."

Dean is just two years older than me, yet it would be hard to imagine two more disparate styles of leaf-catching. We begin in the same way—two slight boys with hazel eyes, rushing out the front door, looking very much alike except for his light, sandy hair contrasted with my dark brown. Yet Dean doesn't stop rushing. He is all bustle and bluster, jumping at leaves one after another like a young golden retriever dropped unexpectedly into a frenzy of skittish waterfowl. His misses far outnumber his makes, but this doesn't seem to faze him. He moves so quickly from one attempt to the next that I would question whether he is even aware of the results, but for the fact that he proclaims his total catches after each successful one.

"Seven!" he calls, crumpling a yellow oak leaf in his fist. For Dean, leaf-catching is neither meditation nor exultation. It is a competition, pure and simple—one in which disrupting your opponent is perfectly fair, and loudly tallying your points is good strategy. "How many do you have?" he asks, while simultaneously diving for a catch, a feat that, I admit, is pretty impressive.

"Five," I tell him.

I'm lying. I don't know exactly how many leaves have been diverted from their paths and into my pockets, but it's at least fifteen. Don't get me wrong. I like winning. Winning feels better than losing, but both are necessary ingredients of the playing itself—if the playing is a competition, which it is to Dean. The truth is that my brother likes winning much more than I do, and I like playing with my brother. I enjoy watching him tumble around the yard like a happy clown.

"Nine!" he shouts.

The game continues until a flash of sheet lightning kindles the horizon. We stop and count the passing seconds. Five, before the sound of thunder reaches us, which we know means the heart of the storm is five miles away. The sky darkens, and what light remains grows softer and sharper. The world around us appears etched in bronze, yet it moves and breathes. Unnaturally so, it suddenly seems to me. The clouds gather so quickly they appear to have a purpose. The trees nod and tilt emphatically, full of urgent whispers, until I am certain they are aware of us.

"Dean, look!" I say, laughing. "The trees are alive. They're trying to grab us!"

"Weirdo," he says, not pausing to look. "They're not alive."

I am about to argue when the first raindrop strikes my head with a firm plunk. More follow—big, fat beads that multiply as the sky opens up. We are soaked within seconds. Dean is already running for cover.

"Game over," he calls. "I win. No more catches. They won't count."

But I am done with leaf-catching now. I lie down on the grass, face upward, and open my mouth as wide as I can. Gathering raindrops is a decidedly passive pursuit.

"Dean, c'mon," I say. "Catch the drops in your mouth."

"I already caught like a billion," he says.

He heads for the house. The rain falls in a mass, with a clamor like the sound of a restless crowd, so that I barely hear the screen door slam behind him. My mouth fills with raindrops, and I laugh when I realize I am essentially drinking the sky. The storm intensifies. Lightning splits the air, followed instantly by a deafening crack of thunder that shakes the earth under my back. Only the wind has lessened, as if to make room for the deluge. All the leaves but one hold fast to their branches. This last one, a defiant red, weaves and twirls toward me like an aerialist struggling to remain graceful through the bombardment of water.

"Elliot," calls my mother. She is standing behind the screen door, next to my brother. I can just make out the puff of her hair, surrounding her head like a little cloud. Her voice is an urgent mixture of anger, love, and fear. "Come inside, please."

The thunder rolls again, and again the earth rumbles in response. I feel it along my spine like the heartbeat of the world. The lone leaf pushes on through the storm, bravely persevering through the last of its acrobatics until it is just above me. Once there, it takes a final bow, turns a shapely pirouette, and lands softly at the center of my chest.

"Now, Elliot," my mother calls again.

That night I see the first of the monsters. The rain has passed, my parents and Dean are asleep, and the world is silent. I lie awake in bed, staring at the closed door of my room. I'm thinking of the thunder and the awakening of the trees, and how the storm has left my senses heightened, so that as I gaze at the brass knob of the door I can see—even in the near darkness—that it is turning. Slowly and smoothly it rotates back and forth, as if whoever is trying to enter isn't entirely sure how to use it. I suspect Dean—then recall that, though he may not be much smarter than a doorknob, he does in fact know how to operate one.

There is a click, and the door slowly swings open. Its bottom edge drags over the shag carpeting with a quiet rustle. The hallway beyond is empty. No Dean. No anyone, or so it appears at first. But then I notice a patch of darkness that is deeper than the surrounding night. Its edges are fuzzy and fluid, but it is roughly the size and shape of a person, like a shadow without an attendant body. It glides into my room and stops. Though it has no discernable features, I can tell that it's smiling at me.

I immediately think of it as a monster, not knowing what else to call this faceless incarnation of night. Yet the label doesn't really fit. For one thing, I'm not afraid, not even a little. More importantly, the shade just isn't monstrous. In fact, it proves perfectly friendly, even polite. After a respectful pause, it bows deeply from the waist, one dark arm at its back and the other unspooling before it in a way I've only seen in movies. Maybe it's British, I think.

When it completes its bow, the shade begins an elaborate pantomime, leaping and rolling silently through the room, lunging out with its arms in all directions. It takes me a while to realize that it's imitating my brother's style of catching leaves, doing its best to exaggerate what is already high melodrama. Though I find it funny, I don't allow myself to laugh or even smile. I lie motionless in bed, keeping my breathing as shallow as possible to minimize the rise and fall of my rib cage. My stillness seems to confound the shade. It stops and taps its foot, then breaks into a new impression, this one of me—knees bent, arm shooting out like a frog's tongue hunting flies—all with such a theatrical seriousness that I find it even funnier. Yet I remain unmoving. Again and again, from one act to the next, the shade changes the performance. I stay frozen throughout. I don't want to disturb it. I realize that I am, in fact, afraid. Not that the monster will hurt me, but that it will go away.

In the morning, at the breakfast table, everything is so normal I almost doubt the shade visited me at all. My father begins weekdays with coffee and the telephone, which means that Dean and I begin them with cereal and silence. The phone hangs on the wall next to the refrigerator, and the cord is just long enough to reach my father's seat on the opposite side of the room. It stretches directly over my mother's chair, taut as a tripwire, cutting off the table from the rest of the kitchen. But my mother doesn't sit much anyway. She hovers on the other side of the wire like a hummingbird, pouring more coffee into my father's mug or dispensing cups of fruit to me and Dean that we pretend not to see. Each time she crosses back to the table, she bumps the telephone cord—inadvertently, I think—and each time my father rolls his eyes in annoyance.

There is a total of maybe thirty minutes during which my family gathers in the kitchen each morning, and my dad is on the phone for the first twenty of them. He runs a shoe store, and though the store closes for business at the end of each day, my father never seems to. I like listening to him. He has a deep voice that rolls from his throat, unless he's annoyed or angry, when it comes out in short bursts like punches. As a rule, he doesn't say much, so I hungrily take in every word of his morning phone calls. They are always work-related, and almost always problem-related, which is another reason I listen so intently. If I can understand some of these problems, maybe I can help figure them out, give some advice, and then my parents will be worried less and happy more. It's not that I offer up suggestions right there over my Cheerios. At nine years old, I don't presume to have all the answers, but I hope to someday. For now, I take in the sound of my father's voice and do my best to catalog the issues for later examination. On most days, that is. Today all I can think about is the monster.

When my dad is done with his call, my mom takes the phone from him and hangs it back up on the wall, freeing herself from the tripwire. She sits down lightly—I'm not certain her butt actually touches the chair—then nibbles on a piece of toast and tries to engage my father before he leaves. We know it won't be long before he does—ten minutes tops, five if his face is red after his phone call, which means something in particular is troubling him.

"Everything okay?" my mom asks. Her first question is always the same.

"Everything's fine," says my dad. His response, too, never changes, red face or not. He adjusts his tie—needlessly, since it's already as straight as the part in his hair. Then he unfolds the newspaper and spreads it over the table.

In the precious minutes before he folds it back up and leaves for the day, the rest of us will compete to siphon some of his attention away from the news. My mother and Dean are much better at this than me, effortlessly offering up whatever comes to mind.

"Can you believe that storm yesterday?" says my mom. "Pretty late in the year for thunder, if you ask me."

"What if I don't ask you?" says Dean. He grins, pleased with his cleverness. It's not a bad wisecrack. I wonder who he stole it from.

"Well," says my mom, "if you don't ask, I won't tell you." I can't decide if she didn't get the joke and this is her sincere reply, or if she did get it and this is her comeback. She rolls her eyes and glances at my father, but he doesn't seem to be listening. He raises the newspaper before him and turns the page.

"Maybe after school," my mom continues, "you and your brother can get out the rakes and clean all those leaves off the lawn. Then this weekend you can set up your new pitching toy before it starts to get too cold."

"Mom, it's called a pitchback," says Dean. "And it's not a toy. It's for practicing." Dean and I are both in the same baseball little league—or we will be, in the spring, when I'm ten and old enough to join. The pitchback is a small, stiff net in a metal frame, like a vertical trampoline. You throw the baseball at it and it springs right back to you, so you can practice without a partner.

My mother sighs. "Oh, whatever it's called."

The two of them go on talking—my mother of the leaves and the yard and things that need to get done around the house, Dean of baseball and how many hits he's going to get next season. My father remains lodged behind the newspaper as the minutes tick away. Any moment now, he's going to stand up and head for the door. He'll tousle Dean's and my hair, then give my mom a kiss. "Bye, dear," he'll say. "Be good, gents." Then he'll be gone. I realize I'm running out of time to be a part of the conversation. When I finally open my mouth, the words burst from me like some sort of confession.

"I saw a monster last night."

If I was hoping to cause a sensation, elicit some dramatic response, I'm disappointed. My father's eyes stay on the paper. My mom looks at me in a sort of vague, confused way, like she's scanning her internal mom playbook for the right thing to say. Only Dean reacts, with a shrug and a snort.

"Bullcrap," he says.

"Dean," my mother admonishes him. "Language."

"It's real," I say, both excited that someone acknowledged my revelation and frustrated that it was Dean, and that he doesn't believe me. "My door was closed, and the shade turned the knob and opened it from the outside."

"The shade?" says Dean.

"It's like a person," I continue, a bit breathlessly, "but totally pitch-black, so all you can see is darkness, but it's darker than darkness."

"You stole that idea from Peter Pan," says Dean. "It's Peter's shadow."

"No, Peter Pan's shadow was flat."

"Two-dimensional," says my mom.

"Right," I say. "Two-dimensional. It can only stick to walls or the ceiling. The monster was three-dimensional, maybe more."

"Stupid," says Dean. "How could it be more than three-dimensional?"

"Well, three at least."

"If you saw a monster, why are you still here? Why didn't it eat you?"

"It's not that kind of monster."

"What was it doing?"

"I don't know. Kinda dancing, I guess."

Dean nearly explodes from laughter, but his mouth is full of milk and cereal, and he desperately tries to keep it shut. His face clenches and turns bright red. The effort to restrain himself makes him laugh even harder, his whole body convulsing silently but violently, until a Cheerio actually pops out of his nose on a thin jet of milk. Finally he bursts, spitting up the rest of his mouthful.

"Dean!" says my mother.

"A dancing monster!" he squeals. "Elliot saw a dancing monster!"

I feel my face flush, like my father's does when he gets angry. I know this is just Dean being Dean, but it still hurts.

"It's not a dancing monster!" I shout back.

"But you just said it was." Dean jiggles in his chair, like he's about to pee his pants. "You said it."

He's got me there. I don't expect this kind of weaponized logic from Dean, and it stuns me into silence. My face grows hotter, and I feel the tears start to build behind my eyes. My mother notices.

"Okay, you two, that's enough," she says. "Dean, clean that up. Elliot, please don't get so worked up about it. He's just teasing. No need to get emotional." She turns to my father, who is still absorbed in the newspaper. "Richard, I think we should get someone to come look at Elliot's bedroom door. It doesn't lock properly. Any little draft can blow it open."

"This house isn't so drafty," says my father. "And why does he need to lock his bedroom door, anyway?"

"Because of the monsters." Dean is still giggling. "And the trees!"

"What trees?" asks my mom. "By his window? What's wrong? Are they bumping against the house?"

"The ones in the front yard," says Dean. "Elliot thinks they're alive."

"Well, they are alive," says my mother. "All plants are alive."

"No, Elliot thinks they're going to grab him," says Dean. "That's why he needs to lock his door. That and the monsters."

There are so many points I want to argue that I don't know where to begin. First, I want to tell my mom that the trees *did* seem alive—I mean really alive, conscious, not just in a plantlike way. Second, I never said I needed to lock my door. Third, I also never said that the trees were trying to get us in some evil way, or that I was afraid of them. Or that the monster was scary. Why would I want to lock it out? But all of these retorts jumble together in my throat and can't get past my tongue.

I'm still silent, and Dean is still giggling, when time finally runs out. With a deep sigh, my father folds his newspaper, drains the last of his coffee, and stands up from the table.

"There's no such thing as monsters," he says.

And that's the end of that conversation.

The shade only gets bolder after this, though I make a silent vow not to talk about it anymore. It continues to visit me in my room almost every night, sometimes opening the door, sometimes slipping under it. Less frequently, it appears in other places—once, for example, when I'm sleeping over at a friend's house—but always at night, when it can find the darkest, quietest corners to play in. There are other monsters, too. One is like a sparkling crescent in the corner of my vision. Another takes the face of an old man in the tree outside my window. On Halloween, I peer out from under the covers to find a particularly bold incarnation rummaging through my dresser. It's a fat man, dressed in black like a burglar. Unlike with the shade, I can see his face quite clearly, and it's both thrilling and a bit unsettling when he turns and smiles at me, as if he's been caught stealing and doesn't really care.

The menagerie is not confined to my bedroom, or even my neighborhood. In January, when Connecticut has sunk into the deepest part of winter, my family takes its first vacation. Though money is tight, my father insists that we go to Florida, because that's what people do. To be surrounded by snow one minute and on a beach in the tropics the next is a revelation, like waking from hibernation, or crossing into another universe. The monsters feel it, too. They are everywhere—hidden in the palm trees, skipping over the waves.

Dean and I spend more time in the ocean than out of it. My father, prone to sunburn, is often forced to retreat into the hotel's air-conditioned lounge, so my mother draws lifeguard duty. She doesn't seem to mind, though after four days she has yet to dip a toe in the water, which seems wrong to me and Dean. After one especially exhausting bout in the waves, we crash on our towels and cajole her until she finally starts to cave.

"Is it cold?" she asks.

"No," we tell her. This is both true and false. Though the water doesn't feel cold to us, we know it will to her. But I also believe she'll like it once she gets over the initial jolt. So this is a half-truth, combined with a white lie, which doesn't seem so bad.

"Is it safe?" she asks. "Are there sharks?"

"Don't be ridiculous," we tell her. This, of course, is not an answer. We have no idea whether there are sharks. Honestly, I hadn't even thought about it until my mother asked, and now I'm a bit concerned myself.

But she's convinced. She puts aside her magazine, hat, and sunglasses. She brushes the sand off her legs, which seems silly since she's about to go in the water. From our towels, Dean and I cheer her on as she tiptoes across the hot sand and lets the water brush across her ankles. Her shoulders rise at the chill, but she doesn't stop to chide us. She pushes on, steering between two sets of breaking waves, toward a bluer channel where the water is calmer. In a moment she is submerged past her shoulders and swimming.

"Wow, she's really going for it," says Dean.

We realize something is wrong. My mother's head is barely above the surface, and her arms aren't stroking but waving, then thrashing. She's moving quickly out to sea through the narrow channel between the waves.

"What's happening?" says Dean, his voice rising. "What's she doing?"

At my silence, he runs off toward a lifeguard tower that seems impossibly far away. I stand alone, frozen, and watch in horror as my mother gets smaller. My mind goes utterly blank. Fear has swollen my heart near to bursting when suddenly a black shadow under the water approaches my mother from the side. I'm afraid it's a shark, but when it bumps against her, she doesn't react. The shadow stays with her, pushing her sideways until she's out of the channel and among the waves. Her outward drift stops. Her head rises. Slowly, haltingly, the waves carry her back toward the shore. It was the monster, I realize. The shade from my bedroom. The monster saved my mother's life.

By the time my father reaches us, my mother is sitting on the beach, wrapped in towels, shaking with cold and fear. She stares silently at the sand between her feet. She hasn't spoken, not even to respond to our efforts to help. When my dad arrives, Dean and I talk over each other, trying to explain what happened. In my distress, I forget my vow.

"The monster saved her," I say.

My father stiffens. Dean abruptly stops his jabber. My mother's head jerks toward me, her eyes wide, almost baleful. My heart stutters, and I suddenly feel cold.

"That's not funny, Elliot," she snaps.

My voice is small. "But I saw it."

Dean glares at me. "Don't be an idiot."

"You weren't there!" I yell.

"Because I was going for help!"

"That's enough," says my father, instantly ending the argument. He draws me aside, away from Dean and my mother. "Elliot," he says, "Mom was caught in a rip current. That's what was pulling her out. It happens all the time. Okay?" When I don't respond, he rubs my shoulders. "You know what?" he says. "When we get back home, we should work on your baseball. You like baseball. You're looking forward to little league, aren't you? You could be a great baseball player."

I *do* like baseball. I *am* looking forward to little league. That my dad believes I could be a great player cheers me. That he wants to help me warms me even more.

"What do you think?" he asks.

My body begins to unclench. I nod.

"Good," he says.

I look over at my mother. She is still shaking, still staring at the sand between her feet. "Mom's so angry," I say.

"She's just scared," says my father. "She'll get over it." His hands fall from my shoulders. "Still, if I were you, I'd keep this monster stuff to myself."

After

After you die, you find yourself in a room with a single door—
though, admittedly, the room is not a room, and the door is not a
door, but, well . . . Anyway, there you are, in a room with a single
door, waiting. You are not sure for what or whom, until the door
opens and Jollis enters. Of course, you think—you were waiting
for Jollis. He carries a pencil and clipboard, as well as a professional
air that, when he sees you, melts into a warm smile. He collects
himself quickly, however, regaining his businesslike demeanor before proceeding to the body.

You hadn't noticed the body until now. It lies on a table in the
center of the room. It is *your* body, the one from which you
just departed, the one in which you lived your life. It is exactly
as it was—or, rather, exactly as you last left it, since it started out
much different, and kept changing along the way. Most of those
transformations—good or bad—just happened. Bones lengthened,
muscles expanded (later, bones contracted and muscles shrank). You
remember outgrowing your clothes as a child, and years afterward
when your hair started to thin. Other changes, of course, were self-
inflicted. That bit at the end, for example.

Once beside the table, Jollis pauses. He gazes upon the body with
a deep wistfulness that blends into admiration, even reverence. You
find this odd. You yourself can't recall ever looking at your body
that way. Jollis must be half-blind, you think, or at least terribly
nearsighted. He seems oblivious to those particular features of the
body that caused you so much grief. The length, for one, wasn't

what you would have liked. And that nagging softness around the middle was hardly ideal. The teeth might have been straighter and whiter. You could go on, but somehow these things don't provoke you the way they once did. It's as if you can now view your body— your *former* body—through Jollis's eyes, and you like what you see.

Jollis shakes himself from his reverie. He reaches toward the body's head to gently tap the brain itself. At his touch, it begins to emit a stream of light that flows into the room and beyond.

"What's that?" you ask.

"Your memories," says Jollis.

You lean in for a closer look. You discover that this incandescent river is made up of individual filaments of light, innumerable and very fine. Various scenes play out along the fibers, full of faces and moments you recognize, but just as often including ones you don't.

"Are you sure these are mine?" you ask. You point out specific strands. "I don't think I did *that*. Or that. And I can't believe I ever said *that*."

"Whose else would they be?"

"But I don't remember them."

Jollis nods sympathetically. "You will."

Satisfied that the memories are flowing smoothly, Jollis raises his clipboard and begins flipping through pages. Each page contains the same preprinted checklist—tiny lettering compressed into tight columns—but with a different name at the top. Beside each line item is a small checkbox. Though Jollis turns the pages quickly, you notice that a great many of the boxes have been marked— typically with an X or a check, but often with an exclamation point, or a smiley face, or some less evident notation. Finally, Jollis comes to a clean, unmarked page. Your name is at the top.

"Ah," he says. "Here we are." He grips his pencil and begins to examine the body, his look of admiration replaced by one of keen appraisal. He skillfully narrows his attention to focus first on one feature, then another. You realize Jollis is not blind to the details at all. If, for example, the body is in remarkably pristine condition, he notices.

"It's in remarkably pristine condition," he says.

"Thank you," you respond proudly. "I took excellent care of it, at least up until—well, you know."

"Did you?" Jollis peers at you quizzically. "How do you mean?"

"Well," you say, "exercise, for starters. I did just about everything, at one time or another. Running, biking, yoga—you name it."

Jollis carries on his inspection, occasionally looking over at you to show that he's listening. Although he is almost halfway down the body, he has yet to mark a single item on his checklist. You find this puzzling. Surely, you deserve some checks. Maybe he's not seeing what you're seeing after all.

"Then there was my diet," you tell him. "Pescatarian, vegetarian, vegan. No alcohol. No tobacco. I went gluten-free, dairy-free, sugar-free, caffeine-free, soy-free, fat-free, carb-free. Virtually food-free."

Jollis nods vaguely in your direction. His examination of the body is nearly finished now, but still no check marks. You grow nervous. Your voice speeds up.

"And I was very careful with it," you say. "Stayed out of the sun. Never swam after eating. Always wore a helmet. Flossed . . ."

Jollis straightens. With one last glance at the soles of the feet, he moves back. He lowers his pencil. Coincidentally or not, the incandescent stream of memories slows to a trickle, then stops.

"That's it?" you ask.

He nods.

"But you didn't check anything on the list."

"Yes," says Jollis, a bit uncomfortably. "That *is* a bit unusual, but nothing you should worry about. It's not a report card. I'm not here to keep score or anything."

"But what's on it?" you ask. "What are you tallying up?"

"Scars," he says.

"You mean from injuries? Like if I'd stuck my hand in a blender or something?"

"Well, yes, and much more besides. The list includes every way in which a vessel can be marked by usage. Cuts and scrapes, certainly. But also wounded pride, tarnished reputation, guilty conscience— everything from broken bone to broken heart."

"You can see the scar from a broken heart?"

"Sure," says Jollis. "We've had cases where the heart was ripped out entirely."

You look back at the body. It really is marvelous. You wonder why you never noticed. "And I have no scars whatsoever?"

Jollis double-checks his list. "Apparently not," he says. "I admit that it's rare. But, as I said, the body is in remarkably pristine condition."

"But that's good, right?"

Jollis looks at you softly. "Keep in mind," he says, "the list is solely for our internal research. It's not a scorecard. There is no grade." He pauses, wrestling with something. "Still, it's remarkable how often the most rewarding journeys are evidenced by the most check marks. A statistically significant correlation. Of course, a broken bone may result from a purely tragic accident—a traveler is hit by a car while standing at her mailbox, say. But more often it comes about from some daring push—she is scaling a mountain, for example, or riding a bicycle too fast down a hill, and she falls."

"And the other scars?" you ask, though you already know.

"The same," says Jollis. "A broken heart, for example, could be the tragic result of a lifetime of mistreatment. Statistically, though, it's more likely to occur when a traveler loves something so utterly that it shatters him a little—or a lot—when he loses it."

"So you get check marks for pain?"

"Not for pain. For striving."

You stare at your former body. What had a moment before seemed immaculate to you now feels sterile, and the pride you felt in defending yourself from life turns to regret for failing to embrace it. It is too unscathed, this body, too unused. Only one thing mars its perfection. It's your last hope, and you grasp at it.

"What about that final piece?" you ask. "At the end." After all, you think, the body did die. You killed it yourself.

"No," says Jollis gently. "I'm sorry."

"But why not?" you ask. That's a scar, you think. You deserve a check mark for that, if nothing else.

"You get marks for striving to live your life, not striving to leave it."

Your dread swells into full despair. Despite Jollis's proclamations—that there are no grades, no report cards—you discover that you want check marks now. Desperately. Even just one. One scar to prove your life. Without your body you are incapable of tears, but you want to cry, and you find it ironic that you spent your life telling yourself not to. The rest of you begins to unravel, dissipating until it threatens to disappear entirely.

Jollis's look softens even further. "Tell you what," he says. "I'll go ahead and give you a half check for that last part."

"Really?"

"I shouldn't," he says. "Technically, it will throw off our research, but it won't be more than a rounding error. Happy to do it."

You feel saved, as if Jollis has pulled you back from the edge of the abyss. "Thank you, Jollis."

"It's fine," he says. "Honestly, I don't see what the fuss is about. As I said, it's not a report card, and I'm not here to judge. Check mark, no check mark. It doesn't matter now."

Elliot

(1982)

I love to sleep. It is one of my favorite things. That I can't actually verify this—that, by definition, I cannot be conscious of my unconsciousness—doesn't dissuade me from my belief. Some things can be taken only on faith. Besides, I have evidence, circumstantial though it may be.

Exhibit A, I hate getting up in the morning. Hate it. I've yet to see a dawn I wouldn't rather turn my back on, head deep in the pillow, blankets pulled high. Even more so in winter. To save money, my parents keep the thermostat low, relying on a kerosene space heater in the kitchen. When most of me is nestled under the covers, the sharp chill on my nose and cheeks is actually enjoyable. But the prospect of facing it in nothing but my tighty-whities? That's just grim.

Exhibit B, I am an Olympic-caliber napper—or would be, if napping were an Olympic event. I can nap anywhere and for any length of time, from the five-minute catnap on the bus to school (I call it the Blink), to the early-evening snooze that can last until the following morning (the Deep Out). My favorite is the traditional siesta. Many an afternoon finds me on the couch, eyelids drawn and breath shallow, gone from this world if only for a brief time.

Upon our return from vacation, I increase my self-prescribed dosage of slumber. Connecticut is still buried in winter. The front yard is white and deep and cold, making it clear that I won't be practicing baseball with my father any time soon. The weather seems to encourage everyone to burrow even further into their own personal dens. Not that my family is one for games or shared philosophy in any event—our primary group activity is television. There is otherwise little to do but homework and reading, which can only fill so many hours. My mother abides my idleness for about a week, until her sense of duty kicks in.

"You sleep too much," she says. It's Sunday morning and she's woken me up—indirectly yet purposely—by her rustling as she opens the curtains and straightens up my room. It occurs to me that this may be the perfect word to describe my mother. A rustler. She rustles through life. I am sure that her criticism is well-intentioned, but how does she know how much sleep I need? Lions in Africa are unconscious for more than eighty percent of their lives. As far as I know, no one chides them for it, or rustles them awake when they're sound asleep on a Sunday morning.

"Lions sleep twenty hours a day," I say.

"Well, you're not a lion," she says. I should have seen this response coming—the blunt assertion of reality that is inarguable yet also somehow misses the point—but I've just woken up and am still groggy.

"I was having a dream," I tell her. This is not unusual, and I suppose could constitute Exhibit C in the case for my love of sleep. I have wonderful, linear, storylike dreams—the kinds of dreams you don't want to wake up from. This one was a good one, too, though I don't get into it with my mom. In the dream, we were all at the breakfast table—me and my family, also the shade and the other monsters. My mother was pouring the shade a cup of coffee and chatting with it about the weather. I was telling a joke, and everybody laughed, my father most of all. In fact, he couldn't stop, his face getting redder and his eyes tearing up until, finally, a Cheerio popped right out of his nose and into the shade's coffee.

"You can't spend your life dreaming," says my mom.

"When else am I going to get the chance?" I ask.

"Never mind," she says, not one for long arguments or shaped logic. She opens the last of the curtains.

The day is cold and gray and not made for baseball. Anticipating a time when my father and I will be able to play outside, I decide to start practicing in the only way available. I grab my mitt, rummage a tennis ball out of the hallway closet, and head down to the basement. Long, naked fluorescent bulbs shine down from a ceiling that would seem low if I weren't ten years old and somewhat small for my age. The floor and walls are of unfinished cement, perfect for my purpose. I push aside cardboard boxes, old lawn chairs, and other debris to clear a narrow lane from one end of the basement to the other. On the far wall I draw a rectangle in white chalk, hoping it approximates the strike zone of a typical twelve-year-old. Then I start to pitch.

The house is quiet in winter. The basement is dead silent but for the rhythmic thud and pop of the tennis ball as it rebounds against the cement wall and back to my glove. I find it soothing, enjoying it so much that I'm immediately concerned when, on the third day of my practice, I hear my father coming down the steps. I'm certain he'll tell me to stop, that the noise is driving him and my mom crazy. Instead, to my surprise, he presents me with a rubber ball the size and shape of a baseball, complete with raised grooves to imitate the lacing. Better than a tennis ball, he says. More like the real thing. I ask him about my form and mechanics, hoping he'll share some tips with me. He watches a few pitches, then nods.

"Looks good to me," he says, before heading back upstairs. There is a small, empty silence after he leaves, and I can't help thinking that more words might have filled it, but I shrug it off and turn back to the wall.

Days pass. Maybe weeks. I'm not sure, but by the time winter begins to recede, I can put that rubber ball anywhere I want in that strike zone. I am so anxious to play catch with my father that, at the first hint of thaw, I grab a shovel and set out to clear the lawn of snow. This is harder than it sounds. Shovels are made for scraping over asphalt, not clawing at the earth. Even after I've broken through the hard upper crust of ice, the front edge of the shovel keeps catching on the grass. It takes me all afternoon to clear a single strip that is just long and wide enough for two people to have a proper catch. When my arms begin to shake from exhaustion, I concede that it will have to be enough, and am vindicated when the sun comes out the next day, drying the strip of grass until it seems a touch of spring in the frozen heart of winter.

By the time my father gets home I'm already outside, mitt and baseball at the ready. Before he is even out of the car, I am chatting away about what I want to show him, and the questions I have for him—like, what's a two-seamer, and how do you throw a curveball, and how quickly can he lose his briefcase and find his glove. He withdraws into the house, then emerges again a few minutes later. He has indeed left his briefcase inside, but instead of his glove he's carrying a long, flat cardboard box. It's the pitchback. We never did set it up before the cold arrived. My father takes it out of the box and has it assembled in short order—a taut vertical net inside a metal frame.

"Look at that, would you?" he says. "Give it a try."

There is that small silence again. My father seems quite impressed with the pitchback, though he's already moving back toward the front steps. He doesn't seem to understand that I asked him to play catch with me, not set up some contraption so that I could be here without him, by myself. I turn toward the pitchback and throw, but my heart's not in it, and the toss is feeble, nothing like the flamethrowers I was hurling in the basement. Still, the ball strikes the center of the net and springs back to me like it's on a string, and that seems good enough for my father.

"Even better than the basement wall," he says, before disappearing into the house.

The door barely closes before it opens again, spitting out Dean. He bounds into the long strip of grass. He has his glove on, and opens it toward me expectantly.

"My turn," he says.

"I haven't even used it yet. And I was the one who shoveled all the snow."

"Fine. How much longer are you going to be?"

"I don't know," I say. "Do you want to have a catch?"

"A catch? Why? This thing is so cool! If you don't want to use it—"

"No," I cut him off. "I'm using it." My face burns. I feel the urge to either cry or punch Dean in the face or both. Instead, I once again turn toward the pitchback. I heave the ball with all of the might my body has managed to garner in its ten years. But I've lost all focus now, and I miss badly. The ball sails over the top and across the yard before burying itself in the snow. Dean laughs all the way back into the house.

"Nice pitch, ace!" he calls over his shoulder.

So, for the rest of the winter and into spring, it's me and the pitchback, with the basement wall occasionally pinch-hitting during heavy rainstorms. Unlike the wall, the pitchback allows you to work on your catching as well as your throwing. If you throw the ball toward the top of the netting, it comes back as a grounder, and if you throw toward the bottom, it comes back as a pop-up. This is how Dean uses it. He plays shortstop for his team, so he cares more about hitting and fielding than pitching. But I stay focused on the center, where a cord is weaved through the netting in the shape

of a rectangle. This is my strike zone, and I pound the corners with
pitch after pitch until I could do it blindfolded.

It is not a matter of determination. I am not out to prove my
prowess to my father—or to Dean, for that matter. Rather, despite an initial sense of bitterness toward the pitchback as a poor
substitute for flesh and blood, I eventually become as enthralled
with it as I was with the basement wall, my spirit eased by the
melodic flow of the repeated toss and return. Dean likes to say
that sport is combat. He says that for thousands of years people
have killed each other in war, and that we've evolved to need this
conflict. Sport, he says, is a modern, bloodless substitute. This is
big thinking for Dean, and he may even be right, but as the days
and weeks go by, and my pitching becomes more and more fluid,
I begin to think of sport not as combat but as dance—the beauty
of the body in motion, where the mind quiets to the point of
vanishing.

My solitary training ends when little league season begins. I tell
my new coach about my pitching, but as a rookie I'm relegated to
the outfield. It is not until halfway through the season, when our
scheduled pitcher is home sick, that I have a chance to test my skills.
We are facing my brother's team. Though this somehow feels right
to me, I'm nervous. Terrified, really. With my parents watching
from the stands, I accidentally hit the first two batters before I'm
finally able to control my pitches. I project myself back onto that
strip of grass in winter. Behind home plate, the catcher becomes
the pitchback. His mitt moves from one corner of the strike zone
to another, and I don't miss.

My brother leads off the second inning. I know he doesn't like
pitches high and away, so that's where I throw them. He watches
one go by for a strike, then another. I can see him getting anxious. When he crowds the plate to reach for the next one, I throw

it down and in instead. He swings awkwardly and misses. Strike three. He bangs his bat on the plate and barks at the umpire before stomping back to the dugout, staring me down the entire way.

Our little drama repeats itself in the fourth inning, the only variation being the location of the three strikes and the even deeper scowl Dean gives me as he stomps back to the bench. He doesn't come to the plate again until the final inning, with two outs and a man on second. I've pitched well, and we're up by a run, yet my brother can tie the game if he gets a hit. He strides from the dugout, all swagger and bravado, but as he digs into the batter's box I see that his face is flushed, and he avoids my eye.

The first pitch is low and away, and Dean flails wildly at it. Strike one. His composure has crumbled, and his normally athletic swing has broken down into an angry hack. He curses loudly enough for our parents to hear. The second strike sails by. Dean steps out of the batter's box to collect his thoughts. When he finally looks at me, the mask of his anger has cracked, and the fear shows through.

I understand. He's one of the twelve-year-olds, in his final year of little league. Striking out to your little brother, especially when the game is on the line, would be humiliating. I think about the two of us catching leaves together, and how I let him win, and that joyful look on his face. I realize that I can let him win now, too. I can throw a pitch down the middle and he'll hit it, and tie the game, and smile that happy smile of his. But to let him win at leaf-catching required only that I lie about my tally of leaves, not that I purposely fail to catch them. Now, I'd have to fail on purpose—abandon all my winter practice, all the long hours with that goddamn pitchback and that goddamn basement wall. I'd have to tell my body not to do its best, not to be itself. And I can't bring myself to do that. I decide to pitch the way I know how. If my brother can hit a fastball on the outside corner, I'll be the first to congratulate him. If not—well, he can go suck it.

He misses. He swings himself nearly out of his shoes, and ends up on his knees. From there he stares back at the catcher's mitt, where the third strike rests snugly, safe from the now empty menace of Dean's bat. The game is over. My brother's shoulders give one small heave as he fights back tears. Then he stands up and hurls the bat against the fence. His outburst silences the crowd, so that when he turns and jeers at me, everyone can hear.

"Lucky pitch, weirdo. Who taught you that—your dancing monster?"

This is the beginning of the end of my undistinguished baseball career. By the following week, Dean has told half the league that I believe monsters visit me in my room each night to dance and sing and perform plays in flowered dresses. My relationships with the other players—most of whom are also classmates of mine at school—had previously ranged from friendship to, at worst, indifference, but are now transformed into ridicule or, at best, avoidance. Even my own teammates snicker behind my back. After a month of this, the flush in my face and ache in my chest start to feel permanent, and I decide I don't need it anymore. I tell my mom that my shoulder hurts from too much throwing. In fact, it does hurt a bit, though whether the pain is from throwing is an open question. She lets me skip a practice, then a game, then another game, and without anyone declaring it, we come to the understanding that I'm not going back.

By the time summer arrives, I am spending more and more time alone. When I tire of the thin strip of trees behind our house, I venture into our neighbor's more expansive woods. This is not the best idea. Mr. Harding is a notoriously mean human being.

He is so thoroughly cantankerous that you get the feeling it was not the events of his life that made him so but rather that he was born hostile, and remained true to form throughout every one of his eighty-plus years. The woods behind his house are thick with leaves and mysteries, including the presence of old, rusted farm equipment—a hand plow, the shell of a tractor—which in my mother's opinion makes the woods dangerous and is another reason why I shouldn't be there.

It is late afternoon, and I am deep within these forbidden woods, when I find a group of low stones arranged into an unnaturally perfect ring. Resting on an old tree stump near the center of the ring is a book. Or most of a book—its cover and first few pages have been torn away. Without stopping to ponder its origin, or the incongruity of its presence here in the undergrowth, or even why I haven't stumbled upon it sooner, I pick it up, sit down with my back to the tree stump, and begin reading.

At that time in Neverene, there was a giant, with a giant heart.

A shiver runs through me. I am suddenly disoriented, though I don't know why. At the moment I finished reading these words, it seemed to me that there was a click and, for a fraction of a second, a darkening of the world around me, like the fall of a camera shutter. The sensation is so strong that I look around to see if someone is there, or if anything has changed. Yet everything appears in its place. The afternoon sun dapples the lap of my dirty jeans. The leaves sway in an imperceptible breath of wind. I shrug off my jitters and open the book again.

This time, when my surroundings disappear, I let them. For a moment there are only the letters on the page, and then they too are gone, and all that exists is the world they conjure. Neverene. From the beginning, a medley of tales seems already under way, featuring a motley collection of players. But it is Neverene itself that captivates me. It is fantastical, mystical—and somehow conscious.

Everything in Neverene—animate or inanimate—is awake. Trees speak, rocks feel, even the weather has intentions. And then there is the giant, with a heart so big he can commune with all of it, whether flesh or wood, stone or sky.

I stop reading only when the failing light demands it, when the white pages seem to glow and the black letters shuffle and blend into one another. I look up. Hours have passed. The sun is gone, and the woods have fallen into half-light. The crickets start their chorus. Tiny sparks pulse in the air around me as the fireflies come to life. I rise on stiff legs and look for the path home, but the way is dark and my head is light. I'm chilled and, admittedly, a little scared. I don't want to try to find my way back through the woods, so I opt for the shorter route that cuts across Mr. Harding's back lawn. A risky move, but I hope the darkness will cover me.

I leave the woods and race across the open grass, hunching over as if this might somehow make me less visible. I am close to Mr. Harding's house, and have almost reached the edge of his property, when a voice calls out.

"Hello, traveler."

I freeze. A small glow ignites in the dark. Unlike the fireflies, it is steady and motionless, and for an instant I believe that the light itself is calling me. Then the glow brightens until I can see that it is a flame in a glass lantern, resting on a table on Mr. Harding's back patio. To my relief, it is not Mr. Harding sitting there, but a woman I don't recognize.

"Hello," I respond.

"What are you up to?" she asks. Her voice is clear and light.

"I was . . . nothing."

"Oh, I doubt you were nothing," she says. "And I doubt you were up to nothing, too. But you don't have to tell me if you don't want to."

Something about her relaxes me—whether her voice itself or her gentle teasing. I stand up straight, no longer looking to run. "Why did you call me traveler?"

"I figured that's what you are," she says. "Either that or a leprechaun."

"A leprechaun?" I bite back a snicker. "I'm not a leprechaun. I'm a boy."

"Well, isn't that just what a leprechaun would say! Now I'm really suspicious. Step into the light so I can get a look at you."

I draw closer, and can see her better now. She has calm eyes and a pale, smooth face. Her hair—brown with fine streaks of gray that glitter in the lamplight—falls messily down to her shoulders. She seems neither old nor young.

"It's hard to tell by the lamp," she says. "Is your skin green?" Now I can't help but giggle. "Did I say something funny?" she asks.

I immediately stop. "No, sorry."

"It's okay," she says. "You can laugh. I don't mind." She smiles, the skin around her eyes crinkling into elfin wings. "I'm Esther."

"I'm Elliot. I live next door."

"Very nice to meet you, Elliot. I think I've met your parents—the entrepreneurs?"

"No, the Chances."

She laughs. I'm confused by this, and would probably be offended except that it's a beautiful, almost contagious sound—bright and shiny, ringing from her throat like a little bell. It occurs to me that you're not required to be offended when someone laughs at you. You can just let them laugh. Still, I'd like to know why.

"Did I say something funny?"

She stops. "I'm sorry, I didn't mean—"

"It's okay. I don't mind either."

Esther nods, then leans forward in her chair. "An entrepreneur is someone who starts a new venture," she explains. "Someone who takes a chance. So you see, we were kind of saying the same thing. Your parents own the shoe store, right?"

"Yes." Talking about my parents reminds me that I should probably get home. It's officially dark now. My mother will start to worry soon, at which point she'll open the back door and loudly call my name until she can see me coming. For some reason I'd rather Esther didn't witness this summons, but I'm also not eager to leave. My family and I aren't saying a whole lot to each other these days, and the more I think about it, the more I realize we never really have, as if there were only so much oxygen in the rooms of our house, and too much talking would threaten our ability to breathe.

"Do *you* want to be an entrepreneur someday?" Esther asks.

"No." The quickness of my reply surprises me, but all I can think of is the shoe store and my mother's perpetual state of anxiety and the blood rushing to my father's face after his morning work calls. "I want to help them."

"How so?"

I want to explain to Esther about how I listen to my parents' conversations and try to catalog their problems so that I can find solutions for them, but my head swims in a fragmented sea of worries I don't understand—mortgages and personal guarantees, interest rates, employee turnover, supply chains. My shoulders hunch up toward my ears as helplessness sets in, and I can't gather my thoughts into any kind of coherent response. "I'm not sure," I finally say. "Maybe I could be an advisor?"

"That sounds like a great idea," says Esther. "I bet you're gaining all kinds of valuable experience just by watching your parents, and someday you'll be able to put it all together and give other entrepreneurs wonderful advice."

Instantly, my shoulders release and the helplessness subsides. At the same time, my throat tightens so that I can't reply. Yes, I want to say. Yes, that's just what I meant.

"And what do you have there?" Esther asks, nodding toward the book in my hand.

For a moment I had actually forgotten about the book. Now my mind lights up with memories of Neverene, and my heart with a desire to return. "It's about a place," I say. "A really cool place."

"Ah," says Esther. "That sounds wonderful."

I grip the book a bit more tightly, as if someone might take it from me. Esther doesn't seem to notice. She just looks at me patiently. Reluctantly, I remind myself that the book isn't mine, and I hold it out to her. "I found it in the woods. I was just going to borrow it."

"From whom?"

"From Mr. Harding, I guess."

For the first time since I've met her, Esther's face falls and the light in her eyes dims. "Mr. Harding passed away," she says.

I stiffen. Outside our circle of lamplight, the darkness suddenly feels dangerous and empty. I've never known anyone who has died. I may not have liked Mr. Harding, but his death unnerves me, and I feel guilty for having been relieved that he wasn't on his patio tonight.

"I'm sorry."

"Me, too," says Esther. "But he had a long life, and one that he could call his own. And that means a lot."

"He didn't like us playing in his woods."

Esther nods. "He cherished his solitude. Also, he was a jerk." At the look of shock on my face, she laughs. "It's true," she says, "but he was my uncle and I loved him all the same." I am even more surprised to hear that Esther was Mr. Harding's niece. It's hard for me to believe that two such different people could share the same genes.

"Anyway," she continues with a sigh, "I suppose the woods aren't his anymore. There's nobody here but me. As far as I'm concerned, you may play in them as you wish, and the book you found is yours."

My chest warms. Though the tightness returns to my throat, this time I'm able to speak through it. "Thank you."

"You're very welcome," says Esther. "Now I wonder if maybe you should get home so your parents don't worry about you?"

I nod, give a little wave, and go. When I reach the crumbling stone wall that separates our yards, I pause and turn. "I was glad to talk with you," I call back.

From within the circle of lamplight, Esther raises her hand. "Farewell, traveler who is not a leprechaun."

In the Future

Bannor says that in the future you can talk to the dead.

Which was inevitable, he says, once they figured out how to seamlessly connect a computer to the human brain. He says biochip implants are commonplace in the future, and their usage has graduated from the vulgar, like the chip in your wrist that allows you to pay for groceries, to the profound, like the one in your skull that combats the onslaught of dementia.

It was a dementia patient who was the first to communicate from the grave. Her name was Rose. She had a garden-variety biochip in her head, connected wirelessly to her computer, which monitored and maintained proper brain function. At the age of ninety-four, Rose died peacefully in her sleep. Her daughter found her body the next morning, and nearly jumped out the window when the computer broke the silence by asking what was for breakfast. There was a long, anxious moment before Rose and her daughter realized that Rose had died and was somehow speaking through the computer. Their conversation lasted exactly three minutes before the process fried what was left of Rose's neural pathways, but it was a breathtaking, if unintended, achievement—one that the public quickly and rather boorishly labeled "Rosurrection."

It also unleashed a series of absolute shitstorms. The first, following immediately on the heels of the discovery, was the widespread and unauthorized exhumation of corpses. In addition to fistfights, riots, and a villainous stench, this craze led to significant public health hazards, if not moral ones. Fortunately, the gravediggers mostly hung up their shovels once scientists discovered that Rosurrection wouldn't work if the brain had been dead for more than a few days.

The second major flap was over whether the technology—or the practice, or whatever you wanted to call it—should be permitted. A vocal minority demanded that it be outlawed altogether, based on an uneasy (and often self-contradictory) combination of religious, ethical, legal, patriotic, economic, and other grounds. But the future is a permissive place. Given that Rosurrection didn't seem to be harming anyone, this quarrel soon withered on the vine.

In its stead arose the debate over whether we are really speaking with the dead at all. By all accounts, that initial conversation between Rose and her daughter had been coherent and personal, but the process doesn't always run so smoothly. Sometimes the deceased don't recognize their loved ones, or they speak nonsense, or sing the same song over and over, or say nothing at all. These apparent failures represent a small minority of cases, yet detractors take them as evidence that Rosurrection is not actually a conversation with the living consciousness of the deceased but rather just a random firing of synapses prodded by electrical stimulation. As to why many Rosurrected minds seem so lucid, these detractors hem and haw. Put a thousand Rosurrected brains in a room for long enough, they huff, and you'll eventually get Shakespeare. In truth, it's hard to prove whether we're speaking with the deceased or just marvelous simulations, but most people don't seem to care. There is a near universal ache to talk to the dead.

Which has led to blistering feuds over who has the right to do so. Though Rosurrection methodology has improved, scientists still haven't figured out how to extend the process beyond just the same three minutes that Rose and her daughter were originally granted. Three minutes—no more, no less—which means there's only so much time with the dead to go around, and everybody wants some. Laws are passed, repealed, and passed again. Courthouse hallways are clogged with litigants. In order to spare their descendants from years of fighting and legal fees, many people include provisions in their wills dictating whether they can be Rosurrected, and when, and by whom.

Despite its attendant chaos, Rosurrection has proliferated in the future. Bannor says that it has come to be viewed as one of those prosaic wonders, like childbirth or indoor plumbing. People speak with the dead every day, all around the world. But it's always a little awkward. The dead themselves aren't typically very chatty. So, after the obligatory last goodbye, the living usually end up asking a bunch of questions, from the practical to the provocative to the inane—What's your email password? Where'd you put the kitty litter? Do you still love me? How come Jonathan got the house and the car and the money, and all I got were the rosebushes? For the suicides, an additional line of questioning inevitably awaits, always along the same lines—Why did you do it? How come you didn't say anything? Was it something I did? This inquisition has become so frustratingly rote that the majority of suicides spend their three minutes mostly silent, quietly saying "I'm sorry" and leaving it at that.

Of course, there is another question—often the final one—that everyone asks the dead, and it has fomented the most intractable controversy of all, one so monumental that its two antagonistic factions have received (or appropriated) proper epithets. On one side are the Foreverists, who claim that Rosurrection proves once and for all the existence of an afterlife and an everlasting soul. Death, say the Foreverists, is dead. On the other side are the Corporealists, who maintain that, while Rosurrection does indeed allow us to communicate with the dead, consciousness resides only in the physical body. They point out that Rosurrection requires an intact, undamaged brain in order to work, and insist that when the brain is no longer functional, the person is gone. Once your three minutes are up, say the Corporealists, death is alive and well.

The Foreverists counter that the dead sometimes tell strange tales, ones that they could not have experienced in their lifetimes. Some deceased describe looking over their former body, or waiting in a long line with other deceased. The Corporealists dismiss these rumors, likening them to the near-death experiences that have been claimed for centuries and never substantiated. Dying is stressful, say the Corporealists, and coming back—even for just three minutes—can't be any easier. Of course the imagination goes berserk.

That final question—the one that incites this endless debate between the Foreverists and the Corporealists—is predictable enough. "Where have you gone?" we ask the dead. "And what's it like there, where you are?"

Bannor says the dead are always confused by this query. "What do you mean?" they respond. "I'm right here."

"No," we say. "You've moved on, but to where? What comes after this?"

Yet the dead, whether in ignorance or subterfuge, do not change their tune. "I'm here with you," they say. "We're all here together. Always."

Elliot

(1982)

I spend days and days in Neverene. Not that it takes that long to actually finish the book. Hardly twenty-four hours after bringing it home from Esther's, I regretfully turn the last page. There in my bed, late at night with my back against the window, my heart takes a moment to settle. I look around the room. Despite the thick orange carpet, the posters covering the walls, the books and toys and other trinkets on the shelves, it all feels bare now, and plain, and those walls seem much closer and the ceiling much lower than they did just yesterday morning. Behind me is the window, but its panes are dark and it seems an exit to nowhere.

I turn back to the first page—that is, to *my* first page, given the book's missing leaves—and begin again. This time I linger. Days. Weeks. Wherever I go, the book is by my side, the key to a door I unlock over and over. Every spare moment finds me digging the book from my backpack and opening it with a mix of excitement and desire and joy. I read late into the nights—compromising my precious sleep—but also at the breakfast table, and at dinner, and through the long, hot afternoons after Dean has gone to camp for the day and I have the shelter of the back porch to myself.

My mother doesn't seem to notice my sojourns to Neverene, until I make the mistake of opening the book in the car while accompanying her on her errands. Though my mind is transported, my stomach refuses to follow. The act of reading in a moving vehicle doesn't agree with it, and I vomit all over the stick shift. In a panic, my mother slams on both the gas and the clutch simultaneously, and we stall just in time to avoid crashing into a phone booth outside the post office. Scared and angry, my mother forbids me from ever reading in the car again, but otherwise lets it go. Unfortunately, a few days later, I make my second and last mistake. Walking with my mom through town, my head down in the book, I step directly into the brisk traffic of the street. My mother's scream eclipses even the blare of the car horns. A station wagon swerves violently into the opposite lane to avoid me, its faux wood paneling passing inches from my face. I don't have time to feel relieved before my mother yanks me back onto the sidewalk and rips the book from my hands. The fear on her face reminds me of the beach in Florida, after she nearly drowned.

"That's enough, Elliot," she says coldly. "Your fantasyland is going to get you killed, and I'm not going to stand by and watch."

Whether my mother throws the book away or just hides it, I am strictly forbidden from seeking it out, and I know I won't see it again. The key is lost, the door shut. A deep anxiety overcomes me, banishing hunger and sleep. My eyes and ears stop registering colors and scents, until the emptiness is complete. After two days in this vacuum, thoughts of Neverene pull me back into the deep woods behind Mr. Harding's—Esther's—house. It is approaching evening on another slow, warm summer day as I make my way to the ring of stones. When I reach the tree stump at its center, I freeze.

On the stump is a rock that wasn't there before. It's about half the size of my fist, its surface ridged and faceted like that of a crudely cut gem. Where the afternoon sun hits one of these facets, the rock's dark surface shines bright white. Where it misses, the rock is as black as the void. It's unlike anything I've ever seen, and I know immediately that it's from Neverene. I was wrong—the book was not the entrance to Neverene. The book was just the map. This ring of stones is the doorway, and this rock is the key. I pick it up. It's surprisingly light. I cradle it in my hands, then sit down on the tree stump with my legs crossed and eyes closed. In Neverene, the rocks and trees are alive, and the giant with the giant heart is able to call forth that life, that power. I resolve to do the same, bending my will to the dark stone, silently beseeching it to open the door to Neverene so I can cross over.

So engrossed am I in my entreaty that I fail to notice the twins from down the street. Their names are Kurt and Dave, but in my mind I've always thought of them as Dirt and Cave. I don't know why. They've never done anything to me, though they've never been particularly friendly either. They're sort of just there. But they're my brother's age and bigger than him, which means they're older and bigger than me, and therefore a bit menacing by default. They also play baseball in the same little league as my brother and, until recently, me. So they've heard all about the—

"—monsters," one of them is saying. "Are you listening to me, Chance? Come in, Chance. Earth to Chance."

I open my eyes. Above me loom the twins—identical in almost every way, right down to their buzz cuts and cargo shorts, their only differentiating features being Cave's extra freckles and the teams on their otherwise matching football jerseys (Dirt likes the Jets, Cave the Cowboys). Each stands astride a brand-new dirt bike, which surprises me because I didn't hear them approach. I feel like I'm in a trance, as if the world has been muffled. The sound of my own voice is unusually measured and calm.

"What did you say?" I ask.

"I said, are you out here dancing with your monsters?" says Cave.

"Doesn't look like he's dancing," says Dirt. "Looks like he's beating off with a rock."

I look down at the black stone in my hands. "The rock is the key."

"To beating off?" laughs Dirt.

"No," I say. "To making monsters."

The twins' laughter dies. In the surrounding trees, the buzzing of the cicadas cycles from reticence to crescendo and back again. "You can't make monsters," says Cave.

"Of course I can. Why do you think I see them when Dean doesn't?"

The twins stare at me. Years from this moment I'm sure Dirt and Cave grow up into rational, sensible adults with concrete minds like my mom, but for the moment they're still kids, and can't fully escape the nagging suspicion that things like monsters might, in fact, exist.

"Prove it," says Dirt.

"Five bucks," I say. "Each."

"Why would we pay you?" asks Dirt.

"Because I'm going to show you how to do it," I say. And why shouldn't they pay me? After all, I'm a Chance, which means I'm an entrepreneur, at least according to Esther.

As if with one mind, the twins think about it, though not for long. "Fine," says Cave. But when I hold out my hand, he scoffs. "We don't have it with us."

"Well, go get it," I say. "And bring two paper cups, and a pack of matches."

"Why?"

"You'll see."

The tires of their bikes kick up dirt as they leave. My hope that they might reconsider is dimmed by the urgency of their departure, then dashed entirely when they return just a few minutes later, dropping their bikes in the undergrowth and holding out two crisp five-dollar bills. They're hooked. I take their money and stuff it in the pocket of my jeans.

"Now listen carefully," I say, lowering my voice. "You must each fill your cup. First with rainwater, since monsters, like us, are made up mostly of liquid. Then with earth or stone, to give it form and structure. Third, with strands of your own hair, so that it will be bound to you. And finally with something living, so that it too will have life."

To their credit, the twins don't ask any questions, but immediately scatter to gather their ingredients. They scoop up leftover rainwater from the hollow of a large stone, pinch some dirt, pluck their own hair, and abduct a pair of bewildered black ants from a nearby colony, mixing all of it in their Dixie cups.

"Now what?" they say.

I rise from the stump and look up at the large branch of a beech tree that extends out over the ring of stones.

"We climb that tree," I say.

I lead the twins up the beech tree, and the three of us shimmy our way toward the end of the branch, the twins careful not to spill their cups. The branch is thick and strong, easily bearing the weight of three boys. Still, we're a good ten feet off the ground, and far enough from any other branches for me to be a bit nervous. When the ring of stones is below us and we're nearly over the stump at its center, I stop.

"Now you have to pour out your cups over the stump."

With a collective deep breath, Dirt and Cave do just that. The evening shadows have grown long in the woods, and it's hard to know whether the jettisoned concoctions actually hit the stump, but I assure the twins that they were on target. We cling to the branch a moment longer, not exactly eager to inch our way back along its precarious length.

"There's no monster," says Dirt. "It didn't work. What a load of crap."

"We're not done," I say quickly. "Climb down."

When we're back on the ground I lead the twins inside the ring of stones and have them place their now-empty paper cups on the tree stump.

"You have to burn them."

The twins nod in unison, acknowledging the logic of this instruction as only children could. They solemnly strike their matches and light the cups on fire, illuminating the dome of leaves above us with a magical glow. We watch the tiny pyres in silence, until the flames are almost out. Beside me, Dirt begins to fidget. I can feel the protest bubbling up from his throat, and am already plotting my next move, when a deep, haggard moan freezes my heart.

"What the hell was that?" hisses Cave.

"The monsters?" says Dirt, his voice quavering.

The moan sounds again, seeping from the bushes on the far side of the ring of stones. It grows louder, until we can no longer pretend that it's not coming from something very real and very much alive. I can't move. My mind howls for escape, but my feet might as well be rooted in the earth. The twins, either more brave or more cowardly, don't suffer from the same ambivalence.

"Run!" screams Cave. "Holy shit goddamn, run!"

And they do. Fast. In seconds, they are gone as if they never existed. Left alone, I stare at the bushes in terror. The moaning has stopped, but the branches begin to shake and rustle, until finally a form steps out.

It's Esther. In the shadow of evening, laughing like a little girl, she seems both older and younger than when I first met her by lantern light. "I'm sorry," she says, though her giggling belies her words. "It couldn't be helped. The looks on their faces!"

My circulatory system slowly resumes normal function. "And on mine too, I'm guessing."

"Yes," she admits. "I'm sorry, Elliot. Are you okay?"

I shrug, but I'm not really mad. I find myself laughing instead. "You're kind of strange, aren't you?"

"Only with people I like," she says, still smiling. "You were helping your friends summon a monster?"

"Make a monster. And they're not my friends. I charged them five bucks each."

She laughs. "So you're a budding entrepreneur after all."

"I guess."

She looks down at my hands. "That's a beautiful rock."

I hold up the Neverene stone. Its black facets shine dimly in the last light. "I found it right here."

"It's called anthracite," she says. "Pretty rare for this area. Is that what you use to make monsters?"

I give her a sharp look, on guard against any hint of ridicule. But there is none. Esther's steady gaze is as open and genuine as ever. "You believe in monsters?" I ask.

"Maybe," she says. "Or maybe I just don't disbelieve in them. Or maybe I believe in you and what you think, and don't consider the existence or nonexistence of monsters as relevant to the discussion."

I think I may love this woman, who somehow manages to embrace my childness while simultaneously inspiring me to grow up a little, who is the kind of person I don't want to keep secrets from. "I don't know how to make monsters," I admit, which of course is the truth. In fact, after the whole baseball fiasco, the monsters seem to have disappeared. Or maybe I'm not looking as hard. At any rate, I haven't seen them, and I certainly can't conjure them up at will. I suppose when the twins figure this out, I'll probably be in some sort of trouble.

I'm in trouble. After three days of heavy rains and deepening dread, the twins' mom finally calls. I listen to my mother apologize so many times that I wonder if she's speaking to the entire family, one by one. When she hangs up, she gives me a stern glance, then proceeds to catalog my offenses. One, I lied. Two, I took money based on that lie, which is stealing. Three, I embarrassed her, which I suspect may be the worst of my crimes.

"And you know I don't like you going into Mr. Harding's woods," she adds.

"Mr. Harding's dead," I say.

My mother stops, temporarily suspending my indictment. "I know." There is an awkward pause in which my mother softens, her maternal instincts threatening to throw the proceedings into mistrial, but her inner magistrate soon regains control. She moves to sentencing. I am to return the money. I am forbidden from ever again setting foot in Esther's woods. And I am to earn enough money through chores to pay for the damage to the twins' bicycles caused by the rain.

"That'll take years," I say.

"Oh, please," my mother huffs. "Don't be so dramatic."

"They didn't have to leave their bikes out there for three days."

"Well, they were scared, Elliot."

Damn right they were, I think. No such thing as monsters, my ass. I would find satisfaction in this, even humor, but for the bleak future to which my mother has just condemned me. Being banned from Esther's woods hurts the most. I have now lost both the map and the doorway to Neverene. I have only a key and no lock to put it in. Nevertheless I keep the dark stone with me until the inside of my pocket turns black. I even succumb to the temptation to show it to Dean. My brother took a certain amount of pride in the fact that I conned money from the twins, and my hope is that the Neverene stone will interest him. But he proves this a fool's hope.

"It's just a dirty lump of coal," he says.

"It's not coal. It's anthracite."

Dean takes the rock and turns it over in his hands. We are standing on the front steps of the house, and he bends down to scrape the stone roughly across the slate, leaving a thin black line.

"No, weirdo," he says, handing the stone back to me. "It's coal."

Whatever it's called, the rock stays in my pocket, my only ballast in what comes to feel like a desolate sea of interminable summer days. I miss Neverene, and begin eating my meals on the back porch, peering into the woods, trying in vain to glimpse the ring of stones. I pace the edge of our backyard until I finally locate a spot from which I think I can see the tree stump at the center of the ring. When rain drives me indoors, I envision building a little fort at the spot, the better to keep a vigilant eye on the gate to Neverene. With pencil and graph paper, I attempt a crude blueprint of the fort, but quickly realize I have no idea what I'm doing. All I know is that it should have a door to get in, and a window—facing the woods—to see out of. Otherwise, I'm clueless. Keeping my true purpose to myself, I nervously ask my father for help. To my surprise and relief, he agrees.

For two solid weeks, it is just the two of us—through the late afternoons after he gets home from work, from morning to dusk on the weekends. We make trips to the hardware store, teaming up to haul our building materials—cinder blocks, two-by-fours, plywood. We even buy shingles for the roof, which my father says we'll need or else the rains will destroy the whole thing in no time. Side by side, we level the ground and set the cinder blocks in the earth. The scent of sawdust fills our nostrils as we measure and cut beams of wood and bind them together, raising up first one wall and then another until my vision begins to take shape. *Our* vision, really, because I can sense my father's passion for the project, and I no longer feel alone in my quest.

Not that my father has changed his colors. Through all of our efforts, he says little to nothing—there is no sharing of heart-kept secrets or dispensing of fatherly wisdom. Yet it is time spent together, and the fellowship of a shared goal. In moments, I completely forget my original intent—the lookout on Neverene—and

instead imagine my dad and me hanging out inside the fort together. I think even Dean might want to join us—especially because, by the time the last shingle is laid, the fort is even more
impressive than I could have hoped.

"All finished?" asks my mom. It is Monday morning, and we are
back at the breakfast table.

"Came out great," says my dad from behind his newspaper.
"Elliot may have an architectural career in his future."

"The only thing left is to put in the window," I say.

"A window?" says Dean. "Why would you need a window in a
toolshed?"

"It's not a toolshed," I tell him calmly. I take no offense. I am
magnanimous, buoyed by my newfound solidarity with my dad
and my confidence in our work. "It's a fort."

"That's not what Dad called it," says Dean. "He said you guys
were building a shed to store his yard tools."

My father looks up from the paper. "Dean—"

"But that's what you said!"

My father shoots a glance in my direction. By the look on his
face, I know that Dean is telling the truth. My father fumbles at his
coffee. His mouth begins to move. He is speaking, but I'm having
trouble hearing him. He is saying something about how he only
meant that if I didn't end up using it as a fort, then he could put
some things in there.

"Why wouldn't I use it as a fort?" I finally ask. I mean, that's
what we were building, right? We were a team, right?

"I don't know," says my father. "Sometimes people imagine something one way and then realize later that the reality is different."

I want to protest. I want to tell him that the fort is exactly what I
imagined it would be. No, that it's even better. But it's clear that my
father doesn't see it that way, that by "people" he means children—
more specifically, me—and not himself. He was building a toolshed,

not a fort in which we might have played together. My own ideas now seem laughable, and I'm embarrassed by them. My imagined fellowship with my father evaporates, a cloud formation that loses its shape just as you begin to pretend it is anything other than what it is—vaporous, untouchable, incapable of bearing the weight of even a small hope.

"Look," says my father, "it's fine if you want to use it as a fort. If you want to put the window in, then we'll put the window in."

"No. Forget it." I look around the room—my father behind his newspaper, my mother rustling at the sink, Dean hunched over his cereal bowl. Everything is as normal as ever, and yet these people suddenly seem like strangers to me. Distant, cold, almost inert. My eyes—hot and wet—sink into my lap.

"I'm going to put it in." My father states this definitively, as if he's the one who decides when conversations are over, and as if—once again—that's the end of that one.

"No," I say. If you can cry without shedding tears, without allowing your body to shake, then that's what I'm doing, a molten mass inside a frozen shell. "I don't want you to."

"Okay," says my father, "but don't get all mopey, Elliot. You've got nothing to complain about and a million things to be thankful for. Nobody has time for one of your moods."

And that really is the end. Something in me is either stunned or killed outright. I'm not sure which. I stop crying, if crying is what I'd been doing. I stop talking. My breakfast is left unfinished. I spend the rest of the day on the back porch, gazing vaguely in the direction of the ring of stones, motionless until evening, when darkness doesn't so much fall as collapse in exhaustion over the earth. The stars seem impossibly far away, and I realize I don't want to be here anymore. I want to be in a world that is awake, with so much life and love in it that the people there need giant hearts to contain it all. I want to be in Neverene.

I sneak out the back and over the wall into Esther's yard. She catches me, despite the darkness. Part of me knew she would— maybe even hoped she would, though my destination is elsewhere.

"If on a summer's night a traveler—" she begins. I stop and wait for her to finish, but she doesn't. She simply sits there as before, on the back patio, within her circle of lamplight.

"What?" I ask.

"What?" she says, playfully imitating me. "Are you not still a traveler? It's a bit early for leprechauns."

Yes, I think to myself. I am a traveler. "I'm going to Neverene."

"Is that your really cool place?"

I nod. "Do you think that's weird?"

She frowns slightly, as if this is a silly question. "I think if you find a place where you feel alive, you should spend as much time there as you can."

"What if that place is just a dream?"

"One way or another everything is a dream."

"Not to my parents."

"It's harder for grown-ups," says Esther. "But even the most practical of us believe in magic, whether we want to admit it or not. Do your parents ever knock on wood?"

I frown, unable to remember, and not bothering to try. "I lost the book. My mother took it away."

"I'm sorry," says Esther. "I see you still have the anthracite."

I look down. In my hand is the Neverene stone, though I don't remember taking it out. I shove it back into my pocket. "It's just a piece of coal."

She laughs lightly. "Anthracite *is* coal," she says. "What you call it is up to you. The names aren't true. What's true is the thing itself—and the fact that you see things one way, and other people see things in other ways."

"Or not at all."

Esther considers me for a moment, smiling as if she's spotted someone she recognizes. "When I was little, my grandmother would never let me hug her. She didn't like to be touched in that way. But she loved giving me foot rubs. She'd peel off my socks, plop my feet on her lap, and go to work. They tickled at first, but I came to love them, even if I never stopped wishing she would give me a hug."

"Why wouldn't she?"

Esther shrugs. "If you're lucky, people will love you in the way they know how. And if you're really lucky, the love they can give will be the love you need."

"What if it isn't?"

"Then I guess you'll have to settle for just being lucky."

These seem like good thoughts, and I'm sure there is wisdom in them, but they don't touch me. I am deep within the well now, and the words pass over like distant birds in a halo of irretrievable sky. I don't even reach for them. I think only of getting away. To Neverene. Time and mind being what they are, I cannot know that this is the last I will ever see of Esther. If I could, maybe it would be different. Maybe it wouldn't.

I thank her, do my best to return her smile, and continue on toward the ring of stones. A gibbous moon sheds just enough light for me to find my way through the woods, until I'm kneeling in the dirt beside the old tree stump. I take out the black rock and rap it against the hard face of the stump, willing the stump to turn into a door and for that door to open. When there is no response, I grow fearful that I'll never know the way to Neverene, and desperate enough to hazard a final guess.

The crickets are caroling madly as I climb the beech tree and scramble out to the end of the long limb from where the twins released their potions. I stare down at the undergrowth until I can just make out the stump. Then I rise to my feet, balance for one precarious second, and jump. The fall is long and dark and heavy.

As I strike the ground, I hear a loud, unnatural crack. In the last moment before the world fades, I allow myself to believe that it's the sound of the earth, splitting open to reveal the passage out.

I was wrong. If the doors between worlds make a noise when they open, I'm not aware of it. The crack I heard was the sound of my leg breaking—more specifically, the multiple fracture of my right tibia. It's unclear whether it was the impact of the fall or the pain of the break that caused me to black out. Either way, I was still unconscious when my parents found me. The first doctor I saw after the incident was a surgeon in the emergency room later that night. He set the broken bone and encased my leg in plaster, but could do nothing for the constriction of my chest or the darkness at the corners of my vision, dismissing me with a pair of crutches.

The second doctor now sits before my mother and me—or, rather, we sit before him. His office is both more casual and more insidious than the emergency room. More casual in its wood paneling and plush sofa and the doctor's own attire of polo shirt and khakis. More insidious because, unlike at the emergency room, I don't know why I'm here, except that my mother thought I should "talk" to someone, and that my father shouldn't know about it. I am too defeated to point out the irony in this.

Yet the doctor's smile feels genuine, his voice calm and light, so much so that when he asks me to tell him about Neverene, I oblige, describing it as best I can. I even take the anthracite from my pocket and show it to him. When the tightness in my chest makes me short of breath, he waits patiently. And when I finally finish, he nods deeply, as if he understands.

"And the monsters?" he asks.

I hesitate, glancing at my mother, but she motions for me to continue. I describe the shade, and the fat burglar and the others. None of this seems to faze the doctor. He goes on, asking about my family, and school, and friends. I talk about Dean and leaf-catching and baseball and the twins.

"Do you ever feel like you're vanishing?" he asks. "Disappearing?"

I suppose this would seem like a strange question if the answer was no. But I remember losing myself in the thunderstorm, and melting into the rhythm of pitching practice. I think of how the world faded away when I opened the book about Neverene.

"Yes," I respond.

"Do you sometimes wish you were somewhere else?"

"I guess."

"Do you want to go to Neverene?" He poses the question casually, generously, as if extending an invitation I'd been longing to receive. I see no reason to decline.

"Yes."

The doctor nods again. He pauses, letting my answer linger for a moment before continuing. "Elliot," he says, "you understand that Neverene isn't real."

His words fall flat and heavy, no longer an invitation but a proclamation, a decree calling for only one acceptable response. The room turns, tightening the vice around my chest. The innocence and ease of the doctor's questions now seem like tools of treachery along a subtle path of interrogation. I feel as if he's lured me into a trap. If I agree with him, I destroy Neverene and the monsters. I banish the spirit in the thunderstorms, kill the giant with the giant heart. If I disagree, I will be outcast—cut off from my parents, my brother, even Esther. I feel like I'm being asked to build a wall where no wall needs to be. Unwilling or unable to answer, I fall silent.

I am relegated to the waiting room while my mother stays behind to speak with the doctor. I can hear their hushed voices—my mother's anxious and hurried, the doctor's still calm but now ominous. The muffled syllables float in from his office, passing through like bubbles—unintelligible, and not meant for me.

In the car, my mother struggles to collect herself. She seems scared. My better judgment tells me to leave her alone, but my anger and confusion win out.

"What did he say?" I ask.

"Nothing," says my mother.

"I don't understand why we had to go there," I say.

"Because it's time for you to stop with all these fantasy worlds."

I would ask why, but I've come to the conclusion that she doesn't really have a reason. "But if you take those other worlds away, I'll be left with just this one."

"Good," says my mother. "It's the only real one."

"You don't know that."

"Excuse me?" Her voice grows sharp, but I ignore it. As if looking for support, I take the Neverene stone from my pocket.

"You don't know," I say.

"Give me that." She holds out her hand. I hesitate. "Now!" she yells. I place the stone in her hand. She rolls down her window and throws it into the street. I fight back a howl.

"Why did you do that?" I yell. "Now I'll never—"

"Never what?" she demands.

"It's real!" I say. My throat thickens until I feel like I'm choking. "All of it! The monsters, Neverene. Even Esther says so. She said if I want to go to Neverene, then I should go."

"Esther? The neighbor?" My mother's knuckles whiten on the steering wheel. "Since when is some lonely old divorcée qualified to give advice to other people's children? You are never to speak to her again. Do you hear me? Never."

I am lost. My breath comes in a clipped staccato of weak gasps. I don't know what else they can take away from me, and I can't understand how it came to this. "I want to know what the doctor said."

"Nothing. He doesn't know what he's talking about."

"Why can't you just tell me what he said? Why can't you just tell me one thing?"

My mother reaches the end of her restraint. "He said you don't really want to go to some fantasyland," she says. Her eyes fill with tears. "He said you want to kill yourself."

PART II

We will now discuss in a little more detail the Struggle for Existence.

—Charles Darwin, *On the Origin of Species*

Before

"That's a terrible idea," says Jollis.

"There's nothing else for it," says Merriam. She is tidying up the room in preparation for her departure—sweeping up stray bits of cloud, packing away the bottles of emotions, all now empty save the last.

Jollis looks at the bare table at the center of the room. "What about the prototype? What if we stuff some—"

"It's too late," says Merriam. "Each traveler's empty space is unique. Only the travelers themselves will know what they need to fill it."

"Merry, you can't just waltz down there and start granting wishes."

Merriam brightens a bit. "That's it, Jollis. That's what we'll call it. The granting of wishes." She appraises the room, nods in satisfaction, and moves to the window. She pulls back the curtain. The distant Earth shimmers in the frame.

"You can kiss that promotion goodbye," says Jollis.

Merriam looks back at him. "I suppose you're right." She shrugs, then rises to the windowsill. "There's nothing for that, either."

"Or worse," cautions Jollis. "The brass won't stand for it." Though the brass are neither short-tempered nor unreasonable, when they get angry you know about it, and Jollis has a feeling this would make them angry.

Merriam pauses. "You're right," she says. "I'll need a disguise."

———

The genies are Merriam's idea, as are the fairies (godmother, tooth, or otherwise), and the spirits of water and forest and sky. In truth, all of the disguises are Merriam's idea. Jollis admires her virtuosity. His favorites are the leprechauns. He likes that they must be captured before they will grant a wish. Make the travelers work for it a little. Plus, Jollis looks good in green.

Jollis goes with her, of course. He cannot let Merriam venture down there alone, even if her plan is beyond ill-advised, and even if she is the one who put the empty space there in the first place. The two of them don their guises and ramble the globe, moving nimbly and changing often to hide from the brass. They reside in lamps, or under bridges, or in the bark of trees or the banks of rivers. From mountaintop to dell, jungle to desert sand, from bygone hamlet to modern metropolis, Merriam and Jollis hear the wishes of humankind and make them come true. And it works! Merriam was right. Whether hopeful or desperate, people come to them longing— for something or somehow or some way—and depart fulfilled and happy. With every human smile of gratitude, or cry for joy, or sigh of relief, Merriam shines. Jollis is glad they came.

Though, once within the bounds of time, Merriam and Jollis realize they don't have enough of it. The sea of wishful humans seems endless—Caleb wants a bountiful harvest, Anahera a child, Jack a new car. Demand becomes so great that Merriam and Jollis devise other means of wish fulfillment, ones not requiring their presence. Travelers wish on shooting stars, on coins tossed into fountains. They pluck four-leaf clovers, fling fallen eyelashes, blow out the candles on their birthday cakes.

Other complications arise. While many wishes are simple enough (most people simply ask for treasure in one form or another), others are vague or difficult to interpret. Katarina wants to be "beautiful." Takeshi wants "revenge." Still others are diametrically opposed to one another. If Obasi wishes to win the love of Babatunde's wife, chances are Babatunde will wish to win it back. Even when they think they understand, Merriam and Jollis sometimes just get it wrong, or fail to anticipate the undesired repercussions of a wish fulfilled, leading a small collection of naysayers to disparage the whole process. "Be careful what you wish for," they say. "You might get it." Though this backlash upsets Merriam, it is no more than a faint eddy in a mighty river. The vast majority of travelers are enthralled by the granting of wishes, and Merriam and Jollis carry on, managing the challenges as they come.

Until the addiction begins. Jollis is surprised when the first recidivist returns to them—a lovely woman who asked for beauty in her youth and got it. How elated she had been! Yet here she was, back again, with yet another wish. Discouraged but undaunted, Merriam grants it, and the woman departs, once more euphoric. Again and again, travelers whose wishes have been granted come back for more, until there seems no end to it—a second wish leads to a third, and a fourth, and so on. The time between fixes varies. Depending on the wish, and even more on the supplicant and the size of the empty space, a wish fulfilled will gratify different people for different lengths of time—anywhere from forty minutes to forty years, but rarely for a lifetime. Jollis begins to fear that no traveler will ever be sated, that it is not just the sea of wishful humans that is endless, but human craving itself.

Merriam refuses to surrender. For her sake, Jollis perseveres, though they struggle to keep ahead of the swelling tide. The genies start granting three wishes at a time, as do the leprechauns (when they're caught, that is—Jollis refuses to waive that requirement). The tooth fairies begin to fulfill wishes on *every* lost tooth, not just the first. Yet people keep coming back. "Wish junkies," Merriam calls them affectionately, though her glow recedes as her mission takes its toll.

The final straw is Wilfred. The worst of the wishful recidivists,

Wilfred in his lifetime has encountered three leprechauns, six genies, and no fewer than twenty-seven fairies. He has tossed a hundred coins into a hundred fountains, stumbled upon eleven four-leaf
clovers, and wished upon countless stars—shooting or not. Wilfred
has to be the luckiest person in the history of people, with the most
charmed of all charmed lives. Yet when he finds his way back to
Merriam and Jollis, he is perfectly miserable, as despondent and
wretched a traveler as ever walked the earth.

"What is it?" Merriam asks him. "What do you wish for?"

"I don't know," says Wilfred, staring at her with hollow eyes.

Merriam's shine dims even further. No traveler has ever failed
to wish for something (other than a few naysayers who refuse on
principle, though even they usually cave). She looks to Jollis with a
hopeless air, as if Wilfred's despair is contagious.

"Just state your wish, traveler," Jollis says to him.

"I can't," says Wilfred. He sits down on the ground and stares at
his palms in bewilderment. "I've gotten everything I ever wanted,"
he says, "yet there's still this hole in my heart that I fear will never
go away."

Jollis falls silent, the truth suddenly clear—the travelers don't
know how to fill the empty space. They've no more idea than Jollis
himself. Merriam was wrong. And by the look on her face, she
knows it.

"It's not a hole," she says, but her words are a ragged whisper,
and her light is nearly extinguished. She slumps so low that Jollis
fears she will sink into the earth forever.

"That's right," Jollis says to Wilfred, raising his voice to make sure
Merriam can hear him. "It's not a hole at all. It's an empty space."

Merriam stirs. She looks at Jollis gratefully.

"Isn't that the same thing?" asks Wilfred.

"Not even close!" roars Jollis. Merriam manages a weak smile.
"And it's not in your heart," Jollis continues. "It's nestled in *beside

your heart—quite artfully, I might add. Your heart is perfect. Nothing wrong with it whatsoever. And your spleen, by the way, is spectacular."

"But it feels—"

"Yes, yes, I know," says Jollis. He takes hold of Merriam, dismayed by how insubstantial she has become, how faded by her labors. He pulls her close and draws her away. The earth grows distant, until its edges appear and it is once again a shining orb in the starry darkness. From here, Wilfred is no more than a speck on the thin surface of the world, yet Jollis has not lost sight of him.

"We're really very sorry," Jollis cries. "Just do your best."

Elliot

It is a damp, drizzly November in New York City. A dense mist doesn't so much fall as hover, thickening the cold air and deepening the evening gloom. On the lower east side of Manhattan, an old building crouches at the edge of the East River. Its windows are shadowy blanks, save for one illuminated square near the door. I stand between them—the building and the river—facing the light but heeding the dark tide at my back. I am twenty-two years old. I am thinking about that doctor.

He tricked me, of course. With honeyed tongue, he led me seductively down one path—where my world was important, worthy of belief—before pulling the rug out to reveal another, where there was a bright line of truth, and I was on the wrong side of it. Fine. Maybe that's what my mother paid him for. The betrayal stung, but what unnerved me was how easily I had been taken in. The doctor's questions had been so pointed, so personal, like he was inside my head. I mean, who asks if you feel like you're vanishing? Is that a standard psychiatric inquiry? Or did he know something I didn't? One might almost suspect that he really could see into my mind, and that he saw something he recognized, which would naturally lead one to wonder whether his diagnosis was correct.

Except that, when you are a ten-year-old boy with an imagination so fertile you believe a monster saved your mother from drowning in the Atlantic Ocean, and when that same mother brings you to a professional psychologist who declares that you want to take your own life, the first thing you do with that information—if you are a Chance—is bury it. Deep. Under an ocean of denial. Then you leave it there, letting the years roll over it, until it is all but lost.

In the process, other things get submerged. I stopped walking in the woods. The ring of stones was forgotten. I gave up the idea of ever asking my mother for the book about Neverene, ultimately surmising that it no longer existed, and wondering at times if it ever had. Even Esther moved away. Somehow this surprised me. She had seemed at home there, in her uncle's old house. I thought she genuinely enjoyed those summer nights on the back patio, watching the fireflies—even, maybe, talking to me. Not wanting to forget her along with everything else, I took paper and pencil and made a crude attempt at drawing her face, but her features had already faded into abstraction. Maybe I had imagined Esther, too.

When the weighty parts of your life are jettisoned, you either soar or drift, depending on your metaphor. I drifted. Middle school passed vaguely by. High school began in much the same way, though neither period was technically devoid of incident. Life has a way of occupying the days, if you let it. There were classes and homework. There were sports—after my ill-fated baseball career, I focused on tennis, eventually making varsity. There were blundering sexual encounters, halting half romances, and other milestones of adolescence. But mostly there were the Shipmates.

The four of us—Roberta, Josh, Christopher, and I—were assigned to be a study group by our English teacher in our sophomore year. And though our first mandated journey together was an aquatic one—wading through nineteenth-century prose in pursuit of a white giant under the Atlantic—that is not why I thought of us as shipmates. Rather, as we spent more and more time together, as the *I* slowly disappeared into the *we*, it occurred to me that maybe my new companions had also been caught in the drift, and that the four of us had come together to form something greater than each—a ship that could more ably navigate the eddies and cross-currents of life.

Which is not to say that we were all hewn from the same wood. Roberta was a member of the cross-country team, Christopher a budding artist, and Josh an avid computer programmer at a time when few of us even knew what that meant, while I myself was most likely to be found with my nose buried in a book. Yet the gravity of these pursuits fell away when we were together. From our earliest study sessions, a collective banter regularly bubbled up between us. Together we were jovial, irreverent, silly. Buoyant, even.

In other words, we laughed a lot. We poked fun at everything, especially each other, which is probably why we never talked about anything of real significance. To raise a deeply held fear or confidence—say, that one had once harbored a belief in monsters, and perhaps still did a little—would have been to offer oneself in sacrifice at the altar of our collective sarcasm. No, we stuck to lighter affairs. Roberta teased the rest of us for acting like boys, and we did our best to tease her back, though she had superior ammunition, and we were more interested in convincing her to reveal the secrets of her gender, no matter how many times she insisted there weren't any. With slightly more sincerity, we vetted each other's love interests, though in truth there weren't many of these, and they tended to be short-lived. We preferred spending time with just us, and mocked whatever romantic comedy was currently in the theaters, even if we went to see it anyway, and even if we privately hoped something similar would one day happen to each of us. But not yet. Later. When we were older.

The days when we *would* be older—our futures—were also not something we talked about. I never shared my dream of becoming an advisor to entrepreneurs. As far as I could tell, Roberta aspired to be a professional runner, which seemed like a risky career choice, and Christopher wanted to be a sculptor, which was perhaps even more preposterous. Josh had no plans, and didn't want any. He decided he'd rather not grow up at all, or at least not any more than he already had, and the rest of us wondered if maybe he had the right idea—so much so that when it finally came time to apply for colleges, we resisted.

"Why would I want to go to college?" Josh would ask. And—because there was no adult in the room to answer him, no one to declare that a higher education was not only the gateway to a more prosperous life but a rewarding experience in and of itself, not to mention a privilege that some of our parents, mine included, never had—the rest of us asked ourselves the same thing.

"Yes, why?" we said. "Why shouldn't we stay here?"

Spoken aloud, the proposal aroused our indignation. "Are we not happy?" we asked. "Are we not home? We will get jobs. We will rent apartments. We will be locals and put down roots and be together forever. Yes, why shouldn't we stay?"

There was a pause. Someone mentioned money. Someone else, the expectations of family members. Neither was a categorical reply, nor an absolute reason why things had to be the way they were. Nevertheless, we did not stay. As applications were completed and offers of admittance accepted, I realized I had been wrong. We had not created something greater than ourselves. There wasn't much binding us together at all—we were less a ship than four corks bobbing down the same stream, if near to one another for a time. We would each face the ocean of the world alone.

The laughter faded. Bags were packed. One by one we succumbed to the momentum of our separate currents. Goodbye, and goodbye, and goodbye.

And the *we* once again became *I*.

The mist grows heavier, bearing down as if trying to sink Manhattan into the sea. A single drop falls, then another. The rain begins to fall in earnest, beating a solemn rhythm on the concrete. The suit my mother bought me is drenched. I can almost feel it shrinking, and it was too small to begin with—she hasn't fully accepted the fact that I finally sprouted to six feet tall and am no longer small for my age. If that's even a thing, once you're in your twenties.

In the growing downpour, the building's lone lighted window seems to contract, and I fear it may wink out entirely, before it comes to life with movement from within. Bodies circulate, chairs are arranged into a circle. Strange faces greet each other with restrained benevolence. Most are dour, but not all. One of them even laughs—not a polite titter but an honest, full-throated guffaw—which I find curious, given that this is a support group for potential suicides.

Though there was no laughter when the Shipmates disbanded, there wasn't any ranting, either—nor any struggle, really. We vowed to stay in touch, but didn't. During our freshman year, a few early letters and phone calls rippled weakly across the distance between us, then dissipated entirely. Christopher spent the following summer in California, where his parents had moved. Roberta stayed on campus in Colorado. Back at home, I saw Josh once or twice, but it wasn't the same. The two of us alone weren't able to achieve the same banter, and couldn't seem to find much else to cling to.

I lapsed back into the drift. In college I stuck to the customary script—drank a little too much, stayed up a little too late. I became a half-hearted member of the junior varsity tennis team. After flirting with literature, I decided to major in economics, primarily because my father thought I should, but also because I hoped it might someday help me start my advisory firm.

For this reason, too, I strived to keep my grades up, passing untold nights hunched over the desk in my dorm room, or in an empty classroom, perched in the most uncomfortable seat I could find so that I'd be less likely to drowse. More often than not, however, I could be found burrowed in the stacks—those deep corners of the library where row after row of books ascended to the ceiling—because that was where Amy liked to study.

Amy and I had been in two classes together—or one and a half, before I abandoned literature by dropping a course on Romantic-era poetry. Both had been in large halls with space enough, and students enough, that Amy and I never bumped into each other. I had been content to admire her from a distance, or at least what I could discern of her—an easy laugh, an electric smile, the kind of beauty that, well, that could inspire you to write poetry. If you were a Romantic.

Until I later noticed her studying in the stacks, my lingering image of Amy was of her staring at me intently as I recited my first (and last) poem. But then I had felt like everyone was staring at me, which I guess they probably were, given that it was my turn at the podium. I was nervous, having been blindsided by the assignment from the beginning—the course description had promised we would be *reading* poetry, not writing it, but our professor insisted that we would never understand the verses of others until we composed one of our own.

I wrote a sonnet. About avalanches. I don't know why, except that I had never seen one, and was fascinated by the thought of all that snow—one moment resting on a mountain, pristine and still, and the next moment plunging downward at two hundred miles an hour with the mass of the Empire State Building. I imagined how awesome it would be to stand in its path and witness the snowpack hurtling toward you. At least until it killed you. Which it would. People generally don't like that sort of thing. One way they prevent big, devastating avalanches is to intentionally set off little ones, by dropping explosives in just the right spots.

"Hi." After weeks of mentally circling Amy's favorite desk, I had finally stopped to speak to her.

"Hi yourself," she said, looking up at me, smiling. "You dropped poetry."

"You noticed," I said, surprised.

She leaned back and brushed her hair from her forehead, her eyes staying on me. It was as if my lingering image of her had come to life. "You hit us with that love poem and then disappeared," she said. "It was very dramatic."

"Love poem?" I assumed she had misremembered. "It was about avalanches."

She arched an eyebrow and looked at me keenly. "If you say so."

I realized she hadn't misremembered a thing, and that there was more to her than a showstopping smile. There was kindness, and wit, and subtlety. That smile, too, though. I suddenly felt unnaturally light, almost weightless.

"Anyway," I said, "it was awful."

"I didn't think so," she said. "It was raw—like you opened your chest and offered up your heart."

"That doesn't sound good at all."

"No, it was attractive," said Amy. "It made me wonder what it would be like to date you."

"Oh." I checked myself, wanting to make sure I'd heard her correctly. "In that case, I'd like to revise my position on the quality of my poem."

The fall was swift. Amy and I became inseparable, consumed with each other—or with whatever it was that filled the narrow fragment of space we suffered between us. She wrote me songs and read me poetry. I made her mixtapes and prepared candlelight dinners using the hot plate in my dorm room. We spent countless hours in bed. When she went home for winter break, I sent her a letter every day. The night she came back, I stood in the snow and threw pebbles at her window—heedless of the punishingly cold winter air—until she appeared at the glass, her smile floating there for just an instant before the pane fogged over with her breath. In the stillness afterward, while I waited for her to come down and open the door, I stared up at the radiant stars and felt that I was one of them. And if it occurred to me that I had become a character in one of those romantic comedies I used to make fun of in high school, I didn't care.

I even brought Amy home to meet my parents. I'm not sure why, exactly. Maybe I just thought it had to happen sooner or later. Or maybe I wanted to share with them the feelings Amy and I had for each other, even if the visit amounted to nothing more than shallow pleasantries. Maybe love makes you more generous. I didn't even mind that Dean showed up, though I hadn't expected him. He was living in New York, having moved there after college to work as a sales executive for an accounting firm. He and Amy had little in common, but they got along well enough. It wasn't until Dean and I were left alone for a moment that he reverted to form.

"She's hot," he said to me. "You bang her yet?"

I punched him in the stomach so hard that he crumpled to the floor. To his credit, he didn't make a fuss, just silently caught his breath and picked himself up before Amy and my parents rejoined us. We haven't mentioned it since, though my reaction clearly surprised us both—neither of us had ever hit the other. I guess love makes you more protective, too.

More everything, really. Stronger, braver, free of imprisonment by the self if not imprisonment by the other—because you

are now for her and she is for you—invincible, unburdened, at-
tuned to a world that keeps expanding not just because you now
see it through two sets of eyes but because you appreciate details
to which you had been blind—the divine intricacy of the hand as
she plays the guitar, the steadfast miracle of the heart, which beats
on even after she falls asleep beside you—until the universe is no
longer an absurd heap of colored spots flecked across a canvas but a
Pointillist masterpiece revealing a whole and graspable truth, made
meaningful—made possible at all—by the fact that someone else
is standing with you, experiencing it exactly as you are, feeling all
the things you feel.

Until she's not.

"It's been magical, Elliot." We stood outside Amy's dorm while
she waited for a taxi to the airport. It was the week after graduation. College was over. Apparently, so were we.

"Then why end it?" We'd already been through this, of course,
but I asked again anyway.

"It just feels like it's time for . . . real life."

"This *is* real life," I said, but I didn't sound convinced, not even
to myself.

Amy plucked at my sleeve. "Oh, Elliot," she said. "This hasn't
been real life at all. That's why it was so wonderful. It's like a dream
we shared. Our little college fantasy."

A searing pain tore through my chest. I didn't know which was
worse—Amy labeling our love a fantasy, or the little voice in my
head telling me she was right, that life is not made up of love songs
and poetry and candlelight, that romance doesn't make you invincible, that human beings weren't meant to be stars.

The taxi arrived. Amy hugged me goodbye, kissed me, and
hugged me again. Then she was gone. And while I can't prove that
the universe was altered in any other way, it seemed to me that it

disintegrated back into an incoherent swarm of colored spots, and that the gaps between the spots were wider than before.

There is not a breath of wind. The rain pummels New York with an intensity bordering on violence, stabbing at my skin until it feels like my thin gray suit has been flayed from my body and I now stand naked—too exposed, certainly, to go inside and join a circle of strange faces. The people in the window begin to take their seats in the circle, but the dark river at my back feels more familiar, safer. I shift my weight to ease the pressure on my right leg. Years later, and it still sometimes aches where it was fractured. It's the rain, I tell myself, though my leg doesn't always ache in the rain, and I know it's more about my own inner weather.

How many times can a heart break before it's, well, broken? If losing the Shipmates was strike one, and losing Amy was strike two, I guess unemployment and moving back in with my parents . . . but I quit baseball years ago. I don't know how many strikes you get in life. Maybe there is no limit. Maybe you just stop swinging.

I don't talk to my family about my heartache, but rather allow them to focus on my lack of gainful employment, which is something they can appreciate as a cause of my melancholy—or "funk," as my mother calls it. Turns out that colleges do not, in fact, hand out prosperous livelihoods at graduation. The economy is weak and prospects are slim, diploma or no. I briefly considered starting up the advisory business I'd been dreaming about. My family wasn't exactly supportive—my father told me I didn't know anything yet, Dean offered me an entry-level position at his accounting firm, and my mother bought me a suit for job interviews.

On weekdays, I don the suit and take the train into New York. I tell my mother I have interviews, though typically I just walk through Central Park until evening, before boarding the train back home. This afternoon I sat and stared at the Alice in Wonderland statue, thinking I would like to join her among the bronze mushrooms, when I noticed a flyer stuck to the side of the Mad Hatter's top hat. It was an invitation to a suicide prevention therapy group, the one now gathering before me inside the lighted window.

I don't think I can accept. Behind me, the river's whispered appeal grows deeper, more seductive. I suspect that if I turn to meet it now, the faces in the window may be lost to me. I turn anyway.

As I do, a yellow taxicab sweeps into the drive, its tires hissing over the sodden asphalt. The beams from its headlights cut across my knees before it lurches to a stop and the rear door pops open. A young woman in a blue suit leaps out into the rain, shielding her head with a large notebook. She slams the door behind her and rushes toward the building, her shoes clicking on the pavement. When she draws even with me, she abruptly stops, pausing to consider me from beneath her makeshift canopy.

"Something wrong with your umbrella?" she asks.

I look down at my hand, still clenched around my unopened umbrella. I'd forgotten I was holding one.

She almost smiles, her dark eyes gleaming with some combination of perplexity and amusement. She lowers the notebook. The rain quickly soaks her suit and flattens her short black hair. For a moment she just stands there, getting wet and almost smiling.

"Right," she says, her eyes flashing toward the lighted window. "Let's do this."

Elliot

(1993)

I like to think the room was meant for music. The bare walls and ceramic-tiled floor seem built for reverberation, though now the only sounds are the shuffling of feet and the thrumming of the rain. Stacked nimbly along one wall are straight-backed metal chairs that look ready to line up into rows—or, in our case, a circle. Recessed spotlights cast bright beams down from the ceiling, but there are no music stands beneath them. Perhaps the musicians have no need for sheets full of notes. Perhaps they know their songs by heart.

There are twelve of us in the circle—a ragtag bunch of all sizes, ages, colors, and shapes. Unlike my imaginary ensemble of virtuosos, we are more silence than song, and could probably use a little sheet music. We carry no instruments but our confusion and sorrow and fear—and the rituals we perform to avoid the stillness in which they're inclined to play. A teenage boy cracks his knuckles. A wizened woman cleans her glasses with a handkerchief. The girl with dark eyes runs her hands through her wet hair.

Our conductor is the last to arrive. He is a tall, lanky man with red hair and a face full of freckles that proceed to make way for his broad grin.

"Hello, everyone," he calls out from the doorway. "Wow, it's bright in here." His hand brushes over a bank of light switches, and the room falls into an ominous gloaming. Deftly lifting a chair from one of the stacks, he swings it into the circle, then takes his seat and looks us over.

"New faces," he says eagerly. "For those—three—of you who haven't been with us before . . . welcome to group." I cringe a bit at the word *group*. Or at least the way he uses it, like he's informing us that we've caught some form of communicable disease, as in "Welcome to chlamydia." But no one else seems to mind.

"I'm Gareth," he continues. "While I'm technically your leader, we like to keep things informal. Tonight I'd like to invite our newcomers to tell us a little about themselves. You can tell us where you're from, or why you're here, or anything at all that you feel like sharing. First, though, let me just say that I'm not a doctor, and we don't prescribe medication—either one of which you may or may not find helpful in this battle you're fighting. What I think you'll find here is a gathering of people like you, and not like you, who are ready to listen, and who are grateful that you're here." He looks around the circle. "Okay, who's first?"

I stare at the floor, wishing myself invisible. I'm still not convinced I want to be here, and I'm certain I don't want to be the first of the newbies to spill his guts in front of a bunch of strangers. There is a short, pregnant pause before someone else finally volunteers. His voice is rich and resonant. I immediately recognize it as the source of the incongruous guffaw I heard from outside.

"Good evening," he says politely. "My name's Bannor. I suppose the first thing I'd like to tell you is that I've been to the future."

I lift my head to look at him—a middle-aged black man with steeply arched eyebrows and deep creases in his forehead that give him a bemused air. His beard and mustache are black but for a silver band along his jawline. His hair, too, is silver, and so closely cropped that you can just see his scalp. He wears a tweed suit and vest, with a burgundy tie that matches his shoes. Resting on his lap is a brown homburg hat, with a band of even darker brown. The single crease of its gutter crown seems to have deepened with age.

Bannor's formal bearing and dapper attire seem more relics of the past than testaments to the future, yet from the ensuing silence and the looks on everyone's faces, I can see that I've heard him correctly.

"You mean you feel like you've seen your future?" asks Gareth. "It can seem that way sometimes. When we lose hope, we can lose our sense of the possible, and we get fooled into thinking that there's only one path forward."

Bannor nods. "I don't doubt the truth in that," he says. "But, no, I mean to say that I've traveled to the future. Not my body, you understand—that would be ludicrous. But my mind, my consciousness."

There is a long pause during which I'm certain each of us is sizing Bannor up, trying to determine if his particular brand of crazy is the dangerous kind. Yet, in addition to being courteous, he appears calm and lucid. It's hard not to take an instant liking to him.

"Wicked," says the knuckle-cracking teenager. "What year did you travel to?"

"The first time, 2162."

"You've been more than once?"

"Eleven times," says Bannor. "So far."

"What's it like?" asks the teenager.

"The future?" says Bannor, shrugging. "It's a mixed bag."

The teenager's mouth hangs open, but he appears out of questions. The room falls into a hush, broken only by the patter of the rain. The group seems unsure what to do with Bannor's revelation. Gareth himself appears befuddled, his composure as group leader shaken. I guess the suicide therapy handbook doesn't cover reports of time travel.

"So why are you here?" asks the girl with dark eyes.

Bannor chuckles, a deep sound from his chest that gently fills the room. "Cut to the chase, and no mistake," he says. "As it happens, during one of my sojourns, I learned that I end up killing myself."

Gareth nods, almost too earnestly, his balance apparently restored by the fact that the discussion has returned to the topic of suicide. I half expect him to exclaim "Aha!" and shrewdly tap his fingers together, but he only looks at Bannor with compassion. "Would you like to talk about that?" he asks.

Bannor's forehead crinkles a little more deeply, and then relaxes. "No," he says, abruptly ending his narration. "Thank you."

"Of course," says Gareth. Clearly more accustomed to reticence, he doesn't push Bannor further, but instead scans the circle for a new secret sharer. "Who would like to go next?"

Before he can focus on me, another hand is raised. It belongs to the elderly woman with the glasses, which have now been thoroughly polished and perch on the bridge of her nose. The thick lenses and wide, circular frames make her eyes seem a bit too large for her face, like those of an owl. Her birdlike semblance is enhanced by her delicate frame and a colorful scarf that enshrouds her neck like plumage.

"I'm Pearl," she says. "I haven't been to the future, though I'm afraid I can't seem to get out of the past." She attempts a smile. "It was wonderful, my past. Just wonderful. Oh, I know it wasn't perfect, but I guess I miss it. My husband died in June. We'd been married forty-nine years. Can you imagine? I can." Her eyes drift past the faces in the circle, toward the benighted windows and the rain beyond. "It's *this* world that doesn't seem real now. This world without him . . ."

She trails off, eyes glazing over. Her hands rest uneasily in her lap, worrying at her handkerchief. Gareth nods, but doesn't try to fill the silence, as if he knows that she has more to say.

"I have this dream," says Pearl. "Not a goal. I mean an actual dream, at night, when I'm sleeping. I have it all the time now. I'm walking by a river, and I come upon all these moments from my life, glistening memories hanging from the trees or just lying in the grass. There are so many—big ones, like our wedding day, and stupid little ones, like the way the floorboards squeaked in our first apartment when we danced to the radio. I walk along and gather them up, one by one, filling up the pockets of my long coat. Then the river rises, and I'm in the water. When I look down, the memories have all turned into stones. They are so heavy. My pockets are full of them . . ."

Her gaze breaks away from the windows and she blinks at us, as if she'd forgotten we were there. She takes off her glasses and begins cleaning them again with her handkerchief. "My, but I can't seem to shut up about it," she says. "Please, let the next person go."

"There's no rush," says Gareth. "Do you want to continue?"

"Oh, no," says Pearl. "For goodness' sake."

Gareth smiles kindly at her. He's still smiling when he finally turns to me. The others follow his lead, their faces swiveling in my direction.

I introduce myself. Unlike in my clichéd imagining of a group therapy session, there is no responding chorus of "Hello, Elliot!" A few heads nod. Bannor squints at me strangely. I hesitate, suddenly feeling like a fraud. What can I say to justify my presence? To convince the others that I have any right to be here? I'm not crazy, like Bannor. Nor has the love of my life for the past fifty years just died, as for Pearl. I'm not sick or starving or destitute (yet). My life is fine. Isn't it? I don't know how to explain this ache in my chest, or why tears come to my eyes out of nowhere, or why I find myself involuntarily drawing a little too close to the edges of subway platforms.

"I'm not sure I have a good reason . . ."

"Reason's got nothing to do with it," says the girl with dark eyes.

I might disagree, but I don't feel I'm in a position to argue. I clear my throat, stalling for time, unsure how to begin.

"I guess it started with the monsters," I finally say.

I brace for laughter, or jeers, or the rolling of eyes, but the group doesn't blink. Maybe their stillness unnerves me, or maybe my initial confession provokes in me the need for more. Regardless, once my mouth starts moving, it doesn't want to stop. The words pour out in a breathless rush—secrets I haven't shared with anyone since my unhappy session with that doctor years ago. I tell the group about the monsters, and my mother nearly drowning, and the pitchback, and striking out my brother. I speak of Neverene and the giant with the giant heart. Of the shed that was meant to be a fort. Of Esther and the anthracite and the twins. Of breaking my leg by jumping from a high branch onto a tree stump I hoped was a door. Of the Shipmates, and friendships so fleeting you question whether they existed at all. And of Amy, and love that wasn't so much love as the idea of love, which makes you question that too.

And all the while, as my oration threatens to degenerate into babble, a smaller voice in my head asks why I'm still talking. When this voice grows loud enough, I stop. My mouth shuts. My senses return. I hear the quiet drip of water. I see the room and the shimmering circle of faces.

Gareth waits a breath to make sure I'm done. "Thank you, Elliot," he says. "And Pearl, and Bannor." He leans forward to rest his elbows on his knees. "What wonderful introductions! We'll talk more, about all of this. For now I'd just like to say that a common theme I'm hearing tonight is one of submission. And I want to remind all of us that we have choices. For example, Bannor can choose not to travel to the future, but to stay here instead, in the present. Pearl can choose to turn her memories not into rocks that weigh her down but into stepping-stones that lift her up."

"Oh," says Pearl. "I'm not sure I like the idea of stepping on my memories."

"You can turn them into something else," says Gareth. "Like birds."

"Or bubbles," says Bannor.

Pearl wrings her handkerchief. "Bubbles are so fragile."

"So are memories," says Bannor.

The girl with dark eyes raises her hand. "What about Elliot?" she asks. "What can he choose?"

Gareth looks at me and smiles, his freckles bunching together at the edges of his grin. "Elliot can choose not to submit to the caprice of an indifferent universe. He can choose not to look to other places or other people to provide him with bliss, but to seize it for himself. Right here, right now. Elliot—all of us—can choose to go out there, grab happiness by the balls, and squeeze!"

Laughter ripples through the circle, but the girl raises her hand again. "Are you sure happiness would be into that?" she asks. "Because a lot of guys aren't."

After the session, I stay behind to help Gareth stack the chairs along the wall. We work in silence, his initial vigor apparently spent. I wonder what he does for a living, and why he would spend his spare time listening to people like Bannor—or me, for that matter. Perhaps he lost someone, or was once lost himself. We finish clearing the chairs, and I thank him. He encourages me to come again.

Outside, the rain has passed, and the girl with dark eyes is waiting for me.

"You're Elliot," she says, reaching out to shake my hand. "I'm Sasha."

"Nice to meet you."

"Is it?" she asks. "C'mon, I want to show you something."

We follow the river south, passing a series of older high-rises. Sasha's pace is brisk but unhurried. The fabric of her long skirt swishes back and forth against her legs. Though she can't be much older than me, she seems more at ease in her corporate garb. Her heels click along the pavement until we stand outside an apartment building facing the water. Above us, a fire escape inches its iron way up the brick facade. Sasha eyes the bottom of the ladder, then takes off her shoes and drops them to the sidewalk along with her soggy notebook. She hikes her skirt above her knees. "Cup your hands together," she says.

I lace my fingers and lower my arms to form a step. Sasha is tall but slender, and I'm able to boost her high enough for her to grab the lowest rung and hoist herself onto the first platform. Once there, she pulls a lever, and the ladder drops noisily down to the sidewalk.

"Don't forget my stuff," she says.

We climb ten stories before Sasha stops and sits down on the wet metal slats of the platform, resting her back against a darkened window. I join her, wondering if I'll have to dry-clean my suit, and what it will cost. The East River stretches like a black moat between us and the distant glow of Long Island. Beacons from the two bridges—the Manhattan to our left and the Brooklyn to our right—cast smudged reflections off the water. Between them, a more diminutive, truncated string of lights ticks silently down the river toward the sea.

"There," says Sasha. "That's what I wanted to show you."

"What is it? A tour boat?"

"Is that what you see?" she says. "I'm surprised. I always think of them as ghost ships, phantoms, sailing off to some far-off place from which they never return. Like your Neverene." I turn to face her, expecting a smirk, but she looks at me earnestly. "Do you believe in your Neverene?" she asks. When I don't respond, she poses an easier question. "Where did you grow up?"

"Connecticut."

"Do they have crickets there in summer?"

"Tons."

"South Dakota, too," she says. "I used to sleep with the window open so I could listen to them. Summers were lovely. People just seemed happier, and for some reason I associated it with the crickets.

It's soothing, you know? That sound?" She looks over to see me nod in agreement, then turns her gaze back to the river. "Winters sucked," she continues. "My father couldn't find work, so he'd get angry, and my mom would get angry, and they'd fight like jackals. We'd be buried in snow and freezing our butts off because they didn't want to waste money on heat. They'd only turn it up when it got dangerously cold, and then the radiator in my room would make this chirping noise, just like the crickets. On those nights, I chose not to hear my parents scream at each other, and instead just listened to the radiator. As far as I was concerned, it was the sound of the crickets, and it was summer, and everything was okay."

The soft hum of traffic rises up from the city. Out on the water, the drifting lights of the ghost ship disappear under the Brooklyn Bridge. The night is still and solemn, as if we ourselves were perched in the lookout of a great vessel that had left the mainland behind and set sail into the vast unknown.

"Do *you* believe in Neverene?" I ask.

Sasha turns to me with wide eyes, then breaks into high, ringing laughter that resounds along the length of the fire escape like an electric current. "No," she says, settling into a sigh. She smiles at me, and her voice softens. "But you can."

To my surprise, her amusement doesn't offend me, even if I'm not inclined to join her in it, or to accept her concession. "No," I say. "I'm done escaping. Gareth is right. I need to grab happiness."

"By the balls?"

"Maybe the horns. Does happiness have horns?"

"Please forward all questions regarding happiness and associated body parts to Gareth," says Sasha. "Though, personally, I don't think he's got the answers."

"Then why do you go to group?"

She draws her thighs to her chest and drops her head, squeezing into a ball. "I guess it makes me feel a little less shitty," she says into her knees. "Plus I get to tease Gareth." Abruptly, she uncurls her limbs, grabs her shoes and notebook, and stands up. "So, you were a pitcher?"

"Briefly," I say. "A long time ago."

"Could you throw a pitch into the river from here?"

I look down, gauging the distance. Below us, along the edge of the island, FDR Drive runs like an artery too near the skin, the crimson glare of taillights flowing like blood. Somehow I hadn't noticed it until now. I could probably clear the distance, though I'd need to step into the throw, and the fire escape is narrow and cramped. "Not from here," I say. "I'd need room to wind up."

"Fine." Sasha opens the window and slips inside before I can ask her whether she lives here or has a penchant for burglary. My question is answered a few minutes later, when she returns in jeans, a sweatshirt, and sneakers that fit her too well not to be hers. Not so comfortable in her corporate garb after all. She starts to climb farther up the fire escape, pausing briefly to look back at me. "You coming?"

We climb to the roof—a flat expanse of fractured tar, ringed by a parapet just low enough to trip over. The serrated incandescence of Manhattan unfolds to the north, but Sasha has her back to it, her eyes on the river. From the pocket of her jeans, she pulls out a plastic square the size of her palm, which I recognize as a computer disk.

"Let's see what you got," she says, handing me the disk. Its rigid plastic casing is unmarked.

"Why don't you throw it in yourself?"

She pulls out a pack of cigarettes. With a practiced motion, she tilts one into her mouth and lights it from a book of matches. "I'm not much into sports."

"What's on it?"

She smirks at me. I can only assume it's something important, and that this is the only copy. Still, there are easier and more certain ways to destroy a floppy disk. Launching it into the East River bespeaks a sense for the dramatic that makes me wonder about Sasha's intentions.

"Are you getting rid of all of your things?" I ask her.

"Not tonight."

"Sometime?"

"We all get rid of our things sometime."

"It just feels like you're preparing for something."

"Like my suicide?" The tip of her cigarette flares as she takes a drag. "I have a problem with the aftermath," she says. "The body, specifically. It seems like such a mess, and I don't want anyone to have to deal with that. When I do think about it, I imagine myself taking a little boat straight out into the Atlantic. I sit on the edge, lean over a little, and then shoot myself in the head so that I fall overboard. Of course, this would require both a gun and a boat, neither of which I currently possess. So, no, I'm not preparing for something. What about you?"

Despite having just bared my soul in group, I'm a bit stunned by Sasha's candor. And her specificity. An image of a subway train passes through my head. "No," I say. "I'm grabbing happiness, remember?"

"Right. What's that look like, exactly?"

"The standard prescription, I guess. Career, money, health, love."

"Sounds like you've got it all figured out."

"It's all up from here," I say. "An ascendant trajectory."

"Gareth will be happy to hear it," says Sasha. She takes another puff of her cigarette, then flicks the ashes over the parapet. "So, you going to chuck that thing in the river or not?"

I look out toward the lights of Brooklyn. They don't seem far now, and the river seems even closer. With a running start, I might even be able to throw myself in. I think of baseball, of a strike zone drawn with chalk on a basement wall, of a narrow strip of green grass in a field of white snow. The disk rests lightly in my hand. I pinch it between my thumb and forefinger, then wind up and lunge forward, hurling it like a fastball on the outside corner. It sails into the night and is gone.

After

After you die, you find yourself in a room that is not a room, at a table that is not a table. Across from you are Merriam and Jollis, and before each of them is a manila folder. They ask if you're ready for your exit interview.

"It's not mandatory," Merriam assures you.

"Yes," says Jollis. "Entirely up to you. Still, we'd appreciate your input."

Merriam nods. "Everything you tell us will be kept strictly confidential."

"Unless," says Jollis, "you give us permission to share it with management."

"Management?" you ask.

"You know," says Merriam. She gives you a conspiratorial shrug. "The brass."

You feel that you know—or ought to know—who the brass are, so you say nothing. Though this whole transition is a bit unnerving, you would like to help Merriam and Jollis. You agree.

"Wonderful!" says Merriam. She and Jollis open their manila folders to reveal a list of questions. Merriam diligently reads the first item on the list—"Can we get you anything to make you more comfortable?" As soon as she finishes reading, Merriam frowns down at the folder, seemingly surprised by her own question. You sympathize with her confusion. It's a strange offer, as you no longer know what it is you might need, or want. You politely decline.

"Certainly," says Merriam. She eagerly moves on to read the

next query from her list—"Lovely weather we're having, don't you think?"

Merriam glances worriedly at Jollis. You assume your own expression matches hers. "Weather?" you ask. "What do you mean? Where, exactly? And . . . when?"

"Oh, I suppose they mean on Earth," Merriam stammers. "I guess on your final—but of course you wouldn't have—"

"We have a confession," Jollis tells you. "We don't normally handle the exit interviews. This whole process is new to us, as you can probably tell. We've never even seen these questions before."

"Sorry," adds Merriam. She looks pained. You beg her not to worry. It's a privilege, you tell her, to be their first interviewee. She smiles.

"Great," says Jollis. "Why don't we just proceed down the list? Next question . . . What was the main reason you originally accepted a position with the enterprise?"

"The enterprise?"

"I think they mean the human enterprise," explains Merriam. "The journey."

"Ah," you say. "Yes, well, the reason . . ." You falter, then try again. "I accepted the position because . . ." Again you stop. There was a reason, you think, wasn't there? There had to have been a reason. One doesn't just blithely accept—but wait. "I'm sorry," you say. "I can't seem to remember accepting the position at all."

Merriam straightens in surprise. "Really?" she says. "Well, that seems inappropriate."

"Yes," says Jollis, thinking it over. He turns to Merriam. "But they wouldn't remember, would they? You know—the Auction, the Fugue . . ."

"Of course," says Merriam. "They couldn't remember. Not yet." She looks down at her folder. "So that was kind of a stupid question, then."

"Let's push on," says Jollis, checking his list. "Now then . . . Were the goals and objectives of your role sufficiently delineated?"

You think about it. There were all kinds of goals and objectives, of course. Everybody seemed to have them, marching stolidly along to one beat or another, and exhorting you to keep pace. But you seem to recall hearing a different drummer—that is, when you heard the drums at all.

"No," you say. "I'm afraid I wasn't clear on them."

Jollis nods sympathetically. "Perfectly understandable. Quite common, really." He makes a note in his folder before reading the next question—"Do you feel you received proper training in order to be successful?"

"To be honest," you say, "I feel like we were just thrown into it. I don't remember there being any training."

"The Fugue," Merriam reminds Jollis.

"Right," says Jollis. "We'll skip that one, too. Next . . . Do you feel you were kept adequately apprised of organizational policies?"

"You mean, like, the rules?"

"I suppose."

"Then I guess, technically, I'd have to say yes." The truth is, you were buried in rules. There were regulations, orders, decrees, axioms, codes, statutes, canons, ordinances, and maxims for every occasion. At times it seemed that, for anything you might do, there was one right way and a hundred wrong ones. There were physical laws, moral obligations, ethical responsibilities, religious commandments, familial duties, philosophical imperatives, aesthetic principles, social norms, political necessities. Yes, people were constantly proclaiming the rules. The real challenge wasn't keeping apprised of them but knowing which ones you really needed to obey and which ones you didn't, especially when some were diametrically opposed to others. "I think maybe we were long on rules and short on guidance," you say, "if that makes sense."

Merriam and Jollis share a knowing glance. "I think we understand," says Jollis. "What was your relationship like with your manager?"

"Manager?" you ask. "I don't think I had one."

"Maybe they mean your mentor," says Merriam.

"I don't think I had one of those either. Was I supposed to?"

Merriam looks at Jollis, who quickly looks down at his folder. "Next question," he says. "What are your future plans?"

"For goodness' sake," says Merriam, annoyed. "How ridiculous. Don't answer that," she tells you, which is a relief, because you wouldn't have known how.

"We'll go with 'Not Applicable,'" says Jollis. He reads the next query from the list—"Would you consider taking a position with the enterprise again, and/or would you recommend the enterprise to a friend?"

"Stop," says Merriam, her frustration bubbling over. "Given the circumstances, you don't need to answer that one either. And I've had about enough of this list." She shuts her folder and takes a moment to collect herself, then looks at you gently. "If you don't mind, I think what we'd really like to know is—why did you choose to leave?"

A legitimate question, you think, and the one you've been fearing. You struggle to formulate an answer. Perhaps if you could take Merriam and Jollis through each moment of your life—but, no, even that probably wouldn't explain it.

"Please be honest," says Merriam.

"That's right," says Jollis. "Whatever the reason, you can tell us—not enough parking, lack of adequate health insurance—"

"No," you say. "Nothing like that. Look, I don't want to sound ungrateful. All in all, it really is a beautiful world. I was just . . . sad."

Jollis and Merriam frown in bewilderment. "Okay," says Merriam. "And . . ."

"That's it." You're not sure how else to say it. "I wasn't happy."

"I don't understand," says Jollis. "You valued happiness so highly that its absence made you quit? What about wonder, or awe, or grace, or intimacy, or sacrifice, or—"

"But that was the whole point," you say. "Right? To be happy?"

"Who told you that?" asks Merriam, her confusion giving way to sadness.

You're concerned now. You have a sneaking suspicion that something important was hidden in the cacophony of all those goals and objectives and rules—and that you missed it. "Pretty much everybody," you say. "Why?"

"We don't mean to upset you," says Jollis. "We're not here to judge."

Merriam nods. "We're just surprised that you left because you weren't happy," she says. "After all, there were so many other things to be."

Elliot

(1997)

This is a day on the ascendant trajectory of Elliot Chance.

7:00 a.m. My alarm sounds with a bold hum, like a double bass heralding the opening of a symphony. I press the off button, studded with clever little beads so that you can find it in the dark. The spring morning and a mercurial radiator have left my studio apartment chilled, but I throw off the covers at the promise of coffee—a taste for which I am actively acquiring, in deference to the medicinal benefits of caffeine. While I shave, shower, and shine, my industrious coffeemaker performs its hum and gurgle, ultimately presenting me with a mug of sixteen hot ounces—or, as I like to think of it, 180 milligrams.

I take it in roughly equal doses, interspersed with the donning of my work attire—boxers and socks (gulp), shirt and pants (gulp), tie and jacket (gulp). I've trimmed the process down considerably, aided by a precisely defined rotation of three suits, two pairs of black shoes, and eleven ties. It's early April, and the air outside is likely to be either cold or wet, so the ensemble is capped off with my father's hand-me-down overcoat, just in case. In Manhattan, when your window looks out on the bricks of the building across the alley, you don't know much about the weather until you're under it.

7:40 a.m. I join the small trickle of suits flowing westward along my street. We turn south on Lexington Avenue, where the trickle becomes a stream. By Eighty-Sixth Street we are a river of blue and gray—a single frictionless body, with hardly a ripple to mar its surface. We cascade down the cement steps of the subway entrance, spill through the turnstiles, and fill the waiting cars of the train.

The ubiquitous yellow taxicab is one of the city's most iconic creatures, but real New Yorkers take the subway. Specifically, from the Upper East Side to Midtown, either the 4, 5, or 6 train. I think of these collectively as the green line, because that is how they're depicted on the plastic, credit-card-size subway map I keep in my wallet. I do not, however, publicly refer to them this way, at least not since Dean helpfully pointed out that only the bridge-and-tunnel crowd does so. (He also helpfully pointed out that "bridge-and-tunnel crowd" refers to anyone who doesn't live on Manhattan Island, particularly the commuters and weekend revelers who pack the roads and suburban rails into the city.)

We islanders are a different breed. The subway doors slide shut, and we dart along in bright cars through dark tunnels, like spies on a joint secret mission that we are forbidden to discuss. I used to smile at my confederates when I caught their eye, though they would invariably avert their gaze (as any good spy would). I stopped this practice when Dean constructively advised that I would some-day get punched in the face for it. At any rate, it's rare to meet the eyes of my fellow travelers. Most bury themselves in the news-paper, or stare thoughtfully into the middle distance, no doubt already beginning the workday in their minds. New Yorkers work hard. As Dean likes to say, "New Yorkers get shit done."

8:10 a.m. The office elevator is decidedly more social, perhaps be-cause the faces are more familiar, or perhaps because everyone's morning coffee is by this time kicking in nicely. The car fills with a collective energy, a shared enthusiasm for the new day's potential that bubbles up in the dependable repartee of my colleagues.

"—the club last night," Dennis is saying. "I've never been so hungover in my life." Dennis is the consummate bacchanal. He's made it his personal mission to verify that New York is, in fact, the city that never sleeps. I don't know how he does it.

"Whatever," says Nicole. She smiles, not quite flirting, but close. She loves to tease Dennis. "You were so home last night. By yourself, as usual—unless you count your cat."

"There were cats, all right," says Dennis. "Why don't you come out next time and see for yourself?"

Nicole smiles again. "You wish." Yep, she loves to tease him.

"Ah, the folly of youth," says Jeff from the corner of the elevator, though we are hardly youths to him. Just a few years older, Jeff is married with two small children, whose finger paintings are proudly displayed above their father's desk. He shakes his head as if to say that he's discovered a happiness that can't be found in any club or bottle. "Someday you'll settle down and see the light," he says. The others laugh.

8:15 a.m. I step into the office that I share with Matt. We don't have windows, but Matt has a poster of the island of Bora Bora above his desk, and it's easy to imagine that those iconic white sands and turquoise waters are just beyond our wall. I take off my suit jacket and hang it from a coat hanger on the back of our door, right next to my office mate's. Matt is always here when I arrive, head down, focused. I don't like to interrupt him, so I keep my morning greeting simple.

"Hey, Matt."

"Hey," he says. Matt's reticence and his enduring absorption in

the task at hand make him somewhat mysterious. Also the fact that
I generally can't see more than the top of his head—the rest of him
is typically hidden behind the cardboard file boxes stacked on his
desk. I can still see Bora Bora, though.

The quiet serenity of our shared space is in marked contrast to the
office as a whole. It's April—tax season—and we're an accounting
firm. Enough said. Most of the accountants have been buzzing with
activity for months, preparing year-end financial statements and tax
returns for our clients, which consist mostly of small-to-midsize
companies rather than individuals. Matt and I, however, work in
audit. Our job is to review the financial statements prepared by the
other accountants, to ensure that those statements accurately and
fairly represent the state of the client's business. For some clients,
this rigorous analysis is an annual rite, but often it is performed only
when a client has a particular need for it—say, because it's requesting
a large loan from a bank. Matt and I often work on these less regular
audits. Our deadlines, therefore, are different, and April has no power
over us.

Though Matt and I work on separate matters, my desk is likewise
littered with file boxes, as is the floor around me. Half of these are
stuffed with documents from the client—everything from financial statements to credit card receipts to angry letters from litigious
customers. The other half contain empty manila folders with as yet
blank labels, which I will use to organize, catalog, and otherwise
bring order to the chaos of paper. When I'm done, our senior auditors will assay the files, examine my spreadsheets, and divine their
conclusions.

You can learn a lot about a business by looking through their
linens, so to speak—what they sell, how much they earn, who they
hire and what they pay them to stick around, who they fire and
what they pay them to go away, even where their executives eat
dinner or take vacation. I absorb all of this data, not just for the

audit but also as research for the inevitable launch of my own advisory firm, the dream I am still determined will someday be a reality. I even offered to audit my father's shoe store, assuring him that my results wouldn't be for public consumption. He politely declined, which was probably for the best.

12:30 p.m. I allow myself forty-five minutes for lunch, though it only takes ten to pick up a sandwich and scarf it down at my desk. Hunger sated, I fill a glass with ice and pour myself a soda, which I will savor through the remainder of my break. As the drink effervesces into a sugary froth, I reach solemnly into the bottom drawer of my desk to retrieve a worn spiral notebook. It is here that I carefully preserve the aforementioned research—along with any conclusions, conjectures, and notions of my own that I feel may be of value to my future clients. I call it the Vade Mecum, a Latin name for *manual* that I feel more appropriately captures its significance.

When finished, I close the Vade Mecum and stash it away, leaving myself twenty minutes to solve Sasha's latest cipher. Sasha works as a copywriter for an advertising agency. She secretly embeds a coded message in every ad she writes, both to relieve her boredom and, I suspect, to assuage her guilt. Sasha detests materialism, and the cipher is often a more or less veiled reproach to whatever is being promoted for mass consumption. An advertisement for candy might ostensibly advocate the scrumptiousness of chocolate, caramel, and other sweet delights. But if you were only to read every third letter, you would receive a different message. "Eat broccoli," perhaps. Or, if the ad were short, something more simple, like "cavity."

As far as I know, I'm the only one privy to Sasha's cryptographic protests. I try to get my hands on whichever publications her ads happen to appear in. Today it's the *New York Times*. I leaf through the paper, my fingertips slowly blackening with ink, until I find it—a large half-page spot for cigarettes. An alluring woman flashes a pearly grin from behind a beguiling wisp of smoke. There's a lot of text, which usually means Sasha's code will be hard to crack, but fortunately I spot the key—the words "second" and "word" both appear in the first line. I write down the second word of each sentence, rearranging them again and again, but to no avail. Changing tack, I put the words back in their original order. When I then take the first letter of each word and string them together, I finally crack the code. The result, while inflammatory, is not terribly original. Still, the puzzle itself was a bit tougher this time. I'm glad, because if anyone else ever deciphers these things, Sasha's going to get fired.

3:00 p.m. Dean performs his flyby.

"Wassup, ladies?" He leans against the doorjamb with a toothy grin on his face. Dean's not in the office much, and I think he's glad to see me. He spends most of his time on the road or in the air, drumming up business. Unlike me and Matt, Dean is neither an auditor nor an accountant. He's an account manager, which means he's responsible for bringing in new clients, then keeping them happy once they've signed on. With his designer suit and sharply coiffured blond mane, my brother is still the young golden retriever at heart, perpetually in motion and eager to please. His misses may yet outnumber his makes, but he does well for himself nonetheless, which is why he had the clout to get me this job in the first place. To his credit, he hasn't lorded it over me, though he's not shy about checking on the work I do for the clients he's brought in.

A typical Dean flyby is brief—just a few words—and always ends with a mangled aphorism that I believe Dean prepares for the occasion. "Remember, dorks," he might say, "there's more than one way to count a chicken." Or, "Remember, dorks, you can fool most of the people most of the time." Sometimes the misquote is close enough to the original that I suspect he thinks he's getting it right, but he never does.

Matt doesn't look up from his desk. He stopped humoring Dean and his flybys long ago, but I lean back in my chair to properly enjoy the afternoon's entertainment. I am by now halfway through my second cup of coffee, in the form of an oversize mug I commandeered from the office kitchen. It's red and black, with the words "Just do it" emblazoned across the side. I take a sip, then look up to let Dean know I'm ready. This time, however, he doesn't immediately unleash his latest customized adage. Instead, he steps into our office and drops an envelope on my desk.

"What's this?" I ask.

"Bonus, baby bro!" He smiles more broadly, pleased with his alliteration and even more by the fact that he's no doubt already opened his own envelope. Though Dean's not responsible for my bonus, he likes to drop it off when he can, as a gesture of fellowship and collective achievement. This is primarily symbolic, since our jobs are completely different, and Dean—who works mostly on commission—receives much larger bonuses than I do.

Nevertheless, I'm grateful. I get paid well enough, and diligently allot my salary according to the proper and accepted ratios—forty percent on rent and utilities (a bit high, but it's Manhattan), fifteen percent on food, ten percent on clothing and entertainment, fifteen percent miscellaneous, and twenty percent to savings. The allotment to savings is higher than normally recommended, but in order to start my own business I'm going to need capital, and relatively soon. Five, six years, tops.

Dean himself doesn't subscribe to these recommended allotments, perhaps because he earns so much more than I do, or perhaps simply because he's Dean—somehow less genetically predisposed to concerning himself with the future. Still smiling, he gives me a salute as he backs his way out of our office.

"Remember, dorks," he says, "if the world gives you lemons, make a gin fizz."

6:15 p.m. I leave work early to meet Bannor for our walk. Every month or so, Bannor leaves me a voice mail indicating a date, time, and particular location in Manhattan where I am to meet him. His choices appear completely random and yet are somehow never inconvenient for me, and I am no longer surprised by wherever we might end up—roving the Bowery, skipping stones over the Harlem River, circling the ice-skating rink at Rockefeller Center.

Bannor had been going on these rambles long before we met in group. When I asked him why he invited me to join him, he said only that he knew we would take these walks together. Because he's been to the future. Obviously. I then asked whether he would have invited me if he hadn't already seen it in our future. He just shrugged and told me he couldn't say. Despite his extraordinary temporal travels, he doesn't really understand how the whole thing works. Regardless, he was right. Though I stopped attending group after a few months, I still regularly meet Bannor for our walks.

Today we convene at the gated end of an oddly quiet lane just north of Washington Square Park. On either side, low-slung carriage houses stand shoulder to shoulder, in marked contrast to the mostly high-rise architecture of the rest of Manhattan. Closed to traffic, the way is paved with cobblestones, which no doubt encourage fast-walking New Yorkers to choose a different path. As a result, Bannor and I have the street mostly to ourselves. We step through the gate as if into another city and time.

"What's this place?" I ask.

"Washington Mews." In his tweed suit and vest—the same ones he wore on that first night of group—Bannor looks at home amid the carriage houses and cobblestones, but then he sports the same outfit on all of our jaunts. He assures me he doesn't always wear it. "Special occasions only," he says, though when I ask him what the other special occasions are—or were—he won't tell me. In general, Bannor doesn't say much, particularly when he's not talking about the future. On most days, we simply walk in silence.

I slow my pace to match his leisurely gait. This gives me ample time to peer into the windows of the simple yet elegant homes, imagining them in their former incarnations as stables for horses. I am just settling into a groove when we abruptly reach the end of the block. Here stands a second gate, beyond which modern Manhattan resumes its rush and blare.

"It's a beautiful street," I say. "A bit short, though."

Bannor stares out through the iron bars. "True and truer," he says.

I'm a bit befuddled. Though my excursions with Bannor aren't always long, this is ridiculous. The second gate, like the first, is open to pedestrians. We could pass through and turn north on Fifth Avenue, or make our way into the West Village, but we would have to abandon the antiquated magic of the mews.

Bannor solves the problem in easy fashion, spinning lightly on his heels and heading back toward where we started. The stroll is just as pleasant the second time, which is a good thing, because when we get to the first gate, we turn around and do it again. I don't mind in the least, and am impressed as always by Bannor's poise. It strikes me that he is the most serene person I've ever met, despite the fact that he's perfectly insane.

"You are unflappable, Bannor," I say. "Incapable of being flapped."

"I don't know."

"You are," I insist. "What's the secret?" I don't really expect him to answer, but we have begun our fourth lap of the mews now, and I'm a little bored.

"Maybe you stop worrying once you've seen your own death."

I am as surprised by the tenor of his response as by its utterance, and I now feel bad for having asked the question. Bannor rarely broaches the subject of his own suicide, or his supposed precognition of it. "But you don't know for sure, right?" I ask. "You can change it. Isn't that why you go to group? To stop it from happening?"

He shakes his head. "Not to stop it. Just to understand it."

"I don't think you have to settle for that."

Bannor reaches his hands behind his back and clasps them together gently. The rhythm of his stride remains slow and steady, though the front curl of his homburg hat dips earthward. "They say a drowning man stops panicking once his lungs fill with water," he says. "Maybe losing things is like that."

"What have you lost, Bannor?"

He slips into silence, one that I don't expect to be broken by anything other than the soft tap of his burgundy shoes on the cobblestones. But he proves me wrong again.

"In the future," he says, "you can talk to the dead."

7:30 p.m. I hit the gym, having fully embraced the view that physical fitness is a critical component of the happiness equation—and also, of course, wanting to look good naked. I'm six feet tall and 160 pounds. I'm not scrawny, but I can't deny that my stomach is a couple abs short of a six-pack, and it would be hard to describe the flexing of my biceps as an "invitation to the gun show."

This is about to change, however. I'm now in the gym six days a week—two days of lower body, two days of upper, and two days of cardio (treadmill or rowing machine). Today is Tuesday, which means I'm all about my upper body. After chugging a protein shake with creatine, it's reps and sets—pull-ups, sit-ups, bench, incline, military presses, extensions, cable rows, shoulder raises, curls, flys, crunches, dips. I shred my pecs, smash my biceps, blast my delts, and destroy my abs. It won't be long before I'm jacked, ripped, yoked. It won't be long before my arms are more pipes than pipe cleaners. It won't be long before I'm a bona fide brick shithouse.

Five, six months, tops.

9:00 p.m. I climb the fire escape of Sasha's building to find her already sitting on the landing outside her window.

"Cancer," I say, settling down into my regular spot beside her.

"You're getting too good at them." She strikes a match and lights a cigarette. "I tried to make that one harder."

"It *was* harder," I say. "Also a bit hypocritical."

Sasha exhales a puff of smoke at me. "Maybe it was meant to be aspirational."

"Are you aspiring to quit smoking, or get cancer?"

She shrugs, and I let it go, turning my gaze out over the river. The lights of the two bridges shine in the adolescent night. "You're not worried that your ciphers are going to cost you your job?" I ask.

"Present company excluded, no one is ever going to read them. For all intents and purposes, they disappear the moment they're written."

"Like a floppy disk tossed into the East River."

Sasha frowns, confused for an instant, then remembers. "Yes, exactly like that."

"You never told me what was on it." As with Bannor, there are some questions I ask Sasha without hope of receiving an answer. Yet today, clearly, something is different.

She takes a particularly long drag of her cigarette. "A novel," she says.

"Yours?"

"No, my neighbor's." Her eyes flash darkly, but she smiles. I'm still not sure what to make of the contradiction between Sasha's shadowy eyes and bright grin. I have, however, learned to ignore her sarcasm.

"That's great," I say. "What's it about?"

"Who knows."

"Still working on it?"

"Not unless you've got a scuba tank."

I feel a small pit open in my stomach. "But you had other copies," I say. "Sasha, tell me you did not write a novel and then throw it in the river."

"I did not," she says, smiling again. "*You* threw it in the river." She seems to think this is funny. "Oh, Elliot," she says finally. "Don't fret. I sent it around first, even got an agent, but it was roundly rejected by the publishing world."

"But it was your first try. You'll only get better."

"It wasn't rejected because it was bad," she says. "Everybody loved the writing. The writing was 'superlative.' It was rejected because it was depressing. Publishers said it would never sell, and that they'd lose money. They told me if I wrote a book that made people feel happy, they'd publish it in a New York minute. They actually said that—'a New York minute.'"

"*That's* what I'm talking about! So you just need to write the happy one."

"Or I could knit sweaters," says Sasha. "People want sweaters, too." She exhales another plume of smoke and watches it dissipate. "And cigarettes."

"It's not the same." I wasn't going to let her off the hook. If I was grabbing happiness by the balls—or horns, or whatever—then Sasha could, too. "If you write another novel—even one that people want to read—you'll still be expressing yourself. And that must mean something to you, or you wouldn't have written the first one."

"Ain't never gonna happen."

"Yes, it will," I insist. "I can see it now—the book will be a masterpiece, critically acclaimed, published in seven languages, and you will become a rich and famous novelist. I'll have Bannor confirm it."

Sasha looks away without acknowledging my joke, which surprises me. Unlike me, Sasha still occasionally attends group, where she still occasionally sees Bannor, and she is not normally opposed to teasing our crazy mutual friend. She crushes the butt of her cigarette and lights another.

"Pearl killed herself," she says flatly.

My throat catches. Thoughts of Sasha's novel evaporate, along with all appeals, argumentation, and cajolery. Instead, I think of Pearl—how she would gently knead her handkerchief in her lap, how she dreamed of gathering memories like stones, filling her pockets until she drowned. I'm not going to ask how she died.

"I'm so sorry. What a shame."

"Is it?" says Sasha. "It was Pearl's decision. Who are we to condemn it? None of us asked to be here. As far as I know, we didn't bid for these lives at auction. If Pearl wanted to leave, that's her call."

"I just meant—it seemed like she had a good life, and it's sad that it ended that way."

"I don't think it's sad," says Sasha. "I think we're obsessed with endings. We can witness or experience the greatest life or love in the history of the world, but if it ends badly, then the whole thing suddenly becomes a tragedy. Or the opposite—one brief moment of redemption at the end of a long life of injustice and pain? Please. All's well that ends well? Bullshit."

"I don't know. Beginnings and endings just seem to carry more weight."

"Why?" demands Sasha. "Why put more weight on one particular moment, just because it's the last?"

"Tradition?"

"It's totally arbitrary," she says. "And painful—because this
weighty, important ending we're so infatuated with? Spoiler alert—
everybody dies."

I am sitting close enough to Sasha that our shoulders touch, and I
can feel her shivering, though the night isn't that cold. A sprinkling
of stars appears in the patch of sky between the bridges.

"This would be a nice ending," I say.

Sasha lets her cigarette slip from her fingers. It drops through
the slats of the fire escape and falls toward the ground far below us.
She watches it go, then lets out a deep sigh and rests her head on
my shoulder.

"Yeah," she says. "In fact, let's just decide that it is. No matter
what happens from now on, let's agree that this, right here, is our
ending. The final page of our story." She sits up and extends her
hand. "Deal?"

We shake. "Deal."

"Good," she says, nodding formally. "Then, Elliot, let me say
that I am grateful to have known you in this life, and I'm glad to
be here with you, at the end." She reaches her arms around my
shoulders and hugs me, pressing her cheek to my chest. "My heart
cares about your heart."

"Me, too," I say. "My heart cares about your heart, too."

"Goodbye, Elliot," she says, still hugging me.

"Goodbye, Sasha."

11:08 p.m. I have sex with my girlfriend. It's tremendous. A first-
year lawyer at a huge law firm, Jennifer doesn't get out of the office
much, so when she's able to make it over to my place, she doesn't

waste time. Her first move is to pour us each a shot of tequila from a bottle I keep for just that purpose. She asserts three reasons for this ritual. One, she likes tequila. Two, it burns away the bad taste in her mouth after a day of lawyering. Three, it is a small tribute to when we first met.

Which was two months ago, in a bar, after she spilled a tequila shot on me. Clearly inebriated, she told me she was a lawyer and that my shirt had committed a tort against her by absorbing her drink without permission.

"It's larceny," she cried. "A wrongful taking."

"Does that mean theft?" I asked.

"Yeah, that."

"I'm no attorney," I told her, "but doesn't that require an intent to steal?"

"Well . . ."

"It seems to me your drink trespassed on my shirt."

She froze, her mouth hanging open in surprise. "Oh my," she said theatrically. "You're a clever one. I imagine you'll be expecting damages to be awarded."

"Oh, I'm damaged all right," I said.

"Is that so?" She stepped back and looked me over in appraisal, searching for some injury other than the stain of tequila on my shirt. "You don't look it," she said. "Emotional distress?"

"Yeah, that."

"Would you consider a reasonable offer of settlement?"

"Never."

"Oh my," she said again, with the same air of affected melodrama. She then turned to the bar and ordered two more tequila shots. "Damages it is!" she cried.

Maybe that's the way to attract a lawyer—with cleverness—or maybe Jennifer was impressed with how quickly I complied with her request to throw back that slug of tequila, or the ones that followed. Jennifer's tolerance seemed as boundless as her energy, which I found even more intoxicating than the alcohol. There's a buzz in the air when Jennifer is in the room. You can feel it.

You can feel it in bed, too. I tend to think of sex as improvisation, but with Jennifer I get the sense there's an elaborate choreography, and that I missed rehearsal. The composition is different every time. Tonight begins with Jennifer perched on the edge of the sink, pieces of our clothing garnishing the cupboards of the galley kitchen like so many holiday ornaments. From the sink, we make our way around the apartment, each new spot demanding a change in position, some of which I later have to look up. In totality, the evening's program turns out as follows: iron chef at the sink, waterfall on the couch, and missionary in bed. It is, as I've said, tremendous. By the time we finish, I have barely enough energy to turn the light off before slipping into a deep and dreamless sleep.

Thus ending a day on the ascendant trajectory of Elliot Chance.

In the Future

Bannor says that in the future there's a pill for everything.

Which is not surprising.

What *is* surprising is that the pills work. According to the scientists, it was just a matter of time. The body, they say, is essentially an electrified skin bag filled with an intricate mix of chemicals, bacteria, archaea, fungi, protists, viruses, and other microorganisms. Though still eons away from deciphering the entirety of this human microbiota, the scientists have come a long way. Far enough, in fact, to be able to concoct biochemical potions—conveniently packaged in easy-to-swallow tablets—to alleviate (if not cure) any ailment.

By this time, of course, the miracle of future medicine had already eradicated most purely physical conditions. Nevertheless, a handful of time-honored bodily complaints remained. Acne in your teenage years, say, or wrinkles in your later ones. Dimples in places you wished they weren't. Malodorous flatulence from that high-fiber diet. Though such conditions proved resistant to any permanent cure, all could now be kept at bay with a pop of the appropriate capsule, so finely calibrated that there weren't even any side effects.

The market boomed, and the fortunes of pill manufacturers soared. Yet the real money lay in the prevention not of physical aches but of emotional ones. Public enemy number one, and the first emotion to fall, was sadness. This venerable scourge of the human condition, this foil to the pursuit of happiness, this pillar of tragedy itself, was casually brushed aside with a glass of juice and a little yellow tablet (though in truth the tablet wasn't so little, but rather the largest of all the emo-inhibitors, with scientists unable to shrink it down to anything smaller than a cashew nut). On the heels of the pill's success, the manufacturers quickly announced a succession of varietals. Sadness, they proclaimed, comes in many flavors—so, too, would its remedy. Grief, anguish, heartbreak, despair? All vanquished.

At which point the manufacturers turned their attention to other hobgoblins of the heart and mind—everything from formidable therapy-session time sucks like anger, guilt, and loneliness to lesser evils such as boredom, shyness, and disgust. No disagreeable sentiment was too great or too small. People even started to coin new emotions. (Some said it was the manufacturers themselves who did most of the coining, in order to sell more emo-inhibitors.) Suffering from a wistful desire to return to a time in someone else's past? That's a condition known as proxtalgia. There's a pill for that. Secretly jealous of your cat's ability to clean itself? That's ablufenvy. There's a pill for that, too.

Dosage regimens varied. Some people chose the preventive route—small but steady doses at regular intervals to avoid the onset of unwelcome vibes. Others preferred a more palliative approach— only taking the pill when symptoms arose, or were likely to (performance reviews, weddings, Monday mornings). Regardless of technique, the effect was the same—when it came to undesirable emotions, if you didn't want to feel them, you didn't have to.

The results were predictable enough. More smiles, fewer tears. More laughter, less screaming and yelling. A decided increase in high-fiving, warm embracing, and other spontaneous acts of affection. Prison populations dwindled, a statistic quickly attributed to the suppression of rage, anger, and hatred. Even violence waned. Boxing, for example, fell to the bottom ranks of the world's most popular sports, while synchronized swimming vaulted into the top ten.

All of which conspired to make life decidedly less unpleasant—which, in the minds of some people, was not the same as more pleasant. In defense of this contrarian view, they pointed to suicide rates. Despite the effectiveness of the emo-inhibitors, the number and frequency of suicides hadn't budged. That is, until one more pill was introduced. The one for fear.

It had been a long time coming, due primarily to the controversy surrounding it, and the . . . well, fear . . . of what might happen. Unlike sadness (which many considered unnecessary) and anger (typically regarded as more detrimental than beneficial), fear was deemed essential for life, or at least for the avoidance of death. Without fear, what would keep people from walking across train tracks, or bicycling without a helmet, or otherwise putting themselves in harm's way? Even when it came to less existential matters, there was concern that people would stop doing things that were good for them. If they no longer feared the consequences of inaction, would they still do their homework? Meet their deadlines? Eat their vegetables?

As it turned out, the answer was yes, to the relief of parents and vegetable farmers everywhere. Rather than being driven by the fear of a bad outcome (getting sick, being chastised by the teacher), people were inspired by the desire for a good one (feeling healthy, learning). What now kept them from stepping in front of trains was the desire to live, as opposed to the desire not to die. Some say it was this change in motivation that was responsible for the precipitous drop in suicide rates. Others claim it was the elimination of fear itself. Either way, once the pill for fear hit the market, people stopped wanting to kill themselves.

Which is not to say they're happier. In fact, sadness is as rife as ever in the future. So, too, are anger, and loneliness, and all the other difficult emotions. If the scientists thought that eliminating suicide meant that everyone would be blissful all the time, they were mistaken.

Even more surprising to the scientists, those who take the pill to extinguish their fear invariably stop taking the other emo-inhibitors—a trend that has sent the manufacturers into utter panic. Worldwide pill sales have tanked, and no amount of marketing wizardry appears capable of reviving them. In a desperate attempt to salvage their profits, the manufacturers have even convened focus groups to try to understand what happened.

"Why did you stop taking the pills?" they ask people. "Do you *like* feeling sad? Do you *enjoy* being angry?"

"No," say the people. "Of course not."

"Then why would you choose to experience these things?" the manufacturers ask, wringing their collective hands.

"Because we're no longer afraid to."

Elliot

(1999)

If the burgeoning frenzy of our office is any indication, it looks like the internet is going to be a thing. Seems like everyone and their second cousin is drafting a business plan, writing some computer code, and forming a Delaware corporation. Why Delaware? I have no idea, but the lawyers have their reasons, and the venture capitalists seem to like it. Start-up companies are raising money faster than you can say "new paradigm." A million here, five million there. Twentysomething founders aren't worried about getting funded. In fact, they don't seem to worry about much of anything. To their apparent surprise, however, investors aren't keen on them applying this nonchalance to the balance sheets, which means these newly flush corporations suddenly need an accountant and, as often as not, a financial audit.

Which leads them to us—or, more precisely, to Dean. Or, even more precisely, leads Dean to them. If my brother had previously been an excitable golden retriever, he is now a Tasmanian devil, a whirling dervish, a compressed cyclone of salesmanship. Whether it's an international business conference at the Javits Center or a booze-addled bash in a studio apartment in Brooklyn, if it has "dot-com" in the invitation, Dean is there—drinking appletinis and gesticulating with his new BlackBerry mobile email device as if it were a golden phallus and nobody else had one (which, for the most part, they don't, since most employers only get them for select employees).

Dean now wears vintage sneakers and knit polo shirts with the collar popped, though Matt and I still reliably come to the office in suit and tie. "Audit needs to look professional," says Dean, which is actually one of his more astute pronouncements (or would be, if either Matt or I ever actually met with clients). It's also one of the more intelligible. Over lunches, brunches, and lattes, Dean has acquired a small thesaurus of new phrases, and isn't afraid to use them, correctly or otherwise. A single Dean flyby might incorporate gems such as "bandwidth," "value-add," "leveraging resources," and "plug-and-play." Possibly in the same sentence. It's all good, as Dean would say. He's far too busy for anything as outdated as established rules of grammar. If new tech clients were falling leaves, he'd be unable to fit them all in the pockets of his designer jeans.

Dean is hardly alone in his newfound passion for the World Wide Web. Tech stocks are booming. The NASDAQ composite index is surging to unprecedented highs, with no sign of slowing. An eight percent annual return has become quaint. If you're not doubling your money every two years, you may as well be lighting it on fire, at least according to the tech investment newsletter that circulates through our office each week. I'm a bit late to the party, but by trading online and also investing in some of our firm's clients, I'm finally able to move my savings into the future—undersea computer cables, optical network switches, and other foundations of cyberspace, along with more prosaic but no less surefire ventures like online pet supply stores.

My coworkers and I check our stocks religiously—watching the dough rise, so to speak. With every click of the refresh button, our portfolios get a little fatter. It's addictive, and intoxicating, like winning a small lottery every day. More importantly, my robust new investment strategy has expedited my progress toward starting my own business, though I'm no longer convinced that consulting for small mom-and-pop shops is the way to go. Instead, I'm working on a high-tech business plan of my own—an internet start-up focused on education. "Giving students around the world the online tools they need to learn more effectively." I even have a name—Socrates .com. I've talked to Dean about it, and he's in. No one wants to get rich quick more than Dean, and it's a perfect team—me on the inside developing the website, my brother on the outside drumming up investors and end users. All we need is a little nest egg to build a prototype, which is where my web-fueled savings come in. At these rates of return, we'll be out of here in twelve months.

Until then, it's audits and more audits. Despite the promise of the internet to save us time, I seem to have less of it than ever. Dean likes having me on the team for his clients whenever possible. "Blood is thicker than the phlegm I coughed up into the sink this morning," he says. As a result, I get into the office earlier these days, and leave quite a bit later. What had been a lunch break is now a rapid infusion of sustenance, still administered at my desk, still composed of a sandwich and soda, but no longer accompanied by ponderings in the Vade Mecum or prolonged efforts to solve Sasha's advertising ciphers. I had so little attention to spare for her last one, I never managed to crack it at all.

Which, come to think of it, was several months ago. Odd that she never gloated over my failure. She's been writing ads for that particular brand of cereal for a year, and never fails to include a secret barb somewhere in the text. And Sasha rarely misses an opportunity to give me shit. But then I've been so buried, I can't recall the last time I saw her. Wanting to check in, I leave her a voice mail, then an email. Days pass with no response, which is also not like her. Though Sasha unapologetically mocks the tech craze, she's no Luddite. I ask Bannor, who tells me that Sasha hasn't been to group in the past few months. I refuse to ask him whether she'll be there in any future ones.

I start to worry. On Tuesday night, I climb the fire escape of

Sasha's building. The rungs are cold with the first hint of autumn. When I reach Sasha's landing, the window is dark and the curtains drawn. My soft taps on the pane scatter into silence. Though I tell myself I'm being ridiculous, my uneasiness grows. Our Tuesday-night rendezvous isn't etched in stone, nor even penciled in. Still, it's been an unspoken tradition for so long that I've come to expect it, despite my own recent run of truancy.

I return the following week, but the fire escape is once again empty and lifeless. No lighted window. No Sasha. Not even a trail of cigarette butts to mark whatever path she may have taken.

Saturday morning finds me at the window of my own apartment— my *new* apartment, the one that I share with Jennifer. She and I moved in together a few months ago. After two years, it seemed like the thing to do. Plus, I thought it might help me save money, though it turns out I'm spending more now. Jennifer wanted an "upgrade," which to her meant a dishwasher and a second bedroom on the third floor of a West Village brownstone. To me, it meant being able to see even a small piece of the sky from my living room, which I can just about do if I press my face to the window and peer over the top of the ginkgo tree gripping the sidewalk outside our building.

At the moment, however, I am not seeking the sky. I'm using my reflection in the glass to adjust my tie—part of the expected attire for someone else's wedding. There have been a rash of these recently. "Welcome to your late twenties," says Jennifer, who seems to genuinely enjoy them. I thought I would, too. The first few times, I looked forward to witnessing the magical bonding of two people in love, until it dawned on me that these affairs had all degenerated into a formulaic sameness, where everyone seemed to be playing a role. Now only Jennifer's enthusiasm makes them bearable—the way she lights up when she sees the bride, her ritual at the reception of touching each table's centerpiece for good luck, the zeal with which she drags me onto the dance floor, where I wouldn't normally go but where I must admit I have fun, at least until I'm too exhausted to keep up.

Today's ceremony features a coworker of Jennifer's who she doesn't particularly like and a man she's never met. No matter. Jennifer has yet to decline an invitation, and we dress accordingly. Though it's the weekend, I wear one of my three business suits. "The least dour one," according to Jennifer, who brushes the lint off my shoulder before commandeering the bathroom. From behind the closed door, the sound of the shower resonates with a dull hum.

By now I could put on my tie with my eyes closed, but I use my reflection in the window anyway. September's morning light slants just so, and there is something about my image—precisely manifest yet completely insubstantial—that captivates me. I stop and stare at it, drifting into reverie, until a hail of small stones pelts the glass. I jump back, biting off a yell, then open the window and look down to see Sasha. She is standing in the street with a fistful of pebbles, bracing herself for another salvo. I call down to her.

"Pretty good throw for someone who's not much into sports."

Sasha considers the rocks in her hand, as if she might still throw them. "I think this is more warlike than sporty."

"Are we at war?"

She drops the pebbles at the base of the ginkgo tree, then stuffs her hands into the pocket of her hoodie. "No," she says.

"I couldn't solve your last cipher," I say. "In the cereal ad."

"There wasn't one," she says. Any comfort my ego might take from this fact is overshadowed by renewed worry. As far as I know, Sasha has never missed an opportunity to secretly impugn whatever it is she's supposed to be selling. I get the feeling that she's stepping back, slowly eliminating traces of herself, if not from the world then at least from what I can see of it.

"Good to know my record remains unblemished," I say. I don't ask her why she failed to devise a cipher, nor why she stopped going to group. "Where've you been?"

She shrugs. "Around." But she hasn't been around. Or maybe *I* haven't been around. "I was thinking you might play hooky for the day," she says.

"It's Saturday."

"Not from work," she says. "From your life."

Behind me, the hum of the shower has been replaced by the whine of the hair dryer. Though wedding duty calls, my concern for Sasha is quickly trumping it. I don't know what playing hooky from life looks like, but my imagination runs dark, and I don't want to let Sasha do it by herself. I suppose I could tell Jennifer the truth, though I'd have to explain my concern, and that would mean disclosing the fact that I used to go to group. Jennifer knows that Sasha and I are friends, but not how we met, just as she knows that I broke my leg as a boy, but not how. I can already hear the alarm bells going off in her head. I don't want her to get all worked up about it, nor do I feel like hearing the inevitable indictment of suicide and those who might consider it. Jennifer's enthusiasm for life isn't terribly patient with those who don't always share it.

So rather than get into all of this, I bury it, like any good Chance would. Instead, I play sick, which is so obvious that it works. When Jennifer emerges from the bathroom, I am facedown on the couch, holding my stomach and groaning into a pillow. The flu, I say. She feels my forehead and says she doesn't think so. Food poisoning, I say. She asks what I ate. I tell her milk and cornflakes. Though I suspect she may be onto me, she doesn't argue. She pours the rest of the milk down the sink and asks if I want her to stay home, too. I tell her that I'll be fine, that she should go enjoy herself. She blows me a kiss on her way out.

Fortunately, fake illnesses pass swiftly. I rise from the couch, lamenting the loss of good milk but not the chance to attend another wedding. Jennifer, I know, will do just fine without me. I shed my suit for jeans and a sweater. It feels good to lose the tie. Moments later Sasha and I are strolling through the narrow lanes of Greenwich Village. In green sneakers with frayed laces, Sasha sets an unhurried, somewhat listless pace, which nevertheless seems bent toward some final destination.

"What should we do?" I ask.

"I want to know what happens after you die."

My unspoken fears begin to breach the surface. "Sasha—"

"So we're going to ask the experts."

This is not the response I had anticipated. In my befuddlement, I ask the first question that pops into my head. "Are these experts still living?"

"I hope so," says Sasha. "I've made appointments."

Before I can determine whether or not she's joking, we are climbing the steps of a small church. The building's dark stone and Gothic archways collect what shadows they can from the morning light. "First stop," says Sasha. Now I really think she's joking. Not that I don't think the church has answers. I just wouldn't have predicted that Sasha would be interested in hearing them. Yet her face bears no hint of her trademark sardonic grin. I grip the curved handle and pull.

To sundrenched eyes, the shadows within are even deeper, the vaulted ceiling lost in darkness. Sasha and I walk down the center aisle toward a raised marble altar, past rows of empty wooden pews on either side. The ponderous stone walls of the nave are punctuated with high windows of stained glass, where solemn faces enact scenes in fractured color.

A door beside the altar leads to a decidedly more mundane office. From behind an old writing desk, a priest emerges and greets us warmly. Clean shaven and relatively young, he could easily be mistaken for one of my office mates, but for his black garb and the white patch of his clerical collar. He graciously pours us coffee while we take our seats. Sasha wastes little time before posing her question.

"Heaven happens," responds the priest. "Or hell, of course. Or purgatory, in those borderline cases." He smiles. "Which likely includes most of us."

"Are there angels?" asks Sasha. I watch her face, looking for any sign of sarcasm, but there is none. This is confusing to me, if not exactly surprising. Sasha wouldn't mock someone else's faith, and certainly wouldn't make an appointment on a Saturday just to do so. Yet if her curiosity is genuine, I fear her motives.

"Yes," says the priest. "I believe there are angels."

"And heaven is forever," says Sasha.

"Yes."

"But not purgatory."

"No," says the priest. "Purgatory is temporary."

"So time exists in the afterlife?" asks Sasha. "How do they measure it? Do they use Earth days?"

"In all honesty," says the priest, "the details haven't been made very clear to us." He sets down his coffee and leans forward slightly. Though his smile fades, his kindness does not. "But make no mistake. You have—you *are*—an everlasting soul. When your journey here is done, you will go on. And you will not be alone." He opens his arms to indicate the room around us. "This is not all there is."

An hour later, Sasha and I have traded the hush of the priestly enclosure for the glare of a neurologist's office. The doctor—a portly man whose jowls have slumped with age—reclines in his chair, his head in line with several model skulls displayed on his desk. He is surprised to learn that we're not here for medical advice.

"Nothing happens," he says. "This is all there is."

"Sounds boring," says Sasha.

The neurologist takes off his wire-rimmed glasses and drops them in the breast pocket of his lab coat. His plump fingers rub at the bridge of his nose. "It would be," he says, "if you were there to experience it."

"How do you know I won't be?" Sasha's tone is even, and I can't tell whether her question is a challenge or a plea.

"Because physiological activity in the brain is not *evidence* of consciousness. It *is* consciousness. When your brain dies, when your EEG flattens, you're gone."

"Gone where?"

"Nowhere. Just gone."

Sasha falls silent, possibly trying to absorb this nihilistic decree. I try to come to her aid. "Things can't just be gone," I say. "Wouldn't that violate some law of thermodynamics or something?"

"It might," say the neurologist, "if consciousness were distinct from the brain and chemicals and electricity. *Those* things aren't gone. They just . . . stop. And then decay, like other matter. *Gone* really isn't the right word to describe what happens to us. It would be more accurate to say that we cease."

"Cease what?" asks Sasha.

"Existing." He looks at us flatly, his dispassionate conviction inviting neither compromise nor debate. "*This* is your life," he says. "This is your story. There's nothing after but a blank page."

"How can you be sure?" asks Sasha.

The neurologist lets out a small sigh. "For the same reason I'm sure there is no elephant under my chair," he says. "Because there is no reason to think otherwise."

The ensuing silence expands until it seems to envelop us, muffling our goodbyes and our retreat from the hospital. Even the clatter of the subway and the clamorous streets of the Bronx feel muted, until we eventually find ourselves standing at the door of the Buddhist meditation center where Sasha has booked our next engagement. As we pass over the threshold into the dim spaciousness within, we appear to bring our quiet with us.

The meditation hall is largely unadorned, with floors of blond hardwood and brick walls painted white. At the far end, a wooden sculpture of the Buddha sits on a low stand. Lining the floor between us and the sculpture are several neat rows of blue cushions, each with a round pillow at its center. All are empty but for the one nearest the sculpture, where a monk in an orange robe sits cross-legged. He would appear to be deep in meditation, but for the fact that his eyes are open and he's looking at us. He raises a hand and beckons us forward.

We leave our shoes by the door and pad softly over the smooth wood until we stand before the monk. Sasha drops unceremoniously to the floor. I sit down beside her and cross my legs. My nose crinkles at the faint scent of incense burning at the foot of the sculpture.

"I want to know what happens after you die," says Sasha.

The monk raises his eyebrows, but says nothing. I wonder if he's taken a vow of silence, or if that's even something that Buddhist monks do. My fears are not allayed when he rises from the floor and disappears through a doorway at the back of the room. A moment later he returns with a box of matches and three small, colored candles—the kind you would put on a birthday cake. The monk resumes his seated position, handing one candle to me and another to Sasha. Then he lights the third candle and sets the box of matches on the floor behind him.

The monk looks at us with shining eyes. His bald head and smooth skin don't suggest any particular age. He is certainly not a child. And not elderly. Somewhere, then, along the ageless plateau of middle life. He nods toward the flame in his hand.

"So," he says finally. "The candle is me. The flame is me. Okay?"

"Okay," says Sasha.

He leans forward, bringing his candle just close enough to Sasha's so that the flame leaps from wick to wick. He then blows out his candle, leaving Sasha's burning.

"Now I have died," he says, indicating first his own candle, then Sasha's. "And you are born. The candle is you. The flame is you. The flame is me."

"And when I die?" Sasha asks.

The monk nods toward the candle in my hand. Sasha reaches out and lights my candle, then blows out her own.

"Just so!" says the monk. "Now?"

"Elliot is born," says Sasha. "The candle is Elliot. The flame is Elliot. But the flame is also me. And the flame is also you."

"Just so," says the monk.

"And this just keeps going forever?"

He nods, tilting his head slightly. "Until nirvana."

"What happens then?"

The monk leans forward, his eyes bright, his lips curled in the hint of a grin. With a sharp puff, he blows my candle out.

The sky has slipped into afternoon by the time Sasha and I are back on the street. We glide through a world of asphalt and concrete and shop windows, of wheezing car brakes and the shouts of children rushing home from school. Sasha seems distracted, and her listless pace has become desultory.

"Just so," I say. "Who's next?"

"That's it."

"Those were all the experts?"

"The ones I could get appointments with." Sasha's mood is pensive, if not exactly dispirited. Nevertheless, I feel the need to try to cheer her up.

"It's like we're inside a joke," I say, affecting a comedic tone. "So a priest, a monk, and a neurologist walk into a bar—"

"It's for a project," says Sasha.

I stop my jest, not knowing where it was going anyway. My worry finally gets the best of me. As fond as Sasha may be of puzzles, I'm unable to let this particular one continue. "Does this project involve ending your life?"

She casts me a quick glance. "No," she says simply.

Sasha has never lied to me, and I have no reason to start doubting her now. I take her at her word and let it go. "Good," I say. "I don't want you jumping from a tree and fracturing your tibia."

She smiles. "Pretty sure I'm coordinated enough to stick the landing without breaking my leg."

"Is that right?" I say. "I think it would depend on the tree. The branch might be so insanely high that no one could possibly stick the landing. Even if, hypothetically, they were an exceptionally gifted athlete."

Sasha laughs, and the tension I've been feeling all day—all week—vaporizes. "I'd like to see it," she says.

"The tree? Or me jumping from it?"

"I'd settle for the tree."

It's easy enough to get to my old neighborhood, though I haven't been back since my parents moved out of the house a few years ago. Sasha and I take the subway to Grand Central, then jump on the first northbound train. The hum of the rails would typically inspire a nap, but today I just stare out the window. As the New York cityscape gradually transforms into Connecticut's leafy suburbs, my mind loosens its grip. Cast aside are thoughts of priests and monks, candles and neurologists, even audits and savings rates. The jetsam fades to black and white as it goes, as if in deference to the kaleidoscopic autumn foliage outside the window. I'd forgotten how beautiful the colors could be.

I become entranced by the blur of it all. When the train stops and my gaze comes to rest on the peak of a distant house poking through the treetops, I see not a McMansion with a mortgage but a hidden castle engulfed in a sea of fire. The two towers rising from its roof are not chimneys but turrets. And the small, winged shadow circling them is nothing if not a dragon soaring over the flames.

"Everything okay?" asks Sasha, retrieving me from my abstraction.

"Yeah," I say. "I just thought I saw a monster."

She looks at me sharply, and I scramble for some way to explain myself. I responded without thinking. It hadn't occurred to me that my answer might disturb her. As it turns out, it didn't.

"Good," she says, smiling. "I was wondering if that guy was going to show up again." She rises from her seat. "This is us."

The streets of my childhood are much the same, though fences now surround the yards. We scale one barrier to get into my old backyard, and another to access the woods behind Esther's house—or what used to be Esther's house. I await the shout that will expose us as trespassers, but it never comes. We pass deeper into the forest, the first brown leaves of fall crunching under our feet. The rusted farm equipment is gone, but the old stump is still there, and the tree beside it. I point out the fateful branch to Sasha.

"That's pretty high," she admits.

"Damn straight."

Sasha crouches down and runs her fingertips over the face of the stump. It is no longer hard and smooth, but softened and scarred by the years. "And this is your doorway," she says with quiet sincerity. "Your passage to another world."

"I don't know about that. My tibia would argue that it's a tree stump."

"Maybe it *was* a door," says Sasha. "And it opened, and you don't even realize it. Maybe we're already in the other world."

"If so, it looks an awful lot like the first one."

"Does it?" she asks, but she isn't looking at me, and doesn't seem to expect an answer. Above us, light from the falling sun catches in the canopy of leaves, setting it afire and dropping the undergrowth into early dusk. My eyes fall to a dark hollow in the bushes behind Sasha. Something shifts in the shadows there—not a squirrel or a breath of wind among the branches but a flicker of deeper black against the gray. My chest flutters when I see that it's the dancing shade of my youth. It seems to be jumping in place and falling, with the same jest and melodrama it brought to its original burlesque, years ago, when it mimicked my brother and me catching leaves.

"What is it?" asks Sasha.

I decide not to further test Sasha's ability to suspend disbelief in me. At least not today. "That's where Esther jumped out from, when she scared me and the twins."

Sasha laughs. "I'm sorry I wasn't there to see it."

"I'm not. I may have peed my pants a little." My mind drifts back to summer and crickets, and Esther on her back patio, sitting with a lantern in the night.

"You had a crush on her," says Sasha.

"Please," I say. "I was ten. And she was fortysomething, I think."

"So what? I didn't say it was sexual. Crushes don't do age."

Fair enough, I think. Maybe I did carry a bit of a platonic torch for Esther. "She was awesome," I say. "You would've had a crush on her, too."

"Maybe we should find out," says Sasha.

Even in this age of the internet, it's not always easy to find someone you've lost. The computers may all be connected, but the people aren't. My mother professes not to know where Esther went, and the family that lives in Esther's old house is no help either. Maybe someday we'll all have chips in our heads that will tell everyone exactly where we are at all times, but for now I'm left scouring the web for a sign. Weeks of searching leave me with a single lead—a list of donors to a small public library in upstate New York. Esther's name is on it.

The white pages for the town aren't online, so I dial Information. For some reason I'm surprised to learn that Esther's number is listed. Perhaps a part of me thought that, like the monsters, she never really existed. Yet if the shade is back . . . Anyway, this may not even be the same Esther—a possibility that seems more likely when I reach an answering machine and don't recognize the voice. But maybe Esther's voice has changed with age. Or maybe it's just been too long.

I leave a message and wait. The next day, when my office phone shows an incoming call from an unknown number, I hold my breath and answer it. It's the woman from the answering machine, and with each word, she becomes more familiar.

"Why, Elliot Chance," says Esther. "You aren't a leprechaun after all."

I laugh. "What finally convinced you?"

"The pitch of your voice," she says. "Everybody knows that leprechauns never grow up. Oh, they may grow beards and smoke pipes, but they're still juvenile. You, on the other hand, have clearly become a man. Not that I'm surprised. I always thought you'd make a fine one."

For some reason I've never really thought of myself as a grown-up. I suppose the hallmarks are all there—twenty-seven years old, college degree, job, girlfriend, apartment. Yet somehow I don't think this is what Esther means.

"I don't know," I say. "I guess if wearing a tie and sitting at a desk in midtown Manhattan makes you an adult, then I qualify."

"Oh, the Big Apple," says Esther. "How exciting. I haven't been in years."

"Are you far?"

"It's just a train ride, really. Though I fear I'm becoming an insufferable homebody."

"Let's fix that!" I say, suddenly excited by the prospect of seeing her. "How about lunch at my favorite Italian place? Best lasagna in the city. I can meet you at Grand Central—"

"Oh, there's no need for that," says Esther. "I'm sure you're busy. Just give me the name of this favorite Italian place of yours. I'd be very happy to meet you there."

"You would?"

"Of course," she says, a smile in her voice. "Am I not also a traveler?"

The week leading up to my lunch with Esther is an unexpected blend of apprehension and tranquility. Though Esther isn't the type to pass judgment, I can't help but worry whether I've become the man she thought I would be. Yet my nervous energy is balanced by a new composure at work, as if my distracted thoughts afford some distance between me and the unrelenting sense of urgency that pervades our office. Though my commute home grows later each night—and darker now, as autumn ages—I don't mind. The long hours seem less so, and the dancing shade haunts my route so merrily that I begin to seek it out. While the eyes of most New Yorkers gravitate to neon and the glow of restaurant windows, mine are drawn to the black mouths of subway tunnels and the hollows beneath brownstone staircases, where the shade pantomimes in playful abstraction.

The morning of my reunion with Esther offers no exception to the general tumult. The office is a bewildering muddle of milling bodies engulfed by a flurry of emails, faxes, phone calls, and memoranda. I sit serenely at my desk, pleasantly occupied with my bagel and paperwork, bestriding the chaos like a mountain of calm. I'm wearing my best suit and most whimsical tie—full of colored spirals—which Jennifer thinks is "childish," but which I know Esther will appreciate. My anxiety about seeing Esther is gone, leaving just a simple eagerness to talk to her about all that's happened since last I saw her, and to hear what she has to say about it.

At midday I promptly rise from my desk, tuck my shirt in more snugly, and brush the last stubborn bagel crumbs from my lap. I retrieve my coat from the back of the door, and even manage to get it halfway on before Dean rushes in.

"Whoa, cowboy," he says. "Put a hitch in that giddyup. I need a redo."

He hands me a file with an audit I recently put together for one of his clients. I recognize it by the profusion of small, colored stickies jutting from its side, each one indicating a potential problem with the client's financial statements.

"What's wrong with it?" I ask.

"Too many flags."

I nod. This is not an unusual request. In any audit, there's room for discretion when calling out possible issues. I tend to be conservative, flagging anything that could conceivably cause trouble. But stickies frighten clients, particularly start-ups, so I'm never surprised when asked to loosen up a bit and let the more innocuous stuff slide. "Sure, I'll take a look this afternoon."

Dean shakes his head. "I need it stat. Client's going to be here in an hour."

"Sorry, I have a lunch." I refrain from pointing out that I gave him the file over a week ago, and that he didn't have to wait until the last minute to actually look at it.

"So cancel it." Dean says this nonchalantly, as if he's telling me to tie my shoe.

"I can't just cancel it."

"Why not? Is it with a client?"

A shimmer appears in the corner of my vision. It is the sparkling crescent monster from my childhood, flashing as if in warning. "No, but—"

"It'll take you ten minutes," says Dean.

"Nothing takes ten minutes," I shoot back. "I'll be late."

"So be late, Elliot." Dean's voice hardens. "I can't show this to the client. They'll lose their shit. Then they'll question whether we know what the hell we're doing, which is going to make them unhappy. And keeping clients happy is the only reason we're here. If that's not a priority for you, we've got other auditors."

Dean's not-so-veiled threat shakes my newfound equanimity. I wouldn't expect him to pull me off one of his clients over this, let alone all of them. But I honestly don't know, and Dean's clients represent the vast majority of my work. He's not wrong when he says that without them, I wouldn't have much reason to be here.

"Fine." I grab the file and rush back to my desk, not even pausing to take my jacket off. Thirty minutes later, I've scrubbed the audit down to a level of alarm that Dean deems acceptable. I race down to the street, forgoing the subway for a cab in the hope of getting to the restaurant faster, but I'm already late. Not that I think Esther will have left. On the contrary, what upsets me is the conviction that she is no doubt waiting patiently for me, and I've left her hanging.

As the taxi makes the final turn toward the restaurant, it's abruptly halted by a line of stopped traffic, which seems odd until I see a flash of blue and red lights ahead. I get out and walk. Nearing the far corner, I see the source of the lights—a police motorcycle parked in front of the restaurant. A crowd simmers at the edges of a cordoned-off patch of sidewalk, where yellow police tape stretches between the motorcycle, a garbage can, and a dented lamppost tilted askew. I scan the crowd and the windows of the restaurant for Esther's face, but don't see her. It occurs to me that I might look right at her and not recognize her, but the thought is quickly pushed aside by a sick, twisted feeling in my gut as I look past the crowd.

Lying on the sidewalk, isolated within the cordon of police tape, is a body. Heeled shoes and long skirt identify it as a woman, and fine wrinkles along the skin of her hands and forearms indicate that she was no longer very young. Her head and shoulders are hidden—shrouded respectfully, if hastily, by the policeman's jacket.

The twisted feeling blooms into a cold fear, corroding my insides. I approach the policeman slowly, almost feebly. He holds a police radio and a driver's license. The rest of him is an indistinct blot in my vision.

"I was . . ." I struggle to finish the thought. "I was supposed to . . ."

The blot shifts. I think it's looking at me. "Did you know her, sir?"

"*Did* I know?"

"She's dead. Hit-and-run."

Dead? Not Esther, then. Not dead. But the words that emerge from my mouth betray me. "She was my—"

The blot shifts again. "Grayston?" it asks. "Esther Grayston?"

I nod. I don't actually believe it, though. There is something unreal about the universe. *One way or another everything is a dream.*

The policeman is speaking. "I'm sorry, sir. Is there someone you can call? Ambulance is on its way." A pause that seems infinite. His voice sharpens. "We'll catch the driver. Don't worry about that. Witnesses say she was just standing here, and the car jumped the curb. Didn't even slow down. Bounced off the lamppost and just kept going."

Sirens in the distance. Angry shouts closer by. A fight. The policeman leaves to attend to it. The faces in the crowd turn away. I slip under the police tape and kneel beside the body. I remove the policeman's jacket.

She is older. Her hair is grayer. Yet I tell myself I would have recognized her. She looks thin, and frail. I don't know if this is due to age or death. Mostly she seems alone, separated from the world by a cordon of yellow tape—a world full of people who have turned their backs, who are already moving on to the next item on their agenda, who are too busy to keep their promise to arrive on time.

I suddenly find it intolerable that Esther's grandmother never hugged her. I think Esther would be exactly the kind of granddaughter you'd want to hug. I lean down and press my chest to hers, resting my arms on her shoulders, embracing her as best I can.

"I'm sorry, Esther."

But she's gone. The shadows cast by the surrounding crowd seem to grow deeper, yet somehow I know that the dancing shade also won't be coming back—the world too stark, too literal, too harshly lit, for its presence. Color drains from the scene, leaving behind the dull gray stain of existence. Though I can hear Gareth's voice exhorting me to grab my brush, I'm getting tired of painting over it.

PART III

If you wish to drown, do not torture yourself with shallow water.

—Bulgarian proverb

Elliot

(2000)

This is a day.

7:00 a.m. My alarm goes off with a grating drone, like a damaged lawn mower, though as far as I can tell they paved the last of New York City years ago, and there isn't a blade of grass for miles. I hit the snooze button. Nine minutes later, I hit it again. This scrimmage continues until I have to piss, at which point I stop the clock, conceding the losing battle against wakefulness and resenting this biological need to rise. Jennifer stays in bed, neither the alarm nor the time giving her just cause to awaken. Young lawyers in New York work ungodly hours. When they sleep at all, they sleep in, and prefer not to be disturbed. At rest, Jennifer's normally tireless demeanor becomes almost serene—inviting, it would seem to me, a good-morning kiss. I refrain, however, knowing it would be less than welcome.

The air conditioner in our apartment is broken. It's August, and hot as hell, but I start the coffeemaker anyway. Because caffeine. I'm up to 720 milligrams a day and there's no going back. The first sip still conveys a whiff of chemical cheer, but it's soon lost in the swill of the remaining ounces. I open my closet and stare at the same three suits and two pairs of shoes I've been wearing for years. My eleven ties hang listlessly, their machine-wrought patterns exposed as a somewhat pathetic attempt at self-expression. I pick one at random and close the closet, leaving behind my father's old overcoat. It's far too hot for it, which is just as well, since it now hangs loosely over my thin frame, calling attention to the fact that I'm losing weight.

8:00 a.m. I step into the street and join the rest of the daily commuters scurrying down Lexington. We are not rats, exactly, nor are we racing. Rats are assertive, resourceful. We are more like hamsters— passive, compliant, scampering back and forth along paths laid out for us like a prearranged network of vivarium tubes, each to his own cylinder, wholly isolated from each other despite our physical proximity.

The subway is merely a more conspicuous segment of the tunnels we inhabit. We crowd together in the artificial light, striving not to touch one another, apologizing when we do. The faces surrounding me are dour, as if we are being sent off to a war we can't win and from which we won't be coming back. Most of the troops stare blankly ahead, the anticipated stress of the workday already in their eyes. Others pore over the newspaper, seeking distraction but only exacerbating their unease. In any event, it's rare to meet the eyes of my fellow travelers. But then, we're not really travelers. You can't be a traveler if you never go anywhere.

8:30 a.m. The office elevator is decidedly more social. The high of caffeine and the imminence of the daily grind combine to fill the car with a contagious anxiety, a barely contained panic in the face of the new day's potential pitfalls, spewing forth in the tiresome drivel of my coworkers, repeated almost verbatim, week after week, month after month.

"—the club last night," Dennis is saying. "I've never been so hungover in my life." Dennis is a drunk. I don't know how he's managed to avoid getting fired.

"Whatever," says Nicole. She smiles awkwardly, trying to hide her discomfort. She hates Dennis. "You were so home last night. By yourself, as usual—unless you count your television."

"You should come out with us."

Nicole forces another smile. "You wish."

"Ah, youth," says Jeff, whose children's fingerprints can still be discerned in paint above his left eye. He huddles in the corner of the elevator as if trying to hide from someone, and he shakes his head as if to say that he would give anything to once again go to a club. "Just wait until you settle down," he says. "Then you'll see." Misery wants company. The others laugh at him.

"Does anyone else think it's weird that we all turn to face the door?" I ask. I don't know why I feel the need to pose this question, except that I *do* think it's weird, and I *do* want to know if anyone else thinks so, too. By the looks on their faces, I probably should have known better.

"Not really," says Dennis.

"I think it would be weird if we *didn't* face the door," says Nicole. "I mean, what are we supposed to do, turn around and stare at each other?"

8:35 a.m. I enter my office, take off my suit jacket, and hang it on the back of the door. Matt is already at his desk, eyes down, ensconced behind a partition of file boxes. The poster of Bora Bora above his head is, quite literally, the very picture of paradise. I've always told myself I'll travel someday. Apparently Matt has, too. Maybe we have more in common than spreadsheets and financial statements.

"Have you been to Bora Bora?"

Matt glances up from his computer. He seems vaguely confused by the fact that I'm speaking to him. "No," he says, turning back to his screen.

"So it's more aspirational."

"What is?"

"Your poster."

Matt's confusion shifts to mild annoyance when he realizes I'm still talking. It takes him a moment to realize I'm referring to the poster. "Oh," he says. "That's not mine. It was here when I started. I think it's covering up a hole in the wall."

He returns to his monitor, apparently concluding that our dialogue has been sufficiently resolved. Which I guess it has. I sit down at my desk and turn my attention to the boxes full of paper, the string of new emails on my computer screen. It is a struggle, this turning of attention. I don't know why. None of this is any different from when I started. If anything, after several years, it should be easier. It's not. What used to take me an hour now takes two. Complex spreadsheet formulas that I used to enjoy crafting now disorient me until the corners of my vision begin to narrow.

The truth is, I just don't care whether the financial statements of some start-up company burning through millions of other people's dollars have been prepared "in accordance with generally accepted accounting principles" or are otherwise perfect enough for rich investors or richer banks. But, as my father says, that's my problem. He says this whole idea that work is something you need to be passionate about is misguided. When I protest that it feels like I'm just working for a paycheck, he frowns. "Someone has to pay the rent," he says. I can't argue with him, but then I wasn't looking for an argument.

12:30 p.m. I eat lunch at my desk—a sandwich and some kind of sugar water. Rumor has it that in ages past, people used to go out for their midday meal. They would sit in restaurants or public parks, eating slowly and talking to each other. Now, if you're away from the office for longer than it takes to pick up a bag of food, you start to feel guilty about it, and vaguely fearful that someone is going to call you out.

The Vade Mecum stays in its drawer. I have no wisdom to add to its pages. Its title now feels pretentious to me, and its contents—as much as I can remember them—naive and ineffectual. Not to mention unmarketable. It seems that somewhere along the way, my firm's clients all became internet companies, whose primary objective is to drive "eyeballs" to their websites so that they can sell the company to the highest bidder and get rich quick. Never mind that the company isn't profitable, that it is in fact hemorrhaging cash. Advice on how to build a better business? Gleaned from years of careful research and analysis? How quaint.

Sasha's latest advertisement has been out for a while now—a full-page display about how an obscenely expensive car will make you sexier and therefore happier. I make a half-hearted attempt at solving Sasha's puzzle, knowing she couldn't resist such easy bait, but I struggle. I look for "greed" and "avarice" and "gross materialism," but the letters jumble on the page and I can't find a solution. I keep ending up with "gratitude," and I know that can't be right.

I give up and take a nap instead. I do this discreetly, in such a way that it could appear to anyone else that I'm actually reading something on the desk in front of me. I turn away from the door and rest one elbow on the desk, then put my head in my hand and close my eyes. I don't have a name for this particular style of nap—or series of naps, really, since I'm not under for more than a few minutes at a time before my elbow slips or my head nods or some noise from the hallway makes me think I've been caught. Still, though nameless, it is perhaps my favorite part of the day, this tiptoeing at the edge of dream, this peaceful carelessness, this nearly slipping away.

3:00 p.m. Dean executes his flyby. Though more anxious than usual these days, Dean hasn't fundamentally changed since before he was old enough to ogle. He continues to attack life in the same breathless way he approached leaf-catching—all bustle and bluster, inefficient and combative. What's worse, I realize that we are all beginning to emulate him. Dean's mindless hustle is becoming business "best practice," and to behave otherwise—to work just eight hours a day, for example, or go out for an hour at lunchtime—is viewed as not being "all in," not being a team player, not valuing your job enough to keep it. So we put our heads down and charge. We are like sailboats without captains—empty vessels crashing into one another as we trace the circumference of a yawning maelstrom of panic.

Whether due to his increasing disquiet, or his coterie of clients barely out of college, Dean's butchered aphorisms have become simple and crude. "The early bird gets laid," he likes to say. Or, "If you can't stand the heat, take off your sweater and show me your boobs." I no longer force a smile at my brother's feeble attempts at comedy. They feel sad to me, almost desperate, as if Dean is beginning to notice that I'm no longer even pretending to be amused.

Do I blame Dean for Esther's death? Rationally, no. He couldn't have known that by making me late for lunch, he would indirectly cause her to be in the exact wrong place at the exact wrong time. He didn't even know it was Esther that I was meeting, and still doesn't, because I never told him. Nor do I ever plan to. I couldn't bear some flippant comment about Esther, assuming Dean remembered her at all, which isn't likely. I look at him now, at his perpetually widened eyes and the beads of sweat on his upper lip. He seems to me like some fearful animal, focused on his immediate surroundings and maybe a moment or two into the future, but not more. I don't think Dean lingers in the past, let alone the sliver of it that included Esther.

He wraps up his flyby. If he said anything of note, I've already forgotten it. But then I wasn't really listening. He gives me one last look, tapping the side of his nose as if he's sharing a secret. "Remember, dork," he says, "if life slaps you, turn the other butt cheek."

8:00 p.m. I meet Bannor for our walk. Despite how long my work days have become, I have yet to miss a walk with Bannor. It is uncanny, really, how Bannor's voice mails never fail to prescribe a time and place that fits my schedule, as if he had access to my calendar and designed our walks to accommodate it. It would almost make you wonder, if you had the energy for wondering.

This evening's venue is Wall Street. I arrive a few minutes early and wait outside the New York Stock Exchange, staring dumbly at its marble columns until my vision blurs and they twist into misshapen dollar signs. I blink and turn away. The summer evening is warm and still light, and the street itself—closed to automobiles— is filled with tourists. They are a colorful, casual, camera-toting assembly, in stark contrast to the gray-suited bankers who occasionally get spit out from the mouths of the stone buildings, like pale corpses from a mausoleum. Pale corpses on cell phones.

If they regard each other at all, these tourists and these bankers, they do so summarily. The tourists snap pictures of the bankers along with everything else, as if these expressionless gray creatures were exhibits at a zoo—reptiles, maybe—released from their enclosures for the tourists' entertainment. The bankers slither through the crowd, their eyes hostile if not predatory at the sight of so many sheep. Animals all, then. Though at least each group has its class in the kingdom. Scaled in my gray suit yet gawking like a tourist, I have no place in either, lost somewhere in the gap between the two.

Bannor arrives. He greets me, as ever, with a silent nod that I've always tried to take as a smile but that I now admit is just that—a silent nod. It has been almost seven years since Bannor and I first met in group. He must be in his late fifties by now, yet time sits lightly on him. A bit more silver in his beard, perhaps. The lines in his forehead slightly more pronounced. He seems no older than when we first met, and certainly no closer to his own death. The only antiquated things about Bannor are his tweed suit and the exactness of the crease in his homburg hat. A century ago the tourists might have mistaken him for a banker, but not today. In this modern age, he is an eccentric, and a—well, I don't know what Bannor is, or does. He never talks about himself. If not discussing the future, or perhaps some small detail along our walk—the call of a particular bird, for example—Bannor is routinely speechless.

Normally I find the silence pleasant, even peaceful. But today it feels like just another form of closing off, of isolation masquerading as companionship, ultimately no different from Dean's inane clichés, or the repetitious blather of my coworkers, or the predictably rote wedding ceremonies of Jennifer's colleagues—all just different forms of distraction from something genuine, something authentic. Bannor may as well be my father at the breakfast table, with a bulwark of newspaper raised to his eyes to ward off conversation until he can make a break for the door. It suddenly occurs to me that I don't know him at all.

"How are you, Bannor?"

He raises an eyebrow. "Fine."

"Are you?" Normally I wouldn't press him, but "fine" is not an answer—or it would be, if everyone didn't automatically say it without meaning it, without even thinking about it, as if we've all agreed that we don't really want to know how anyone else is doing, or whether they are okay. I mean, what if they're not? What then? "Are you really fine, Bannor?" I continue. "How are things with you? What's going on with you?"

Bannor clasps his hands behind his back and keeps walking. We pass Federal Hall, with its thick marble pillars and imposing bronze statue of George Washington out in front. Bannor glances up at the former president with a hint of appeal in his eyes.

"In the future—"

"I didn't ask about the future," I say, pushing further. Something inside me is teetering, grasping for something to hold on to. "I asked about *you*. How are you? What do you do for a living? What are the other special occasions you wear your suit for? What is it that you lost? When, exactly, do you think you're going to kill yourself? And where? And how? Just give me one thing, Bannor. One real thing. For god's sake, I don't even know your first name."

Bannor removes his hat and rubs at the silver sheen of his closely cropped hair. His pace slows to a shuffle, almost stopping altogether, then picks up again as he begins to speak. "My wedding," he says. "I wore this suit at my wedding." He sets his hat back on his head. "In the past," he adds.

"I didn't know you were married."

"For a time," he says. "She left."

"I'm sorry, Bannor." My body crumples with shame, shrinking, wanting nothing more than to melt down to the pavement and escape into Wall Street's ample gutters. I shut my mouth, determined to leave Bannor alone, but he continues.

"Fire and water is what we were. By the end, there was so much smoke, we couldn't even see each other." He pauses, calculating. "That was ten years ago," he says. "Our daughter was five."

"You had a daughter?"

"Have," says Bannor. "I have a daughter, but I don't see her. Not now, at least. She thinks I'm crazy."

"Because of . . . your travels?"

Bannor nods. "My first trip was about six months after they left. I made the mistake of telling my daughter about it. I thought it could be our little secret, but she told her friends at school, where I worked. I lost my job soon after that. Not her fault, of course. She didn't know any better. Really, you'd think I would have seen the whole thing coming, given that I was traveling to the future, but it didn't work that way. That's what you'd call irony."

"What did you do at the school?"

"I was a teacher," he says. "History. Not anymore, though. I lived my whole life in Harlem—now I bag groceries in Alphabet City, and spend Sunday mornings clearing my neighbors' needles and shell casings off the front stoop." He shakes his head. "You'd think I would have seen it coming."

We've nearly reached the eastern end of the street, where a small patch of sky opens up over the East River. The bankers and tourists are mostly behind us. Bannor stops and turns to look back to where we started. At the far western end, just visible through the narrow lane between the muscular towers of commerce, the delicate steeple of Trinity Church points to the heavens.

"I'm sorry, Bannor," I say again.

"Albert," he says. "My first name—it's Albert. Though, if you don't mind, I prefer to use my last. It's the one thing we still share, my daughter and I."

9:15 p.m. I skip the gym. Again.

9:30 p.m. I meet Sasha on her fire escape. Judging by the number of used matches and cigarette butts on the sidewalk, she's been here awhile. I settle in beside her to look out over the water and the lights of Brooklyn. I keep silent, still stinging with guilt over making Bannor talk about his past, and not wanting to do any more damage.

Besides, Sasha's already heard everything I had to say. About Esther's death, I mean. Given that Sasha was the only person I ever spoke to about it, she had to hear it more than once, until even I could see that this fire escape was no confessional, and that any catharsis my tirade may have originally provided had since decayed into masochism. Sasha listened patiently throughout. Now that I've slumped into silence, she bears that, too, at times mirroring my muteness, at times filling the space with words of her own.

Tonight she speaks casually of South Dakota. She's recently back from visiting her parents, in the same house she grew up in. It's a relatively recent development, these trips back home. During most of her years in New York, Sasha almost never went home, not even for the holidays. Especially not for the holidays, she would say. Last summer, though, she finally got on a plane, but not before laying down two rules for herself. First, she'd only stay for five days at a time. Everyone in their proper dose, she says. Even parents. Second, she'd only visit during summer. So she can listen to the crickets.

She doesn't do much when she's there, but I like hearing about it anyway—catching up on local gossip with her mom, watching television with her dad, even taking walks through the woods near her house.

"I found something that made me think of you," she says. "I thought maybe you'd like to have it."

She reaches into the shadows at her side and retrieves a round bundle of cloth that I hadn't noticed until now. She hands it to me. No bigger than a golf ball, it sits lightly in my palm. I unwrap the cloth, and my throat clenches when I see the hard black object within, its dull sheen barely visible in the city's evening glow.

"It's a piece of coal," I say.

"Coal?" says Sasha in mock surprise. "That's bona fide anthracite. I have it on good authority."

I don't know if I want to argue with her or thank her, but it doesn't matter because I can't possibly speak anyway, consumed with the effort of repressing the sobs that well up in my chest, clamoring to get out.

"Elliot." Sasha's voice grows gentle, and I know what's coming. "It's not your fault," she says. She's told me this before. More than once. Yet somehow she knows that she's not done saying it, because somehow she knows that I still don't believe it's true.

11:08 p.m. I don't have sex with my girlfriend. After three years, our sex life is no longer inspired choreography, but a different kind of performance art, where the same show is performed for the same audience again and again. I'm not sure if this is a problem or if it's normal, but we don't talk about it, so we're not likely to find out. Instead, we dutifully make sure we get naked together every few weeks, each of us no doubt suspecting that regular sex is on some "healthy relationship" checklist somewhere. On with the show.

But not tonight. I am in bed with the television on when Jennifer comes home and crawls in next to me, burrowing into the covers on her side.

"What are you watching?" she asks, her voice a disembodied murmur from within her cocoon.

What am I watching? A tearjerker of an old movie that never fails to get to me, never fails to leave me with this vague, fleeting memory of something lost and beautiful.

Jennifer risks a glimpse. "Oh my god, are you crying?" she asks, suppressing a chuckle.

Am I crying? No, I don't think so. My vision is a bit glassy, maybe, but my cheeks are dry enough. That's not crying, is it? And why would I be crying, anyway? What do I have to cry about?

"Elliot," says Jennifer. "It's just a movie. If it makes you sad, don't watch it."

She hunkers deeper under the covers and is instantly asleep, her words hanging in the empty air like the pronouncement of a generation. If it makes you sad, don't do it. If it's not real, don't believe in it. And so on. They mean well, these people. They do mean well, don't they? You can't argue with the soundness of this advice, can you?

According to physicists, everything in the universe exists only to the extent that it relates to something else. This is not metaphor, this is science. Even the most elementary particle, they say, is in essence a set of relationships reaching out to other things. If an electron, then, is separated from the protons and neutrons and other electrons of the atom in which it resides, and is not observed or otherwise acted upon by any outside force, then that electron, as a matter of scientific fact, is not merely isolated or independent. That electron, quite literally, doesn't exist. There is no electron.

A tear finally does run down my cheek. I'm not entirely sure why. I have no defensible reason, scientific or otherwise, to feel this way, or to be so tired—of these people, of this day, of this life. Yet, as Sasha once said, "Reason's got nothing to do with it." To the extent I'm actually here at all, I just don't want to be anymore. I shut off the television. The movie isn't quite over, but I know how it ends.

After

Elliot

(2000)

There are a number of ways to kill yourself. One way or another, they're all bad.

Many are too painful or difficult to even consider. If you are neither a Buddhist monk nor a Japanese samurai, then you probably can't achieve—or even describe—the strength of mind required to immolate yourself or carve open your own abdomen with a sword. Less exotic methods aren't much better. It's nearly impossible to break your own neck by hanging yourself, which means you'd have to dangle there—by your throat—until you suffocate. And if you've ever pressed the edge of a razor blade to your inner wrist, just to see how it felt, you know that some innate sense of self-preservation immediately kicks in to stifle any thought of breaking the skin, let alone cutting deeply enough—twice—to bleed to death. Suicide is hard. Even if you conclude that the end justifies the means, the means themselves may terrify you to the point where you can't invoke them.

Most methods also allow far too much time to abort the process before completion. It can take seven minutes to suffocate by hanging—undoubtedly the kind of excruciating ordeal you'll want to get out of once you're in it. Or, if you pull a very old car into the garage and close the door, you'll have maybe twenty minutes before you black out, during which you'll somehow need to refrain from simply turning off the engine. As to slitting your wrists, if you manage to cut deeply enough, you may still have to watch yourself bleed for over an hour—more than enough time for your survival instinct to take over, whether you want it to or not.

Even if you find the resolve to begin, and the conviction to follow through, the means themselves are liable to let you down. Many methods are frighteningly unreliable. Only six percent of people who slit their wrists actually die as a result. Of those who intentionally overdose, the success rate is six percent for nonprescription drugs and twelve percent for prescription. Failing grades, by any measure. And the consequences of failure can be nothing short of horrific—more so, arguably, than the consequence of success. A drug overdose can devastate internal organs. An aborted hanging will almost certainly result in brain damage. The long-term effects of carbon monoxide poisoning can include memory defects, parkinsonism, dementia, psychosis, paralysis, and blindness.

And then there's one more scenario. The one in which you do everything correctly, nothing goes wrong, and you successfully reach the point when it's too late to abort. A fait accompli but for the waiting. You take the pills, or jump from the bridge, or step off the chair with a rope around your neck. Even then, there's often time—whether minutes or seconds—to contemplate what you've done, to reconsider that which can no longer be reconsidered. Time for an emphatic, resounding voice to rise up from the deepest, most primal corner of your reptilian brain and rage against your desire to be gone, flooding what's left of the vessel of your spirit with guilt and shame and doubt, declaring in no uncertain terms that you've made a terrible, irrevocable mistake. It is a voice you don't ever want to hear.

All of which leaves me with one option.

"A gun," says Bannor, echoing my words back to me, apparently unsure whether or not he's heard them correctly. "You want to steal a gun."

"Yes," I say. It's not easy to surprise Bannor, though I take no pride in having done so. "From your neighbors. The ones who leave shell casings on your stoop."

We are walking through the Ravine, in a fragment of Central Park called the North Woods—a bite-size homage to the island of wilderness since displaced by New York City. Even this tribute is manufactured—streams and waterfalls made by human hands, boulders strategically placed, trees carefully planted to create the disorderly illusion of natural order. Granted, in some spots, away from the main avenues, the North Woods achieve a certain still-ness. In moments, you can almost believe you're deep among the trees of Connecticut, looking for words in a book that no longer exists.

"An unusual request," says Bannor.

I know he's baiting me, but I don't plan on discussing my intent. Telling someone your goal seems a way of trying to prevent it from being reached. A cry for help, or something, which is fine if that's what you're looking for. I wasn't going to talk to anyone about it at all, but I need Bannor's help to make it happen, and I trust him not to judge or argue. I decide that I won't offer up my reason for wanting the gun. If Bannor asks me directly whether I plan on killing myself, I'll be honest with him. He doesn't.

"They're kids," says Bannor. "As often high as not. If you want to relieve them of a gun, that's fine by me."

"I don't want to put you in danger."

Bannor waves this off with his typical composure. I suppose that once you've foreseen your own death, other perils don't concern you much. We climb a short rise to stand before the Blockhouse—a square one-story structure built in 1814 to defend against the Brit-ish. It is more block than house—the few openings in its thick stone walls are just large enough for the business end of a musket. If there's anything inside, I don't know what it is. A sign out front says that the fort once contained a cannon, but that it is now "empty, roofless, and securely locked."

"They go out on Saturday nights," says Bannor. "They don't always bring the gun."

A flicker of warmth passes through my chest. I can't tell if it's gratitude, fear, or something else. "Thank you, Bannor."

He shrugs. "If you say so."

After he left Harlem, Bannor toppled southward down the eastern edge of Manhattan until he landed in Alphabet City, so named because it's bounded and intersected by Avenues A, B, C, and D. "Though if it were up to me," says Bannor, "I'd give it an F." He now lives on the fifth floor of a boxy walk-up that at one time might have been described as a tenement, and hasn't changed much since.

On Saturday night, he meets me at the corner of his street to escort me past several shadowed stoops, where some of the locals gather for the evening's illicit activities. "Everybody knows everybody here," Bannor explains. "Better if they don't take any undue interest in you." The night is warm, and Bannor is dressed casually, in brown slacks and a short-sleeved button-down shirt. It's the first time I've seen him wear anything other than his trademark tweed suit and homburg hat. Evidently he doesn't feel the night's agenda constitutes a special occasion. I don't hold it against him.

The front door of Bannor's building hangs open. Inside is a dark, cramped foyer, illuminated only by the faint light of a distant streetlamp. I try to close the door behind me, but the lock's strike plate has been torn from the doorframe. The bolt protrudes uselessly from the door, with nothing to fit into.

"Leave it," Bannor tells me. "It's been that way awhile."

A narrow and even darker stairwell snakes its way up through the building's core, its walls scrawled with graffiti both strident and

inscrutable. We reach the fifth floor and head down a long hallway toward the rear of the building. Here, incongruously, a well-
maintained row of ceiling bulbs reveals freshly painted walls, both
of which I suspect are Bannor's doing. Most of the doors display at
least two locks, if not three, though Bannor's has but one. "What
do I have that anybody wants?" he asks.

The austerity of Bannor's apartment supports his claim. A single
sparsely furnished room serves as kitchen, bedroom, and living
area. One other door leads to a compact bathroom, and a lone
window opens to a fire escape on the building's backside. Yet the
room's tidy economy, and a few thoughtful touches, belie the pov-
erty of the rest of the building. A vibrantly colored Mexican rug
sets off the kitchen area. Handmade throw pillows adorn the bed.
A large dent in a red teakettle somehow evinces not clumsiness
but character, and a dedication to usefulness over ostentation. The
space contrasts sharply with my and Jennifer's apartment. There is
no Italian espresso machine, no closet stuffed with coats, no extra
bedroom in which no one ever sleeps.

Though the decor offers some insight into Bannor's nature, I
can see just three personal items in the apartment, all hanging on
the refrigerator. The first is a photograph—Bannor in his tweed
suit and hat, standing with his arm around a woman in a yellow
skirt. At their backs is a tall fence and what looks like a lion in the
distance. Nestled between them is a little girl in a blue dress. Her
hair rises in a jubilant frizz above her head, as if electrified by the
wattage of her broad grin. The photograph itself is held in place by
the second personal item—a ceramic magnet that looks like it was
painted by a young hand. It is in the likeness of a miniature black-
board. Written across it, as if in chalk, is the word DADDY.

"The Bronx Zoo," says Bannor. "Have you been?"

"No," I say. "Looks like a special day."

Bannor nods. "A long time ago."

I turn my attention to the third item on the refrigerator—an unopened letter addressed to "Mr. Albert Bannor," with a return address of New Orleans.

"From my wife," says Bannor. "*Ex*-wife."

"She's in New Orleans?"

Bannor nods. "They moved there a while back. Just before you and I met, actually. She said she wanted our daughter to get in touch with her heritage. I told her Harlem is our heritage, but she sees things differently."

"Don't you want to open it?"

He shakes his head. "Not yet." He moves to the door and raises his hand over the light switch. "It's going to be dark," he says. He flips the switch, making good on his prediction. As my eyes adjust to the blackness, Bannor moves past me and opens the window that leads out to the fire escape. "Right," he says. "All set, then?"

I follow him out the window. The rear of the building faces those of its neighbors, as if they were shunning one another. The space between is still as midnight. I'm reminded briefly of another fire escape, and of Sasha, but Bannor doesn't stop to rest his back against the bricks and light a cigarette. Instead, he drops silently down the ladder to the floor below. I shadow him until we are crouching outside the window directly under his. The dark pane reveals nothing.

"Looks like they're out," says Bannor.

"How do we get in?"

In answer, he slides the window open. "They don't worry much about being robbed." He takes a small penlight from his pocket and hands it to me. "And *we're* not getting in. *You* are."

I crawl through the open window and drop into the kitchen— the first of a line of rooms that extend in railroad fashion toward the front of the building. The thin beam of the penlight reveals a rusted gas stove, a metal folding table, dirty dishes piled in the sink. A cockroach scurries behind a coffeemaker. Opening one plain wooden cabinet after another, I find a few pots, pans, and mugs, but no gun.

I slip down the long hallway, passing through a living area dominated by a large flat-screen television that seems out of place in the squalor of the apartment. In the bedroom, splayed carelessly over the dusty floor, are three soiled mattresses, only one of which is fitted with a sheet. I turn to the lone dresser, rummaging through crumpled clothing until I find what I'm looking for—a heavy revolver with a wooden grip and black barrel. With a fumbling effort, I manage to open the cylinder and confirm that it's loaded.

I shove the gun in my pocket and head back toward the kitchen. As I navigate the darkness of the living room, I kick something hard. It yields at the blow, clattering in all directions on the hardwood floor. I cringe at the noise, and fear that I've broken whatever it was into pieces, but the penlight reveals a scattered pile of compact discs. Kneeling down to gather them, I see that they're video games, the kind that teenagers would play. A corresponding game console is hooked up to the flat-screen, with several joysticks lying idly by. Beside them, more ominously, are the needles Bannor had mentioned, along with spoons, a lighter, and two small plastic bags full of brown powder.

"There are children starving in Africa," my mother used to say. "You should be grateful." This was her refrain whenever I was upset in a way or to a degree that she didn't think was valid. She didn't mean that I should be grateful that there were children starving in Africa, of course. She meant that I should be grateful for what I had, particularly because other people had so much less. The theory, I guess, was that you could not be sad if you had something to be grateful for, and that you always had something to be grateful for because there were children—whether starving in Africa or lost to heroin addiction in New York City—whose suffering was unquestionably worse than yours.

It took me years to discover at least two fundamental flaws in this argument. First, gratitude isn't happiness. If it were, the dictionary would just use one word for both. Second, if you follow this line of thinking to its conclusion, it unravels. Ultimately, how bad do things have to get before you are permitted to feel sad, or lost, or hopeless? By my mother's theory of happiness, everyone who still has something to lose should be boundlessly joyful. The only person who can claim any right to feel miserable would be the single unluckiest person in the world, and even he might have trouble arguing his misery with my mother, since things could always get worse for him, too.

I don't know why or for how long I linger there, staring stupidly at the paraphernalia of drug addicts and regretting their misfortune. Eventually I stir myself into motion again—echoes of my mother's words having done nothing to change my mind, just as her well-intentioned reasoning never made me feel better. If anything, it made me feel worse. Grateful, yes—but also sad, that the world could be so unapologetically cruel, and guilty, for not being happier in it.

I creep back into Bannor's apartment to find him sitting at the small dining table, waiting for me. Unwilling to linger, I move toward the door.

"Success?" he asks.

"Yes. Thank you, Bannor."

"You can stay here if you want," he offers.

"Thanks," I say, but I open the door anyway.

"You'll be going home?"

Home. The word sounds strange to me, but it's as good as any other. "Yes."

"Okay, then," says Bannor.

The windows of my apartment are lightless. Jennifer is out of town, and I'm not expecting company. I approach from the far side of the street, my fingers twitching, my skin prickling as if it were on fire. When a figure steps out from behind the ginkgo tree, my hand instinctively dives to my pocket for the gun, then stops when I recognize Bannor. It seems just a minute earlier that I had left him in his apartment, though in truth I don't know how long it's taken me to get here. It might have been quite easy for him to outpace me. In the lamplight, his closely cropped hair is a silvery shimmer.

"Jesus, Bannor. You scared me."

"Odd, isn't it, that you can still be scared? I mean, considering."

"I guess." I don't really want to consider it. I don't want to consider anything.

Bannor gestures toward the front door of my building. "Shall we?"

"I don't think that's a good idea," I tell him. "I think you should go home."

He frowns. "Elliot, if tonight is going to be your last on this earth, I'd like to be there for it. And if not—well, we can order pizza."

I register his joke mechanically, without finding the humor in it, without wanting to find the humor. "I'm not going to be ordering pizza, Bannor."

He nods. "I'm not afraid. You don't need to be, either."

"Of dying?"

"Of anything."

I don't want to argue, or even ask what he means. I turn to climb the steps to my building. When Bannor follows me, I'm too tired to protest. He trails me inside, up the staircase and into my apartment, settling into a chair beneath the living room window. I drift to the center of the room and linger there in the dark, unsure of what to do next. If there was a plan, I've lost it. Perhaps it's Bannor's presence that unnerves me. Or the weight of the gun in my pocket.

The gun. Right. I take out the revolver, daunted by its heft. "It's good that it's heavy," I say, not sure who I'm speaking to, or why I'm speaking at all.

"Okay," says Bannor. His voice is tiny, like a miniaturized version of a voice.

"I should get a bag or something," I say. "For the afterburner." I meant to say *aftermath*, but my mouth seems to be moving on its own now.

"No need," says Bannor. "I'll take care of things."

My free hand grasps a chair from the dining table and slides it to the center of the room. My legs buckle, dropping me into the seat, and my torso bends forward until my elbows are resting in my lap. The other hand grips the gun normally, pointing it at the floor. It hangs from the end of my arm like an anchor.

"It's good that it's so heavy," my mouth says again. "But it's not a rule or anything. There's no animal." *Manual*, my mouth meant to say.

It's easy, really, in the end. The hand turns the gun around, like this, so that its thumb is on the trigger and you're staring down the muzzle. The other hand grips the barrel, holds it steady.

"You are a lonely electron," says my mouth.

The revolver is so heavy. So heavy and so real, its wooden grip slick with sweat, its metallic body cold and dark. The mere sight of it invokes unwanted emotions that threaten your intent. Fear. Revulsion. But it is exhausting to be an electron. All that spinning and spinning through the vast empty space of the atom. It is all so terribly exhausting. It would be pleasant to be done. A relief to be done. And easy, really, in the end.

The hand raises the gun.

"Elliot Chance!" The shout detonates through the room. The voice is familiar, yet thick with emotion in a way I don't recognize. I look up to see Sasha's silhouette in the entryway. Her hands are raised to her chest, clenched into fists, as if she's going to fight someone.

"Bannor, you left the door open," says my mouth.

Sasha steps over the threshold. "No," she says. "Absolutely not. Put it down."

This is not a request but a command, which is all it takes, apparently, to frustrate whatever purpose I thought I had. I set the revolver gently on the floor at my feet. Sasha turns on a lamp, then comes to stand beside me. She's not looking at me, though. She's glaring at Bannor.

"What the hell are you thinking?" she demands. Though I expected the question, I'm relieved to see it isn't directed at me. "You gave him a gun?"

"No," says Bannor. "He stole it."

"Goddammit, Bannor!" Sasha actually stamps her foot on the floor. She seems almost maniacal, her short hair jutting out in all directions as if it had just exploded from her scalp. It occurs to me that she may have been sleeping. I have no idea what time it is.

"Elliot's life does not end tonight," says Bannor.

"You don't know that!"

"I know when I'm going to die," explains Bannor. "And I know that Elliot is there when I do."

This revelation stops Sasha, who seems as surprised as I am to hear this new twist to Bannor's prophecy. She lets out a deep, frustrated sigh. "Bannor, that's—"

"Insane?" he asks.

"Irresponsible."

Bannor nods. "Maybe so," he says. He rises from the couch and starts for the door. On his way out, he pauses beside Sasha, leaning over to give her a fatherly kiss on the top of her head. "That's why I called *you*."

He slips out, closing the door behind him. Sasha turns her ire to me. Her glower sends a bolt of adrenaline through my chest, a surge of energy that clashes with my utter exhaustion like an oscillation of fire and ice, expanding and contracting my senses until I feel myself begin to splinter.

"I don't believe you," Sasha says tightly.

"But you do," I tell her.

"What?"

"You *do* believe me," I say. "We didn't ask to be here, remember? We didn't bid for these lives at auction. You said."

"That was hypothetical."

"Not for Pearl."

Sasha's look hardens further, as if I've struck a blow I didn't intend. "This is different," she says.

"How?"

"Because I'll miss you!"

The brittle edge to her voice stops me. I don't know how I ended up in this negotiation with Sasha, or how she ended up on the other side of the negotiating table. I thought that we were aligned on these matters. The last thing I want to do is worsen the pained look in her eyes. "I'll miss you, too," I say softly.

"No." Her words come at an angry clip. "You won't. Because you'll be dead. You weren't even going to say goodbye."

"I thought we said our goodbyes. That we had our ending. I thought that was the point."

"That you could just go kill yourself?" Sasha's patience begins to fray. She doesn't seem to know what to do with the shreds. "No, that was not the point."

"Sasha," I say quietly. "What if I'm ready?"

"You'd be selfish, that's what."

"Was Pearl selfish? You said it was her decision. You said—"

"Well, I changed my mind!" The breaking of Sasha's voice seems to shock her. She turns and hurries for the door as if to escape further damage. "It's selfish, Elliot," she says on her way out. "Tell yourself whatever you want, but it just is."

The door slams, sending echoes that reverberate through the room before eventually sinking into the dull silence left behind. I lower my head into my hands and stare down at my feet. Sasha's words rattle noisily through my mind, grieving me in a way I hadn't expected. A long moment passes before I realize that she's taken the gun.

Before

So there you are, at the Door of Wonders.

Merriam smiles nervously. Jollis gives you an affirming nod. "Okay, then," he says. "Let's do this." He faces the door, grips the brass ring at its center, and pulls.

On the other side, an open plaza stretches boundlessly in every direction. From one unseen end to the other, hovering at regular intervals just above you, are luminous objects. Stars, you think, until you squint past their initial brilliance. For each is no bigger than a breadbox, and no two are alike, resulting in what you somehow know is an endless array of colors, shapes, luster, and movement. They spin and pulse, glimmer and flow. Most are abstract, but others take on vaguely familiar forms—a flickering lamp, a bubble in a stream, a flash of lightning in a summer cloud.

Directly beneath each of these brilliant curios is a throng of travelers. They swarm and squeeze and jostle, leaping for the light. They bellow challenges and vent supplications. Though their clamor is passionate, there is no ferocity in it, only a collective, joyful yearning. You haven't a clue what it is they think they're doing.

"Bidding," says Merriam. "This is the Auction. They're bidding for lives." Each of the gleaming curios, she explains, is a life yet to be lived, a journey yet to be ventured, awarded in the Auction to whichever traveler desires it most deeply.

You look closer, peering more intently into the dance of each curio until you can make out, in precise detail from beginning to end, the measure of the life within. Some are shorter, some longer, some front-loaded with joy and ending in sadness, others strung with years of injustice before culminating in bittersweet redemption. The variations are infinite, yet not a single life is without its assemblage of petitioners. Nearest to you—shaped like a hornet's nest and pulsing with red-and-gold light—is an unequivocal train wreck of an existence, littered with poor decisions, bad breaks, and tragedies ill prepared for. Yet the press of travelers beneath it is as vibrant as any other, the journey no less desired for its ruinous run of misfortune.

"Why are they bidding on that one?" you ask.

"Why wouldn't they?" asks Jollis.

"It just looks so . . . hard," you say. "Wouldn't they rather have the easiest, most successful lives?"

Jollis shrugs. "Who can say? Some *do* bid on so-called charmed existences. But perhaps a traveler recalls a life of ease that was utterly spiritless, and now longs for one of meaning through hardship. Or a journey without tragedy that ended up feeling superficial, leading them to crave one of loss and depth." Jollis gestures toward the life shaped like a hornet's nest. The bidding for it has grown more frenzied, and the pulsing of its red-and-gold light quickens in response. "Or maybe a traveler is fresh off a life of great achievement, plagued by even greater anxiety," says Jollis, "so that they seek one of failure, devoid of expectations."

Jollis's reasoning is unusual, yet somehow compelling. In fact, even as he speaks, your gaze is drawn to a life off to your left that you find oddly appealing—a green and glittery thing, shaped like a violin, in which a particularly disastrous choice leads to all sorts of mayhem. Still, there seems to be a flaw in Jollis's logic.

"But I'd just avoid it all," you say. "The mishaps, the bad decisions. Knowing the consequences, I'd just make different choices."

Jollis shakes this off. "After the Auction, just before you are born, comes the Fugue. It erases any memory of the life to be lived, and even the fact that you chose it."

Merriam nods. "It's the only way the whole thing works."

"So my choices aren't really choices," you say. "I'd be going through motions that are already determined. I just wouldn't realize it."

"No," says Jollis. "Your decisions in the life are real, original. The fact that we see them here doesn't change the fact that you make them. You are entirely free to decide otherwise. You just don't."

"Then is the life made, or do I make it?"

"Yes."

"That doesn't make sense."

"Sometimes you have to abandon sense for truth," says Merriam.

A cheer is raised among the travelers nearest you. The auction for the hornet's nest has been completed. The winner is congratulated by the others, no soreness or envy to be found. You see, too, that the green and glittery violin has also been awarded. No matter. With a boundless menu from which to choose, you feel certain you'll find a life you like. Or don't like, that is, depending on what you're looking for.

"When you're ready, the Fugue is that way," says Merriam, pointing. "But if you're so inclined, there's a training arena over there. It's a beautiful facility."

"Training for what?"

"For your life."

"Why bother training if I'm just going to forget it all?"

Jollis glances at Merriam. "Some travelers say the Fugue is imperfect," he says. "Others believe that you keep the traits you train for, even if you forget the training itself."

"Like muscle memory?"

Jollis shrugs again. It occurs to you that much of this is a mystery

even to him and Merriam. You consider again the Door of Wonders, the ardent assemblages of travelers, the infinite matrix of curious lives, shining like so many stars in the sky.

"So I won't remember any of this?"

"For all intents and purposes, no."

You nod. Merriam and Jollis warned you that things would get
confusing, and they have. Still, nothing you've been told makes
you want to turn aside now. As your gaze circles back to Merriam
and Jollis, there's just one last thing that troubles you.

"Will I remember *you*?"

"I'm afraid not," says Merriam, smiling sadly. "But don't worry.
We'll see you again."

Elliot

(2000)

New York City. The far edge of December. The first heavy snow of the season is falling—wide, soft flakes, each one intricate and symmetrical. Like the pictures you see of snowflakes in books. Like the way you think snowflakes ought to be.

I step out the front door of my building and pause for a moment, suspended in the cold, windless air. Dense clouds and the wintry tilt of the earth conspire to cast the morning in a twilight that will linger all day, until time itself becomes indeterminate. The snow descends with a leisurely nonchalance, belying the swiftness with which it blankets the city. As the inches accumulate, ordinary sights and sounds disappear—parked cars become hillocks, pedestrians retreat into electric-lighted burrows, even the buildings largely vanish in the mist. The whiteness is so otherworldly, I hesitate to label it white at all. They say the Inuit peoples of the North have fifty words for snow. I think they would need to invent another, were they to experience this winterbound Manhattan.

Normally, I would venture out into this frozen world while it lasts, before New York feels the storm waning and bullies its way out of its forced hibernation. Once the plows and cabs and plodding feet reawaken, the brilliant white will deteriorate into a ponderous gray slush, flecked with soot and car exhaust, threatening to flood your shoes at every puddled intersection. There is little time—hours, at most—in which to wander the fleeting wonderland, to trek the exposed spine of Sixth Avenue as if you were the last sojourner on earth, marveling at the silence of a city that is finally, mercifully, asleep. Or to peer upward with your mouth agape, endeavoring to distinguish the falling flakes from the backdrop of cloud, in the hope of catching one on your tongue. I'm always amazed by the emptiness, by the realization that no one else chooses to immerse themselves in the spectacle. (I once thought I saw a cross-country skier on the West Side Highway. The distant figure, blurred by the falling snow, appeared to stop and wave to me before passing away. By the time I reached the spot where I thought the skier had stood, there were no tracks left, and I can't be sure it wasn't just a dream I had.)

But I do not venture into the ephemeral this morning. Instead, I raise a shovel and clear a path through the snow—down the steps and across the sidewalk to the base of the ginkgo tree—so that Jennifer's Chihuahua can take a shit.

I say "Jennifer's Chihuahua" because it was Jennifer who one day brought him home and informed me that he was staying. She, however, refers to him as ours—or as Henri, which is what she named him. I initially found this funny, since it seemed the kind of name you'd give a French poodle rather than a Mexican Chihuahua. The irony was lost on Jennifer, though, who decided she liked the name after hearing it on her favorite sitcom. I'm not sure how Henri feels about it. I thought about calling him Enrique, but I didn't want to confuse him, and who am I to stereotype him anyway? Maybe he identifies as French. After getting to know him better, I now believe that he has something of the artist in him—the expressive pouts, the fits of delight, the flair and variety of his poops at the ginkgo tree. I've decided to pretend that he was named after the famous French painter, and will even call him Matisse now and then, to which he responds with a look of curious annoyance.

I've tried to point out Henri's aesthetic disposition to Jennifer, but she doesn't see it. "He's a dog, Elliot," she says, quite accurately.

"But he's so expressive," I say. "Look at his face."

She laughs. "He probably has to go potty."

"What about the fact that he refuses to wear the blue sweater you got him, but is okay with the red one?"

"Dogs can't see red," says Jennifer.

"Or the way he'll just stop and stare at some random object?" I say. "As if he's studying it for a portrait or something?"

"He's probably trying to figure out the best way to hump it."

There's no convincing her, but it no longer surprises me that I might know Henri better than Jennifer does. Arguably, based on the amount of time spent with him, Henri has become not Jennifer's dog, nor ours, but mine. Jennifer has been working more than ever, and neither Henri nor I have seen all that much of her. Today she even bucked her lawyer's trend of sleeping late, leaving for the office before dawn in order to get there ahead of the storm. That it may now prevent her from coming back home is a thought that I suppose didn't occur to her.

For several reasons, I've accepted both Henri's arrival and the burden of caring for him without complaint. First, I've grown quite fond of the little French Mexican. After several months of scraping food into his bowl, curling up on the couch with him, and scooping up his stylish turds, I believe we've formed a bond, even if he categorically rejects my attempts to train him to do anything else. ("I am an artist!" I can almost hear him say.) Second, next to the odd blizzard, Henri is the best excuse I have for going in to work late, or leaving early, both of which I've been doing more of recently. Dogs aren't allowed at the office—an exclusionary policy of which Henri disapproves, as evidenced by the pool of urine he leaves on the kitchen floor every Monday afternoon. ("An artist!")

But the primary reason I've embraced Jennifer's dog is because Jennifer asked me to (sort of)—and because, ever since Sasha berated me for wanting to kill myself, I've been thinking a lot about selflessness. Not that Sasha's intervention actually changed my mind, or magically sutured the stubborn and inscrutable rift in my heart. Had Sasha not taken the revolver with her when she left, I can't say that I wouldn't have picked it right back up again. Yet her accusation of selfishness bothered me far more than my mother's insinuations of ingratitude ever did, until I began to wonder whether I'd been going about everything all wrong.

I'm trying, then, to forget about "what Elliot wants" or "what Elliot needs." In other words, and with all due respect to Gareth and his gracious leadership of group, I have stopped trying to grab happiness by the balls. I could never get a firm grip on them anyway, and I'm not sure happiness appreciated my efforts. To paraphrase Sasha, some emotions just aren't into that kind of thing.

If Jennifer's Chihuahua represents my first opportunity to practice selflessness, my brother provides the second. After years of hobnobbing, chumming, consorting, and cajoling, Dean finally received an invitation to join an exclusive men's club in Midtown, complete with smoking room, racquetball courts, Michelin-starred restaurant, and extravagant initiation fee. To celebrate—and, perhaps, legitimize—his inauguration, he promptly started smoking cigars and taking racquetball lessons. After working on his game for months, he's been pestering me to play, I suspect because he's now practiced enough to feel certain that he will win. Instinct tells me to avoid this sort of direct contest with my brother, disinterring little league memories of strikeouts and exile. Yet, in deference to my newfound spirit of altruism, I accept.

I played a bit of tennis back in the day, and have exhibited sporadic glimmers of virtuosity at the Ping-Pong table, but I've never set foot on a racquetball court. Dean graciously takes it upon himself to introduce me to the sport. In the plush locker room of his club, he outfits me with a brand-new racquet, glove, and goggles to go along with my worn tennis sneakers and gym shorts. A deep-carpeted corridor leads us to a glass wall through which I catch my first glimpse of the court itself—a rectangle of blond hardwood flooring bisected by three red lines, two solid and one dashed. The floor is tightly enclosed by white walls stretching up to a high ceiling. As we slip through the glass into the compressed silence, the door shuts behind us like the seal to an airtight box.

Dean explains the rules of the game while hitting the rubbery blue ball against the far wall. He seems to relish the chance to both display his skills and flaunt a whole new panoply of jargon—hinders and rollouts, plums and splats, three-wall serves and high-lob Z's. I'm only half listening. Given my lack of experience—and Dean's recent training—I have no intention of winning, or even trying to. I am more captivated by the spare geometry of the court, by the abrupt, hollow *thock* of the ball as it strikes the wall, by the whiteness of the wall itself.

No surprise, then, that I lose the first game. I honestly don't recall having begun it, and am only aware that it's over when Dean grabs the ball and announces the score.

"That's game," he says, almost contritely—struggling, I suspect, to substitute compassion for condescension. "Another one?" he asks, more eagerly.

Our second game unfolds much as our first, though my brother's ceaseless chatter has evolved from basic explanation to emphatic directive. Some of his tips seem obvious enough—bend your knees, snap your wrist, keep your eye on the ball. Others are more arcane, particularly as Dean continues to brandish his shiny new vernacular. "Pinch!" he yells. "Killshot!" "Dinky-doo!" Whatever it is he's trying to tell me, Dean himself clearly takes it seriously. Ever the golden retriever, he bounds around the court, earnestly struggling to employ the techniques he's learned while simultaneously straining against them, as if they were a leash he's been told is for his own good. His exhortations on proper form are lost on me. If my footwork is shoddy or my elbow flies out, so be it. I let my body do what it wants, my attention rapt by the frantic carom of the ball through all corners of the room, like a proton in a particle accelerator.

It comes as a shock to no one that I lose the second game as well, but as we start the third, a funny thing happens—I get better. My fixation on the bouncing of the ball begins to reveal opportunities for patterns and angles that make the game more beautiful, and also happen to win me points. The match grows competitive. Dean's deluge of instruction evaporates, replaced by a rising tide of trash talk that would, as they say, make a sailor blush. This surfacing of my old adversary triggers a desire in me to beat him, and our contest grows more heated, hanging in the balance until the last few points, when, pausing to wipe the sweat from my brow, I see that old look of fear on my brother's face, and remind myself that this was supposed to be about selflessness.

"You played well." Dean hands me a cigar wrapped in plastic. "Almost took that last game from me."

Freshly showered, we have retired to the smoking room of Dean's club. As one does, I suppose. All dark wood and thick Persian rugs, the room is much like an elegant library but for the lack of books and the faint whiff of pretentiousness seeping from the cracked leather of our antique chairs.

"Just lucky," I say. "I don't have your skills."

Dean attempts a modest shrug. "I'm thinking about changing instructors."

"I like all the ricochets," I say. "It's like a subatomic particle." Dean arches an eyebrow. "I've been reading about electrons," I explain.

"You should take some lessons," he says. "You could really be good."

I refrain from pointing out that maybe I already am good, or else maybe Dean himself isn't. "I don't know," I say. "Seems like a lot of work. I'll probably just hack around once in a while."

Dean frowns. "Remember what Dad used to say—'Do it well or don't do it at all.'"

"I remember," I say, recalling my father's words but not the context in which he spoke them. "That never made much sense to me."

Dean's frown deepens, as if I've profaned some sacred gospel. We sink into reticence. It occurs to me that I've never simply sat with my brother, alone, for any length of time. The silence grows awkward, until a young woman approaches in a white tuxedo shirt and red bow tie, deftly balancing a serving tray on her fingertips. She sets two glasses of brown liquid on the table between us.

"Here you are, Mr. Chance." She smiles, turning on her heels before I've realized that she was referring to Dean.

"Thank you, Teresa." My brother ignores the drinks, instead handing me a small metal tool with a circle in the middle where two opposing blades come together. Like a miniature guillotine.

"Snip off the tip," he says. "One quick motion. Take the plastic off first."

I do as I'm told, dropping the severed tip of my cigar into a nearby ashtray. Dean does the same, then lights a wooden match and holds it toward me. A vision of Sasha's Buddhist monk flashes before me. *The candle is you. The flame is you. The flame is me.*

"Normally, you would never light another man's cigar," says Dean. "But we'll make an exception." I put the cigar in my mouth and crane forward to hold it over the flame. When I see smoke, I inhale deeply, sending a searing bolt of fire down my throat and into my lungs. I explode in a fit of coughing.

"Jesus, Elliot. Don't inhale it."

"What else am I supposed to do with it?"

"Just let the smoke into your mouth and savor it. Then exhale it."

This seems bizarre to me, like foreplay without the final act, but apparently cigar etiquette is replete with odd customs and practices, which Dean proceeds to expound—don't hold the cigar in your mouth, do wait until the cigar is warm before removing the label, don't dip the cigar in alcohol, do let the ash accumulate at the tip of the cigar until it's about an inch long, then roll it—don't tap it—into the ashtray. Don't point with the cigar, or chew on it, or rush it, or smoke more than half of it.

"Is there an official rulebook I can pick up somewhere?"

Dean hands me one of the drinks. "You'll get the hang of it. Here."

"What is it?"

"Scotch."

"You like scotch?"

"Single malt," says Dean, as if this answers my question. "The best. Just sip it."

As with the cigar smoke, I let a little of the whisky into my mouth and keep it there a moment, swallowing rather than exhaling this time. Though the burn is not quite as violent, I struggle not to gasp. The effort brings tears to my eyes, but Dean doesn't seem to notice.

"Great, right?"

I'm about to defend the opposing point of view when I stop myself, realizing that there's been enough conflict and awkwardness between my brother and me this afternoon. I decide that, no matter what I truly think of whatever Dean says, I'm going to respond generously, selflessly, communicating with Dean on Dean's terms.

"Delicious," I say. *I've never had to siphon gasoline out of an automobile with my mouth, but I'm willing to bet this tastes just like that.*

"I tell ya," says Dean, "I could get used to this. I think I could probably be managing partner of the firm within five years."

"You could absolutely be managing partner. You deserve it,

given the business you bring in." *You would run the company into the ground in twelve months. You know as much about the actual workings of the firm as a snake-oil salesman knows about snakes.*

"You wouldn't mind if I was your boss?"

"It would be an honor." *It would be an unmitigated disaster.*

"Thanks, Elliot." Dean lifts his glass in a toast, smiling his broad, toothy golden-retriever smile. "That's big of you."

I raise my drink in return. Our glasses converge with a muffled clink. "You're my brother," I say. "I want you to be happy."

You're my brother. I want you to be happy.

It is Dean who inadvertently reveals my third opportunity to practice selflessness, offhandedly mentioning that our father has been struggling with the shoe store.

"He's calling it a 'rough patch,'" says Dean.

"What do *you* think?"

"I think brick-and-mortar is dead. But don't tell Dad that."

Dean's account of the shoe store feels dubious. My father wouldn't disclose that kind of intelligence if you hung him upside down by his toenails. My mother, however, reluctantly confirms the news. Apparently my father had to let several employees go, and has even started working weekends again himself.

"It's just a rough patch," my mother insists.

Knowing that my father would never accept a blatant offer of aid, I start showing up at the store on Saturdays, claiming that I've come out to Connecticut to get some fresh air, or visit with my mother, or pick up a new pair of wing tips. My father holds down the fort by himself, and even the small trickle of customers is steady enough to keep him busy. Though he doesn't ask for my help, my presence doesn't seem to bother him. I linger in the storefront, perusing the selection of men's and women's dress shoes, recalling the times I'd come here with my mother as a kid. More than twenty years on, the little shop maintains its aspect of dignified comfort, though the walls need painting and there are bald spots in the carpeting, which my father has attempted to conceal with product displays.

On my third visit my father is busier than usual—so much so that when a customer wants to try a different style of loafer, my father asks me to bring out a pair from the back. I duck behind the counter and into the rear of the store, where a staircase leads to the basement. This subterranean, covert section of my father's establishment is equally unchanged since my childhood. Narrow aisles divide rows of shelving, mostly full of shoeboxes but with an occasional gap here and there, which Dean and I would use to climb to the top and press our palms to the ceiling when we were little.

"Thank you, Elliot," says my father as I hand him the loafers. He turns back to the customer. "My son, the accountant," he explains, with a ring of pride in his voice that surprises me.

By week four I have commandeered a fitting stool and started helping customers, side by side with my father, who stays close in order to answer any questions. Together we outfit our patrons with shiny new footwear that I can't help but think makes them just a little bit happier. I imagine them venturing back out into the world with a fresh lightness in their step, even—why not?—discovering that they can leap tall buildings, or walk on water, or fly through the air. As if they were superheroes, and my dad and I the cobblers of magic shoes. As if we were all on the same team.

Which leads me to believe that the seating in the store is all wrong. There are eight chairs, arranged in two rows of four, each row with its back to the other. Yet superheroes would never sit like this. They would need to come together, to associate in some sort of league in order to coordinate their superheroic endeavors. They would need to huddle up. I suggest to my dad that we rearrange the seats into a large square, all facing inward toward one another. I do not, of course, reveal the actual inspiration for this proposal. (*If I were you, I'd keep this monster stuff to myself.*) Instead, I tell him that it might make the store feel more social, more welcoming.

My father shakes his head, rejecting the idea without even looking up from the cash register. "People like their privacy," he says. *I mean, what are we supposed to do, turn around and stare at each other?*

When I was about six years old, my father tried to teach me how to run a race. "This is the start," he said, tracing an imaginary line in the grass of our front lawn. He raised his arm to point toward the far end of the yard. "The finish line is between those two trees." I remember peering over at the trees, unable to discern the line, but taking his word for it. My father then demonstrated the "set position"—crouched forward with one foot behind the other, back knee on the ground, hands splayed across the starting line. As he began the countdown, I examined my hands to make sure I was doing it right. The grass between my fingers was warm with early summer, yet still green and lush with spring—so inviting that when my father yelled "Go!" and started for the far trees, I instead leapt to the side and rolled furiously across the turf. I laughed and laughed. My father patiently lined us up again, though any amusement he may have felt evaporated after the fourth attempt. That was not, he explained, the way to win the race.

Differences aside, I continue to help my father at the shoe store. Each Saturday I stay a little later, eventually locking up after the last customer has gone, at which point my father and I head down to the basement to complete the more menial tasks—restocking inventory, polishing returns for resale. It is simple, restful work, with not much to think about except the various styles and colors of shoes, and why some people prefer the Oxford, others the Derby, still others the chukka boot. It's a mystery, really. You couldn't even begin to guess what a person might like without knowing something about their history.

"You should collect email addresses," I find myself saying.

"From who?" asks my father.

"Customers. You could ask them for their names and email addresses, and keep track of what they buy. That way, when a new style arrives that they might like, you can send them an email to let them know." I brace myself for my father's rebuff. I hadn't intended to make any more recommendations, but this basement work is hypnotic, and the words just sort of came out.

My father looks up from a black sandal in his lap, the strap of which he is struggling to repair. "You know, Elliot," he says, "that's a really good idea. Thank you."

"You're welcome." This time, the ring of pride in my own voice surprises me, and also encourages me. "It's been nice," I continue, "helping out here a bit."

"Glad you think so," says my dad. "Especially since I'm not paying you."

"I was thinking maybe I could come work full-time."

He turns back to the broken sandal. "God, no," he scoffs. "You have a job."

"I'd quit."

"Don't be ridiculous," he says. "You're not going to sell shoes your whole life."

"But you have."

"Exactly," says my father.

And that's the end of that conversation.

There's a particular ache that results when a person is right there next to you but feels a universe away—a loneliness that is somehow unbecoming, given that you're not alone. It's probably my fault for tumbling sideways when others race ahead. Nevertheless, I continue to help my father on Saturdays, just as I continue to play racquetball with Dean and take care of Jennifer's Chihuahua. I guess this is selflessness, though if it's supposed to make me happy, I'm not sure it's working. Maybe it's selfish to expect it to. I suppose I could ask Sasha, but I haven't seen her in months—since the summer, when she stole my stolen gun.

Perhaps selflessness isn't supposed to make me feel better. Maybe that's the point—that it doesn't matter if I feel unmoored, or sad, or empty. Maybe it doesn't matter what I feel at all, now that I'm being selfless.

Or maybe I just need to give it more time.

In the Future

Bannor says that in the future they've extinguished the will to live.

More specifically, a team of scientists researching the human genome identified the specific gene responsible for the desire to stay alive. Then they figured out how to switch it off.

The suppression of the "survival gene" was hailed as a historic milestone of human and societal evolution, which had been increasingly seen as leading toward a goal long since enshrined in the collective psyche—freedom. Over the course of generations, the ideal of individual liberty had become a worldwide obsession. Dictatorships were toppled, oligarchies dismantled. As political independence increased, humanity turned its attention to more insidious forms of oppression, eventually concluding that in order for people to be truly, completely free, they had to be rid of the final shackle—the genetically programmed command to draw breath. Indeed, the phrase "will to live" itself came to be considered an oxymoron. The survival gene, said the scientists, was a tyrant. And we were its slaves. It wasn't a matter of will at all.

Turning off the gene didn't make people suddenly want to die. They just no longer instinctively wanted to live. They became impartial, which did not mean they were indifferent. In fact, they were keenly interested in the question now being put to them, the answer to which had been mandated for them until now: Is life worth it? Most people didn't know how to answer this query, or even how often to ask it. Should it be posed as part of a daily ritual? Should you rise each morning and—after choosing between a bowl of cereal or a plate of eggs for breakfast—decide whether you should live or die? Perhaps it was meant to be an important yet only occasional inquiry, like a high-schooler deciding whether to study for a test or steal a car. Or was it the kind of matter that only needed to be addressed once in a lifetime, maybe on your eighteenth or twenty-first birthday, alongside the casting of your first political vote or your first (legal) sip of beer?

Confusion ensued. In short order, a plethora of experts sprang up to offer assistance. The decision whether to live or die was too important, they claimed, for people to make on their own. Professional guidance was essential, and—for a reasonable fee—they'd be happy to provide it. New certifications were announced, personality tests were revised, and online quizzes proliferated. Various and often conflicting methodologies and ideologies developed, each of which promoted its results as more accurate or "true" than the rest, ushering in a new age of existential uncertainty. Bannor says it was all a bit of a mess.

Eventually two dominant camps emerged. The first declared that the answer to the question of whether to live or die depended on *purpose*. Not, as often assumed, on whether your life had purpose, but on which would have greater purpose—your life or your death. Happily, most members of this camp found in favor of life. A conspicuous minority, however, concluded otherwise. Some of them died for what were widely considered noble causes— the proverbial falling on the live grenade—but those cases were rare, since more often than not people were able to accomplish more by staying alive. The greater portion of these suicides consisted of people in whom perceived wrongs instilled both rage and helplessness—from the religious terrorist hoping to eradicate an entire civilization to the vigilante looking to carry out rough justice to the exasperated bicyclist forced to dodge pedestrians on the bike path one too many times (as in the notorious Selfie-Stick

Incident in San Francisco, for example). Needless to say, the results were unpleasant. Fortunately, the violence abated over time, as the belligerents gradually canceled one another—and themselves—out.

The second camp was larger than the first, with a more nuanced methodology known as the Pleasure-Pain Polemic. Basically, you measure the total amount of pleasure in your life (broadly defined to include happiness, joy, and the like) and the sum of all your pain (including despair, sadness, and so on). You then compare the two measurements and—voilà!—you have an answer as to whether or not your life is worth living. Proponents uniformly lauded the elegance of this approach, but quickly fell into disagreement over how to implement it. At the heart of the discord was one fundamental question—what was an acceptable ratio of pleasure to pain?

Some believed it was simply a matter of preponderance. If there was more pleasure than pain, then life was good, or "net positive," and worth continuing. If the pain outweighed the pleasure, then life was bad, or "net negative." Others gave life a grade based on the classic letters used in academia. In their view, a life below sixty percent pleasure was an F, and not worth the trouble (though among the irredeemable perfectionists, anything less than an A was equally unacceptable). Still others went the other way entirely, determining that a life of even one percent pleasure was still worth living. One, after all, is still greater than zero.

Variety and correctness of measurement styles aside, the ultimate consequences were predictable enough—people who felt their lives were too painful checked out. The existentially inconsolable were the first to go, but they were hardly alone. The list of departees grew long—the lonely and the lost, the heartbroken and the scared, the grief-stricken, the dispossessed, even the just plain sad. To those that remained, the phenomenon was unsettling. Yet, true to their character, they tried to look on the bright side. As populations thinned, there was more space for humanity, and the natural world made a flourishing comeback—the air grew cleaner and the oceans clearer, and the list of endangered species dwindled. Besides, those that remained told themselves, the departees had every right to determine their fates. With the demise of the survival gene, they were finally free to choose, and that was a good thing—an imperative, really—regardless of the consequences.

Nevertheless, the uneasiness of those left behind continued to grow. They weren't unhappy, exactly. After all, their lives were—by some definition—pleasurable. Yet they missed the departees. Even more, they noticed that other aspects of their world started to go missing, or at least diminish. Pathos was lost. Nostalgia. The sober reflection of melancholy. The sublime ache of wistfulness. More tangible realities also became scarce—literature, art, poetry. (Music stuck around, but only the poppy kind, and only for a few weeks at a time.) Eventually people noticed that even some integral emotions—compassion, empathy—were in short supply. Yet the gospel of freedom was sacrosanct. Though the world might not be as rich, people consoled themselves by reminding one another that they were finally free.

That is, until the scientists—the very ones who unveiled the survival gene in the first place—published new studies announcing that their prior research, while not wrong, was incomplete. The gene may be a tyrant, they declared, but it was not the only one. Extensive investigation and thorough analysis clearly indicated that people were subject to emotions beyond their control, in the face of which they could not possibly make rational choices, including but not limited to the choice between life and death. We were as helpless before the whims of our own feelings as before the dictate of the survival gene, said the scientists. More so, even. According to their research, switching off the gene had not made us more free, but less.

Bannor says there were some rumblings and whispers questioning the veracity of the new studies. Where were the peer reviews?

Where were the double-blind clinical trials? But these voices were muted and few. The scientists were widely commended for their diligence. The new studies were endorsed, accredited, and quietly filed away. Any further switching off of the survival gene was flatly prohibited—a necessary evil that humanity would have to bear in order to maximize its own freedom.

Things gradually went back to the way they were. The world once again grew a little more crowded, a little more troubled, and a little more sad.

And a little more wonderful, too.

Elliot

(2001)

March is difficult. Not quite winter, not quite spring, a day like to-day is inherently unsure of itself, and acts out accordingly—a dank mist one moment, a sprinkling of hail the next, a burst of sunshine that might convince you to take off your jacket just before a frigid wind sweeps down the back of your neck. If we humans—we of restless hearts and constant craving—are not built for stasis, neither are we made for these rapid, unpredictable changes, these constant switches and revisions, these petulant, moody days of March.

If the season's fitful weather bespeaks the rousing of the city from its winter slumber, meant to inspire us to do the same, I do not heed the call. In fact, I've been sleeping more than ever, which is saying a lot. The nighttime dreamscapes of my unconscious have neither dulled nor diminished over the years, and I prefer to linger there, even if the occasional nightmare leaves me in a cold sweat. I wish only that I could remember them for more than a few minutes after waking. It seems unfair that they should flee so quickly, while memories of the concrete world stubbornly persist.

It would be easy to blame my hibernation on winter, to ascribe it to some ancient, evolutionary instinct to bed down through the gray season, to lie low and conserve energy, but even my waking hours have been lifeless. A captive of societal inertia, I allow myself to be nudged through the motions of an estimable modern life. Go to work (though later than usual) and return home again (though earlier). Read email, crunch numbers, send email. Pay rent, fill cupboard. Whatever it takes to keep the organism alive. An automaton with a biological imperative.

Essentially, I'm turning into Matt. Lodged behind his desk like a stone golem, my office mate seems only artificially alive—wanting nothing, needing nothing, perhaps even feeling nothing. I begin to suspect that he is a simulacrum, no more real than the island in the faded poster above his head. I want to reach out and poke him, to test whether he is just a mirage, but I refrain. As far as my interactions with Matt are concerned, a friendly jab in the arm would be a gross breach of decorum. We don't even say good morning anymore.

One grows accustomed to numbness—so much so that when Dean appears in the doorway of our office, I'm surprised when my senses discern the old fear in his eyes. I can't tell if this is something new, or if he's been like this for months and I just failed to notice. He hovers for a moment, a thin sheen of perspiration on his brow. I set down my coffee and dutifully wait for the completion of his flyby, but it never comes. Instead he enters the room, dragging a chair toward my desk and taking a seat. I don't need to strain my foggy memory to know that Dean has never done this before.

He has also abandoned his trendy jeans and sneakers in order to reprise his designer suit and monk-strap shoes—something else I hadn't noticed until now. From the inside pocket of his jacket, he takes out a cigar and sets it on my desk.

"I don't think we can smoke in here," I tell him.

"It was going to be a prize," he says, "for if you ever beat me at racquetball." His tone is sunny, belying the shadows under his eyes. "But I got tired of waiting, so just consider it a gift. It's Cuban. Take a whiff."

I run the cigar under my nose. It smells like dirty ash, though I doubt that's the response Dean is looking for.

"Smells like the soil, right?" he says. "Like its homeland. As if you were down there munching on tapas or whatever."

"Yeah," I say. "Just like that."

Dean leans back and crosses his legs as if he's going to be here awhile, though he doesn't seem intent on lighting up. I set the cigar aside, silently considering my options for its future disposal. Maybe Bannor would want it.

"How's Jennifer?" asks Dean.

"Why do you ask?"

He laughs. "Um, because she's your girlfriend—and presumably my future sister-in-law."

"Presumably," I say. "She's fine. We got a dog." I can't remember if I told Dean about Henri. Apparently not.

"Nice," he says. "A black Lab?"

I find it entirely predictable that Dean would assume we got a Lab, though why he would expect it to be black is beyond me. I've no doubt that Dean would hate Henri, who is inclined neither to perform tricks nor just sit there and look pretty, and who wouldn't deign to pick up a stick with his mouth if you fetched it for him with yours.

"Chihuahua," I say.

"Oh." Dean suppresses a grimace, then shrugs. "Well, still."

He pauses—so briefly that I wouldn't normally think anything of it, except that not only does Dean never sit down in our office, he also never gives me gifts, or asks me about my girlfriend. This bit of theater is a clear prelude to something, and after a moment he finally gets on with it.

"So, Satchel has their board meeting tomorrow. The investors are coming in to discuss a potential round of investment. They're going to need the audited financials."

"That's fine," I tell him, somewhat relieved. "We finished last week."

"Yeah," says Dean. "They just need to make one last change. They need to move about five million in revenue from this quarter to last quarter."

My relief evaporates. "You're kidding."

"No," says Dean, his words coming faster now. "It's not a big deal. The company's booked about ten million for Q1. They just need to show five of that in Q4 instead."

"Q4 of the prior tax year."

"Yeah."

"You can't do that," I say.

"It's not a big deal," Dean says again, as if repeating it will make it true.

"It's lying to the investors in order to induce them to invest. That's fraud, and it's illegal. I think it's a big deal by definition."

Dean's sunny tone abruptly morphs into dark clouds. "Jesus, Elliot, don't be so dramatic. It's real revenue. They made the money."

"Then why not book it in the quarter they made it?"

Dean starts to flush. "Look, if Satchel doesn't show that it hit specific revenue targets in the last fiscal year, the next round of investment doesn't happen. The investors will start calling in their loans, and the company will be done. Over. Bankrupt. Just because of the timing of a little revenue. It's absurd."

"Why don't they just explain that to the investors?"

"Because that's not going to happen, Elliot! And nobody's asking you for advice. Just edit the financials. It's not a big deal."

"You keep saying that. It doesn't sound like the investors would agree with you."

"Elliot—"

"It's also tax fraud."

"How the hell can it be tax fraud?" demands Dean. "They're actually declaring more revenue sooner, so they'll pay *more* in taxes. The government should thank them."

"That's not necessarily true, but either way it's still tax fraud."

"Goddammit, Elliot! Just do it." He jumps up from the chair, his face bright red, the sweat on his forehead beading more sharply.

He heads for the door, then stops, apparently awaiting my capitulation.

When we were in high school, Dean would occasionally ask me to help him with his homework. Normally this meant explaining some broad concept, or translating some arcane problem into a question with which he could comfortably grapple, but every once in a while he would simply ask me for the answer. For some reason, I never really considered this to be cheating. Maybe my moral sense wasn't yet fully developed, or maybe it just never occurred to me that my brother would ask me to do something wrong, that he would ever value his success more than my integrity.

I look over at him. He grips the doorframe, glaring back at me with a mixture of fear and aggression. Something in my chest that has been going cold for some time now finally freezes. Then it breaks.

"I let you win," I say.

"What?"

"At leaf-catching. When we were kids. I never counted all of mine."

Dean shakes his head in disbelief. "Who cares?"

"You did," I say. "You cared."

"Well, that's sweet, Elliot, but now it's time to sit at the adult table and act like a grown-up."

"You're a prick."

Dean's eyes go completely dead. His voice is low and withering. "I'm also the only reason you have a job and don't still live with your parents." There it is, the rubbing of this truth in my face. I'm surprised it took so long. Dean continues to stare at me, or at least in my direction—seeing nothing, really, other than himself. I can't speak. I don't want to speak. I want to pick up the chair and smash it over his head.

"I'll do it," says Matt. I'd forgotten my office mate was there, which isn't hard to do. His eager depravity is entirely predictable.

"No," says Dean. "Elliot's going to do it. He's not going to take a nap in the office today, and he's not going to go home early because he's feeling sad. He's going to do his job, by tomorrow morning, like the client wants."

He turns and leaves—no mangled aphorism on his way out, though I can think of a few that would fit. I look blankly down at my desk, waiting for my pulse to settle.

"Matter of time," says Matt.

"What do you mean?"

"Dean hasn't signed a new client in six months. If Satchel goes bankrupt, I don't know who he's got left. All of his dot-bombs are cratering."

"Dot-bombs?"

"Internet companies," says Matt. "The crash. Not even Dean can deny it anymore. Live by the sword, burst your bubble, as he might say. Though of course he wouldn't, because he's screwed."

My gut clenches, my stomach compacting into a mass of lead. I turn to my computer and log in to my investment accounts. One look confirms Matt's report. It's all gone, or virtually so. Thousands of dollars in savings have become hundreds.

"I can't believe it."

Matt laughs casually, almost haughtily, as if he saw this coming. "Dude, where have you been?"

There has to be a mistake. I pull up the stock charts for the past year. The NASDAQ looks like a profile of the Himalayas—March is a soaring peak, May a deeply cut ravine, with another sharp crest in July. Yet the market was still at high altitude as late as August, at which point it became a sheer cliff face running straight down to today—maybe not rock bottom, but well below the levels at which I invested. Seven years of savings have been eviscerated in eight months. I was just too numb to feel the blade. The last time I paid attention to my investments was over a year ago. Just before Esther died. The only mistake was mine.

And if my public company stocks are basically worthless, then no doubt my firm's dot-com clients are completely so. If Dean's accounts are disappearing, all the money I put into them is gone, too, along with any hope of starting my own business. Of course, regardless of savings, the idea of founding an internet company with my brother was a joke. But now even the dream of my own advisory firm is just that—a delusion. I have no seed capital, and no right to ask business owners to take my advice. What would I say? "You can trust me. I lost all of my savings in the stock market."

No, that dream is dead now, to the extent dreams ever live at all. And with the stock market crashing, it's safe to assume that the job market will, too. Any thought I had of quitting suddenly seems naive, if not laughable. The moral dilemma posed by Dean's demand no longer seems like a dilemma at all, but rather an inevitable result of "sitting at the adult table and acting like a grown-up." The heaviness in my stomach grows, and my breathing becomes shallow, as if whatever oxygen they see fit to pump into our windowless cell is finally running out. Though it's barely noon, I head for the elevators, making sure to avoid Dean on the way. I tell myself I just need to step outside for some air, though once I'm on the street, my feet begin to head for home.

I don't know why. Jennifer won't be there, and I don't normally ask her for guidance anyway. Though, now that I think of it, maybe she can help. She is an attorney, after all, and this is basically a legal question, or an ethical one, or both. Maybe she'd have some insight based on her training or experience. She won't be home until late tonight, but that's fine. I'm scheduled to meet Bannor this evening anyway. He wants to see the Manhattan skyline at night from the George Washington Bridge. I have yet to miss one of our walks, and I'm not going to start now.

Unsure what to do with myself between now and then, I'm drawn to my apartment by a sense of familiarity, if nothing else. It's Monday, so I'm not surprised to find that Henri has already pissed on the kitchen floor. I am less prepared, however, for two new details. The first is the presence of a man's suit jacket draped over the back of our lounge chair. The second is a series of feminine moans escalating to a pitch I recognize, though it's been years since I heard it last. I fight back sudden nausea and move toward the bedroom, where two bodies writhe beneath the sheets.

"Wow." My voice is dull, searching for anger or even glibness but finding neither. I stand in the doorway, trying not to lean too heavily against the frame. For some reason, I don't want to show weakness. As if I were a dominant male in a nature show, fighting to keep his mate. As if there were something left to fight for. As if I actually cared to fight for it.

"Jesus, Elliot!" Jennifer's scream conveys mostly shock, but also a touch of annoyance. She leaps up from under the covers, which is remarkable because she was flat on her back with a man between her legs. His head, too, pops into view—small, glassy eyes peer out from an otherwise unremarkable face.

"Dude," he says. Really. Verbatim. I guess lawyers can be morons, too. Or bankers, or whatever this particular suit is.

"Before you get upset," says Jennifer, "let me—"

"Don't bother." I'd rather not hear Jennifer state her case. There's nothing she can say, of course. I'm not even sure why I'm still standing in the doorway, except that my legs won't heed my command to move.

"Elliot, this . . ." Jennifer waves her hand to indicate the bed or her dude or both. "It's not a big deal," she says, a phrase I've heard one too many times today already.

"But it is." I am only partially speaking to Jennifer. "It is a big deal."

"C'mon, man," says the dude. "It's just sex."

"And cheating," I say. "Don't forget cheating."

Jennifer drops her shoulders. "We're not married, Elliot."

I can't quite believe this is her argument. Isn't it just like a lawyer to hide behind that kind of technicality. But I don't mean to bash lawyers. I'm sure there are plenty of attorneys who are decent and kind and good. It's just that I only happen to know one of them, and—as it turns out—I don't actually like her very much. I did, though, at one point. Didn't I? Maybe I liked us. Or maybe I just liked the surface of us, not realizing—or not wanting to realize—that the core was hollow, and largely empty, and vast enough that Jennifer and I could be both inside it and yet a world apart.

On my way out, I pause at the puddle of urine on the kitchen floor. I realize now that Henri was protesting not my firm's policy against dogs in the office but the presence of a stranger in my bed, which means that the stranger has been coming here every Monday since Henri's arrival, at least. The cold leadenness in my gut spreads up into my chest. Normally, I'd gather a fistful of paper towels and mop up Henri's complaint. But today I leave it where it is. I'm confident that I speak for both of us when I say that this is what we think of the so-called grown-up world.

You can cover a lot of ground in Manhattan before it dawns on you that you might not be getting anywhere. I spend several hours spiraling crookedly out of the Village and into Midtown, at which point I begin to force my feet vaguely north and west. A few hours later, the George Washington Bridge thrusts its girdered gray towers into the open strip of sky above the Hudson River.

A pedestrian walkway flanks the road over the bridge. I follow it out to the middle of the span, running my hand along the short railing to my left. Behind the clouded horizon, the sun is close to setting, and the day has settled into a brooding stillness. I stop and lean on the railing to look toward the city. Hundreds of feet below me, the river is the color of slate, reflecting nothing.

Though I'm not the only one walking the bridge, there aren't many of us. A lone jogger passes, panting heavily. A pair of tourists gawk at the skyline from behind their camera lenses. I am the only one hovering by himself out here at the midpoint, so it's not surprising when I'm approached by a police officer with the Port Authority insignia on her dark blue coat. She slows down, giving me a kind but wary look that reminds me of Gareth on the first night of group.

"How we doing today?" She smiles, though her eyes remain vigilant. Her hands hang loosely at her sides, as if she's preparing to wrestle me away from the edge.

"Fine, thanks," I say, forcing a smile in return. It's the old lie again—two lies, really—the smile and the words. I'm not fine. I'm not fine at all. But "fine" is our favorite lie. We all tell it, all the time. The question itself—"How are you?"—has been neutered. "Good," you are to say. "Great." Or, these days, "busy." People don't want an actual answer.

Though, in fairness, this particular patroller may be an exception. She seems not only interested in my response but dubious of it. "There's a phone about twenty yards that way," she says, "if you need it."

The kind of phone, I think, that dials only one number. I wonder what they would say. What can they do, these well-meaning Gareths of the world? Can they fill the hole in my heart with anything that lasts? Can they alter the journey of my life? Or would they instead strive to change the way I perceive it? Would I want them to?

"Oh, thanks, but I'm good." Trying to ease the officer's skepticism, I offer what I hope is a more sturdy alibi. "I'm waiting for a friend. He's been wanting to see the city at night from here."

"Smart friend," she says, the tension in her stance relaxing a bit. "It never gets old. I walk the bridge at night all the time."

"For pleasure?"

"Sometimes." She glances up at the darkening sky. In the distance, the buildings are just beginning to twinkle. "Not long now," she says. "I'll leave you to it. My name's Rita, by the way."

"Elliot," I respond, surprised by this personal introduction. One last play from the suicide prevention playbook, perhaps. Or just a friendly audible. I can no longer tell. The officer—Rita—gives me a nod and moves away, gradually disappearing along with the last of the day.

By the time I spot Bannor's approach, night has fallen in earnest. I can just make out the cut of his tweed suit, alternately brightening and dimming as he passes under the bridge's procession of streetlamps, as if he were flickering in slow motion. His features are mostly concealed by the brim of his hat and the shadow of his beard. It's not until he's standing next to me that I notice how much older, and fragile, he suddenly looks. His face is drawn and thin, with dark hollows under his raw eyes.

"Bannor, are you okay?"

He shrugs. "I'm fine." Bannor is as conditioned as the rest of us. *Great*, he may as well have said. *Busy*.

"Did something happen?" I ask—seeking, like Rita, something more authentic.

"Nothing to cry about."

It's clear to me that this isn't true. It's also clear that I won't get more out of him, so I don't push. "I hate it, sometimes. This world."

Bannor sighs. "I can't say I've seen enough of the world to hate it." He turns to rest his hands on the railing, raising his eyes to take in Manhattan's shining silhouette. "Well, would you look at that. Like a postcard."

"What you imagined?"

"It was my daughter who imagined it. How she got it in her head, I don't know, but she always wanted to come stand here and see the city at night. I told her I would take her someday." Bannor's hand falls to his side. His fingers clutch at the empty air. "I never did."

"That's not your fault," I tell him.

"Maybe not. Or maybe it is a little. It doesn't matter." He straightens up, running his hands down the front of his suit. "It's time for me to say goodbye, Elliot. This is the end of my road."

If I had thought my capacity to feel had been extinguished, I was wrong. My legs begin to quiver. I nearly fall over before Bannor reaches out a hand to steady me. "No," I tell him, remembering his prophecy—that I would be there when he finally killed himself. "You set me up."

"Stop it."

"I'll leave," I say, scheming. "I'll walk away. If I'm not here, you can't die. You said so." I manage to take one wobbly step, determined to flee in order to save my friend.

"Elliot, please." Bannor's voice is filled with a rare hint of emotion that halts my escape. "I just want someone to see me."

My legs continue to shake, like the shoddy foundation of a structure that wasn't built to last. We struggle so desperately to fabricate a human life. Be a baseball player, be a lover, be a productive member of the workforce. Be happy, be selfless. Declare a truth to your existence and erect it as a monument to the heavens, not realizing until too late that it was never anything more than crude scaffolding, prone to collapse. One or two good shoves is all it takes.

I command my feet to stay. Bannor has never asked me for anything. I won't allow myself to refuse his first and last request. "So that's it?" I ask stupidly. "You're going to jump?"

"Leap," he says. "I'm going to leap."

I feel myself starting to cry. "I'd really prefer that you didn't." My words sound pathetic to me—restrained, trite, shallow, utterly inadequate to express the despair flooding through me. When did I start talking like that? Have I been so well trained?

"Sometimes the past just won't let you go," says Bannor. "No matter how hard you try."

"Is this what you saw?" I ask him. "Is this the future?"

He nods. "Do you think I'm crazy?"

"No," I say firmly, resolutely, hoping my conviction will persuade him to stay.

He steps forward and gives me a hug, patting me once on the back, soundly, as if to prove I'm there. He releases me and sits up on the railing, sweeping his legs over to stand on the lip, where he pauses to look at me.

"I see you, Bannor." My voice is the splintering of wood, the crash of metal bars.

He takes off his homburg hat and presses it to his heart. "Thank you, my friend," he says. "I see you, too." Raising his free hand in farewell, he takes one step backward into the night. Then he's gone.

No one screams. No one runs over to help. It's as if Bannor purposely timed it so that his departure wouldn't cause a fuss, as if he knew the precise moment in which no one would be looking. Except me, of course. I can't tell how long I stand there after he's gone. For all I know, the wheel of the universe completed its final revolution, started all over again, and cycled right back to this moment, so that the world beyond the bridge's end is wholly differ-ent from the one Bannor left behind. But, no, that is just one more childish dream. There is no magic wheel I can spin to change the world. Things are no doubt just as they were. My life savings are still gone, along with my career prospects. My relationship is still over. Dean still awaits my surrender. And my friend is still dead. I will never walk with him again.

PART IV

A man crossing a field encountered a tiger. He fled, the tiger chasing after him. Coming to a cliff, he caught hold of a vine and swung himself over the edge. The tiger sniffed at him from above. Terrified, the man looked down to where, far below, another tiger had come, waiting to eat him. Two mice, one white and one black, began to gnaw away at the vine. The man saw a luscious strawberry near him. Holding the vine with one hand, he plucked the strawberry with the other. How sweet it tasted!

—Zen parable

Elliot

(2001)

It is neither the gathering darkness nor the deepening chill that eventually forces me from the bridge. They are failed stimuli, registering on an intellectual level only. I am cognizant of the generally accepted view that when the sun is not shining on the surface of the earth, it is called night, and when air molecules around me oscillate more slowly, it is called cold. I know these things. I do not feel them.

No, what motivates me to finally head for shore is the fear that Officer Rita may come back around, and that she may start asking questions again. Hard questions, like "Where's your friend?" or "How are you?" What answers could I possibly give her? I am all out of falsehoods, and the truth is as chimerical as ever. *He fell. He was never here. He leapt. I also am not here. I, too, have leapt. I just don't know it yet.*

Most likely, I would say nothing. I have descended into a dumb, empty stillness. There is no longer a lead weight in my stomach, nor any quiver in my legs as they tread south toward the heart of Manhattan. It is well after midnight. The streets are dormant but for a scattering of souls—the unquiet, the restless, the lost. Their stirrings perpetuate the celebrated notion that the city never sleeps. It's a lie. New York sleeps, it just has bad dreams—nightmares that rouse themselves to some semblance of life when the hours get small enough.

I don't know what time it is when I get back to the office. Night may be a passing shadow, but this darkness seems different, outside of time, looking in. Nor is the hour revealed as I slip down deserted hallways or turn on the lights in the cell I share with Matt. It is as if someone has stolen all the clocks. I step behind my desk and stare at the computer, its face gray and lifeless. I leave it be. From the bottom drawer of the desk, I retrieve the Vade Mecum. The notebook is curiously light in my hand, considering the weight I once placed on the thoughts within it. Its mottled black-and-white cover harkens back to those old composition notebooks in which callow hearts penned words they hoped would wrest meaning from the world.

As I turn for the door, I spot the cigar that Dean gave me, the anticipatory bribe for yet another deception. I pick it up and go, killing the lights on the way out. I proceed down one hallway and then another until I reach Dean's office, where the glow of his computer's screensaver illuminates how different the room is from mine—spacious, private, chicly furnished, with windows overlooking the broad avenue below. I sit down at his desk, taking in the view from here, trying on the perspective, attempting to imagine what it's like to be my brother. I can't. He and his world are as alien to me as the deep sea floor. But of course I am the stranger here.

Though Dean leaves the computer on all night, he doesn't use it much. Instead, he keeps a stack of manila folders on his desk, one for each client. There are fewer than I remember, and I am again shocked that I didn't notice how bad things had gotten. In fairness, our start-up clients fail all the time. Their young founders even take pride in it, claiming failure is a necessary step on the path to success. But not like this. This is a bloodbath. The folder for Satchel is still here, at least for now. Inside are Dean's personal notes—a passionate if incoherent scrawl—along with documents prepared for Satchel's investor presentation, the offending financial statements among them.

It would be easy, really, to comply with Dean's demand. Turn to the computer, open the file, change a few numbers. That's it.

Would anyone ever know? Probably not. Does it really make a difference whether Satchel made money in January versus December, or is "year-end" a completely arbitrary division of time, not to mention a purely human fabrication in the first place? No, yes, yes. Would the investors really be harmed if I made the change? More so than the employees who will lose their jobs if I don't? I can't know, and no one else can either, but that's not the point. It's not for me to rig the game, and it's not for Dean either.

I close the file. From a pen holder shaped like a skull, I take a red felt marker. In large letters across the face of the folder, I write my parting words to my brother, keeping it simple so he'll understand—"I quit." Dropping the marker back into the skull, I stand to leave, but the bright red letters stop me. I realize that they will be my final words, not just to Dean but to my parents as well, which is not my intent. I find a new piece of paper. For some time, I just stare at it, its blankness another question to which I have no answer. How can words suffice to say goodbye? I take another pen from the skull, not the heavy red marker but a ballpoint that traces a thin blue line as I leave my parents the message I need to send. "I'm sorry," I write. Then, remembering my mother's age-old plea for gratitude, I leave them the message they deserve to receive. "Thank you."

I address an envelope, affix a stamp, and seal the note inside. In the top drawer of Dean's desk, I find a butane lighter. These things I take, along with the Vade Mecum and the cigar. Everything else in the office I leave behind. There is nothing I will miss, except maybe Bora Bora, but that was never real anyway.

Outside, the wide avenues of Midtown remain suspended in a dreamlike stasis. They carry me southward until they dwindle into the narrow streets of Alphabet City, where a stout blue postal service mailbox opens its wide mouth to swallow my last letter. Near Bannor's building, in a dark corner of a neighborhood park,

I find an open trash can full of newspaper and other garbage. I press Dean's lighter to the newspaper, spinning its flint wheel until the whole pile is ablaze and the flames lick through the wire mesh of the trash can itself. Without ceremony, I toss the Vade Mecum into the fire. Its desiccated pages blacken and curl.

As I raise the cigar to throw it in as well, a disheveled man limps out of the darkness to join me. His dirty clothing bespeaks a life on cold streets—wool hat and gloves full of holes, thick boots, one heavy overcoat layered over another.

"Warm," he says, drawing close to the fire.

I nod.

"Gonna smoke that?" he asks, seeing the cigar.

I shake my head, handing it to him. "You go ahead."

"Thanks." He juts his face toward the flames, deftly lighting the cigar without singeing his eyebrows.

"It's Cuban," I tell him.

His eyes close. He puffs gently on the cigar. "Ain't that something."

Bannor's building is as I remember it—dank and dim and branded with angry words until the fifth floor, where Bannor's influence can still be felt in the form of the clean, well-lighted hall. The door to his apartment swings open without a fuss, as I somehow knew it would. *What do I have that anybody wants?* A Mexican rug, a dented teakettle, a photograph of a family that once was.

Though my destination is elsewhere, I can't help but take a quick look around. There is no suicide note, nor much else to prove that Bannor ever lived here. Clinging to the refrigerator is the abandoned photograph. The little girl in the blue dress is still smiling, heedless of the future. It occurs to me that, on a sunny day at the Bronx Zoo, at some moment years before this one, she is always smiling. I suspect there is a lesson there, about time and the nature of the real, but it's lost on me.

I take the photograph down from the refrigerator and put it in my pocket. On the dining table, a lone leaf of paper rests beside an envelope. The letter from Bannor's ex-wife, opened now. I don't need to read more than a few words to grasp the heart of it—"Remarried . . . adopt . . . change her name." When I've seen enough, I tear the letter into pieces, though Bannor himself chose not to, and undoubtedly handled the news with more resignation than rage. *I can't say I've seen enough of the world to hate it.*

But I'm not here to tear up the past. Dropping the tattered letter on the table, I turn back to my reason for coming here at all. I open the window and crawl out to the fire escape. As before, the courtyard behind Bannor's apartment is desolate, the buildings still obstinately keeping their backs to each other. I descend one floor to crouch outside the neighbors' window. It is again dark and silent, though it no longer yields when I try to slide it open. Apparently Bannor's neighbors have learned to worry about being robbed. I've no way of knowing whether anyone is inside, but I don't care. I bend one arm and swing my elbow sharply against the window. The glass fractures with a muffled crash, followed by the tinkling of shards on the kitchen floor. I wait a moment to see if anyone will respond. When no one does, I reach through the broken glass to unlock the window.

The apartment is too dark to navigate without Bannor's penlight, so I risk turning on the lights in the kitchen. The glare sends something scurrying into a hole under the counter, but nothing else stirs. I move through the living room and into the bedroom. The light reaches just far enough to reveal that two of the mattresses are empty. On the third, two bodies lie nestled together, unmoving. Only the rasp of their breathing indicates that they're asleep and not dead. From the floor beside them, the metallic glint of a needle catches my eye. I've no fear of waking them as I ransack the dresser, then the closet, then the rest of the apartment.

I find no gun, however. This failure arouses neither anger nor frustration. There is no one left here to feel these things. Just a vacant space, a blankness clinging feebly to a human frame. My body moves to the front door of the apartment, where blurry fingers reach out to unlock the slide bolt. The door swings open crookedly, leading to an empty hallway, an empty stairwell, an empty street. I step outside—a void, an absence, a patch of night in the night.

No easy way out, then. No trigger to pull. No button to press. Leaving only one path—follow Bannor's lead. Simple enough, except that my body won't jump from the George Washington or any other bridge. I know this because, after Bannor's fall, I stood at the railing for a very long time, looking down. When I realized he was not coming back, I determined that I would dive after him. My limbs refused, some ancient wiring deep within my skull insisting that bridges are dangerous and cannot be leapt from. But it's incomplete and flawed, this circuitry. It can be bypassed. I know of at least one high place where the wires cross and deem it safe, one high place from which I can jump, if only because I've imagined it so many times before.

I walk south to the river's edge between the two bridges. On the sidewalk, beside a familiar brick facade, a miniature cairn of cigarette butts marks the base of an even more familiar fire escape. I drag a trash can from the street corner, using it to climb to the bottom rung. Iron steps bear me upward, coiling past darkened windows before spitting me out over the low parapet and onto the roof. A subtle wind steals across the fractured tar. It is full of voices.

I suppose the woods aren't his anymore. There's nobody here but me.

Lights on the horizon. An infinitude of tiny, disparate points, like candles. Between us is the dark water, bounded on either side by the glow of the bridges, their spans ablaze with opposing veins of red and white. Luminous bits of filament traverse the gulf between the bridges. Ghost ships, sailing away, never to return. They are the way out, and this the point of departure, the last port of call, my welcome here long overstayed.

Maybe we're already in the other world.

I step to the far end of the roof, stretching the distance between myself and the edge. Plenty of runway. From here I cannot fall. From here I can only fly.

At that time in Neverene, there was a giant, with a giant heart.

The wind dies. The ghost ships stay their procession, waiting. A great calm descends, here at the margin of life, at the border between worlds.

Step into the light so I can get a look at you.

But it is fragile, this equilibrium. A ripple of movement at the edge of the roof disrupts the stillness. A bird, I think, until the shadow grows and rises, etching a hole in the backdrop of candlelight. The dancing shade of my youth, perhaps, come to see me off. Or the ferryman, seeking his toll. I watch in silence as the silhouette crosses over the parapet. It drifts to the center of the blackened tar, looks at me, speaks.

"Are you hurt?"

No. Yes. I don't know.

"There's blood on your suit."

I look down. Why am I wearing a suit? Corpses wear suits. But no, the blood is from deep cuts across the knuckles of my hand. I am not a corpse. And the apparition facing me is neither bird nor shade nor toll collector, but a girl I recognize—a young woman with dark eyes and short black hair. She seems to have a knack for appearing at the extremities of my days. This time, however, Bannor could not have called her. And this time I am not holding a gun. She is.

"What's that for?" I ask.

"I heard someone," says Sasha. "On the fire escape. I wasn't sure if it was you." She sets the revolver down by her feet. A hint of daybreak begins to color the eastern sky. I can just make out the grip and barrel of the gun, recognizing it as the one I stole from Bannor's neighbors, when they still had a gun to steal. "Anyway, it's yours," she says. "I'm sorry I took it."

"Even if I'm going to use it?"

"Yes."

"You said it was selfish."

"It is," she says. "It's also selfish for me to try to stop you."

In the rising light, Sasha grows more substantial. She is barefoot, wearing a tank top and loosely fitting pajama pants, as if she were still asleep in her bed and we were sharing the same dream.

"I was going to jump from your roof," I say.

Sasha's mouth twists in a wry expression I can't quite unravel. "You think you could throw yourself into the river from here?"

A memory of rain and cigarettes, of a computer disk launched into the night. "I'd need room to wind up."

"I wrote another one," says Sasha.

"Another novel?"

She nods.

"I was hoping you would," I tell her. "Did you submit it anywhere?"

She shakes her head. "I'm not going to publish it."

"How will people read it?"

"What people?"

"You know," I say, but I shrug my shoulders, because I'm not sure if I know myself. "The world."

"I didn't write it for the world."

I nod. That sounds about right. About perfect, really, for a woman who sows the fields of public discourse with coded messages—ciphers in plain sight, meant for everyone and revealed to no one. No one but me, that is.

"What's it about?"

"Do you remember the research project?" asks Sasha. "A priest, a monk, and a neurologist walk into a bar?"

"I thought you were planning your suicide."

"No," she says. "I used to plan it. You convinced me not to."

"I don't remember doing that."

"The night we met—when you talked about dancing monsters and sentient trees, and giants, and a world you hoped to get to some-day. You reminded me that it's okay to pretend, to see things that aren't there. That I wasn't the only one who experienced things differently from everyone else. That maybe if life doesn't seem a little weird to you, you're not looking closely enough." *As far as I was concerned, it was the sound of the crickets.* "I realized that if someone like you could be terribly unhappy sometimes, then being terribly unhappy sometimes couldn't be wrong."

I scrape my foot across the tarred roof. "You said you didn't believe in Neverene."

"Maybe I just call it something else."

Compassion is perilous. When there is nothing left of you but an empty vessel, a black hole, immune to the blows of life—the lone-liness and confusion, the profound disappointment, the anger—it is the kind word that breaches the event horizon, that rips your heart back open, that compels you to once again suffer the concussion of your existence.

"It hurts," I say.

"I'm sorry," says Sasha. "I can't fix that, and maybe you can't either. Sometimes I think it's supposed to hurt." Her eyes begin to shimmer. "And if you need to leave, I understand." The shimmer gathers, concentrating until it falls in silent drops down her cheeks. "Except that I wrote this book," she says, "and it's nothing, really. Just a bunch of words. But I'd be curious to know what you think of it, and I was wondering if maybe you'd like to give it a read? Or, really, do anything at all? Before you go?"

As Sasha speaks, the rush of pain intensifies. My gaze moves to the revolver. The sun has risen in earnest, and the stark lines of the gun's barrel and cylinder are no longer nebulous, whereas life seems as murky as ever. Maybe I'll always feel a little lost, a bit apart. Maybe, as Sasha suspects, the heart is meant to burn, and life will always be a question to which I don't have an answer.

Yet here in the calmness at the edge of the world, I realize I don't need one. In this moment, I am not obliged to sit in judgment upon my life, to determine whether it is good, or bad, or worth the effort. In this moment, there is only one question being asked of me, one to which I do have an answer.

"Yes," I say. "I'd like that very much."

After

After you die, you find yourself at the end of a very long line.

"What are we waiting for?" you ask the traveler in front of you.

"To lodge complaints," she says. "There's a counter."

You peer down the row of travelers toward the front. There you see a booth with an open window above a counter. In the window, listening patiently to the traveler at the head of the line, is Merriam. She nods earnestly, now and then attempting a smile.

"That's thoughtful," you say. The protracted length of the queue now seems like a blessing. Considering how things ended, you expect you'll have a lot to complain about. You're going to need some time.

You almost don't know where to begin, so you decide to start with the big stuff. War, you think. War was terrible, as were its less newsworthy variations—clashes and skirmishes, battles and brawls, feuds and fisticuffs. All violent conflict, really. And meanness. Mean people sucked. In fact, people could be complaint-worthy in all kinds of ways. They could be unfair, and selfish, and just plain rude, not to mention pushy, greedy, dishonest, arrogant, self-righteous, pretentious, shallow, materialistic, and willfully ignorant. Whew. You wonder how much time you're allowed at the counter. You fear you could fill it with grievances about other travelers alone.

Then there was pain. Pain was, well, painful. Cuts, scrapes, bruises, breaks. That agonizing toothache you had when you were eight. The time you dropped that metal door on your toe, and the nail turned black from the blood building up beneath it, throbbing unbearably for days, until your father finally took you to the emergency room, where they lanced it with a sharp needle, releasing the compressed pocket of blood in a sudden spurt. There was that kidney stone you passed in your twenties. And the harrowing fever you got in high school, forcing you to miss the field trip that all your friends went on.

Come to think of it, missing that field trip was a major disappointment. That's another complaint right there. You also never ate fresh pasta in Italy, or heard a lion roar, or looked at the night sky through a telescope. You didn't become an astronaut when you grew up, or a firefighter, or a pirate. There were enormously wide swaths of reality you didn't get to see, hear, taste, or feel. A whole host of things you didn't get to be.

The line to the complaint counter slides forward, more swiftly than you anticipated, growing ever shorter as your list of complaints expands. You press on with the composition, eventually moving from the weighty stuff to the littler things, no less bona fide for their smaller stature. There was airplane food, and junk mail, and inclement weather, and stale movie popcorn, and twenty-four-hour news cycles. There was traffic and acne and bills and work and mosquitoes and—

"Yippy little dogs!" you exclaim, not realizing you've broadcasted this remark until the traveler in front of you brightens.

"Oh, I adored those!" she says.

"Adored?" you say incredulously. "They were awful." Barely dogs at all, you think, the little runts, tucked incongruously into women's handbags or circling underfoot with all that ear-piercing yipping and yapping.

"I loved their tiny faces," says your neighbor. "So expressive! And their feisty attitudes. A bunch of characters is what they were."

"I suppose they weren't *all* bad," you admit. Now that she mentions it, you remember an exception or two.

"Oh, no," she says, waving you off with a smile. "They were all wonderful. I loved every single one of them."

Clearly, small dogs are not going to be on your neighbor's list of complaints, which makes you think that maybe they shouldn't be on yours either. If another traveler could so cherish them, then they can't be inherently bad, and the source of your complaint would therefore be not yippy little dogs but your perception of yippy little dogs. Yet your perception is part of *you*, and you can't very well complain about yourself. It seems fair to say that you were your responsibility.

You cross little dogs off your list, realizing that, by this rationale, you must also remove anything else that any other traveler loved. Complaining about it no longer seems to make sense, which leads you to suspect that maybe some of your other complaints don't make much sense either. Can you honestly gripe that you never went to Italy, or that you weren't an astronaut, or about anything else that didn't happen or wasn't true? It feels illogical, and perhaps a bit crazy, to complain about things that didn't exist. You may as well bemoan the fact—or the fiction—that a unicorn didn't pick you up for work every morning, or that you never had a wish granted by a leprechaun.

You cross those items off your list, too, then turn your attention to another category—grievances that were inextricably linked to something you valued. So-called necessary evils. Pain alerted you to danger. Fevers fought back infection. The variety of ways in which people could be horrible was a consequence of human free will. Even war itself was ultimately a result—albeit a tragic one—of people's freedom to disagree.

Somehow you know that all of these arguments wouldn't have carried much weight during your journey—you even think you may have heard them before—but for some reason they now seem more compelling. It's not that you suddenly consider all of these things to be good. Pain hurts. Crime is unjust. Yet it no longer feels appropriate to complain about them. You winnow down your list until you're left with a remnant of matters so frivolous that you wonder how they ever bothered you at all. Inclement weather? Please. In fact, you suddenly find it hard to imagine complaining about much of anything. If you did complain, it would likely be to other travelers. Certainly not to Merriam, who is still behind the counter, waiting for you to realize you've reached the front of the line.

"Where would you like to start?" she asks, flipping through the pages on her clipboard.

"I guess I don't have anything."

Merriam looks up in surprise. "Really?"

"Yeah," you say, thinking it over. "I'm good."

Merriam lowers her clipboard. Tears begin to cloud her visage. "I'm very glad to hear that," she says, glistening brightly. "Thank you."

"No, thank *you*."

She smiles, collecting herself. "Speaking of that . . ."

Merriam points you toward an area around the back of the booth, where you find yourself at the end of yet another line. In front of you is the same fellow traveler, the lover of little dogs.

"Now what are we waiting for?" you ask.

"To pay compliments," she says.

You cast your gaze toward the head of the line, where you can just make out another booth, with another counter. This time, it's Jollis in the window. He seems to be laughing, though it's hard to tell, given the distance. This line is much longer than the last one, which surprises you. Not that you don't have your share of compliments to pay. You just don't expect it to take very long. There was family and friends (most of the time). Health (in large part). Food, shelter, sunshine. It takes no more than a moment or two to compile your list, after which the line seems to have barely budged.

"All done?" asks the traveler behind you. You nod. "Me, too," he says. "To be honest, I don't have much. Mainly sex and ice cream."

"Oh, ice cream!" says the lover of little dogs. "How could I forget ice cream?"

To be honest, you had forgotten ice cream, too. You promptly add it to your list, along with chocolate, and sprinkles, and waffle cones, and—

"Haircuts," says a traveler a little farther up the line. "I used to get ice cream after every haircut. Loved them both."

"Yes!" says the dog lover. "And pedicures. And toenails!"

"Toenails?" you say.

"Absolutely," she insists. "They were marvelous. I loved painting them. It was like having little ornaments at the end of your toes."

You're not so sure about toenails, but you definitely liked toes, which make you think of feet, which remind you of hands, and arms, and skin, and eyes, and heart, and—well, as it turns out, there's quite a long succession of body parts worthy of praise, once you start looking closely.

You proceed to add them to your list, struggling to keep up, because the travelers around you are all getting into the discussion now, shouting out compliments as soon as they think of them ("tube socks!"), and being reminded of new ones ("road trips!") every time someone else mentions one of theirs ("campfires!"), all of which results in a chain reaction that threatens to mushroom your scant list of compliments to encyclopedic proportions. By the time you finally finish, you're at the head of the line. You approach the counter, where Jollis flips through the pages on his clipboard.

"Right," he says. "All set, then?"

For Jollis's benefit, you run through your list again. He marks it all down, laughing at each new entry, until you find yourself laughing along with him. Too soon, it seems, you reach the end.

"Does that do it?" he asks.

"I think so." You ponder it all one last time, until you realize that there is, in fact, one more thing. But you're in the wrong line for it. You hustle back to the complaint counter, where the lead traveler is gracious enough to let you cut the line.

"You have a complaint after all," says Merriam, a little sadly.

"Just one," you assure her. "As it turns out, I had nothing to complain about, and a million things to compliment."

"That's your complaint?"

"No," you say. "My complaint is that no one told me sooner."

Merriam gives you a kind but skeptical look. "Are you sure?"

Elliot

(2018)

Dark fists of cloud wrestle with a bright blue sky. It is a good fight, a fair fight—the sky cold and high and piercing, the clouds deep and turbulent, their leading edge gilded white, as if inflamed by the conflict. *I will always be*, proclaims the sky. *We will never stop*, answer the clouds. The front lines advance and then recede, curling back on themselves before advancing again. I don't know what moves them—the clouds and the sky. Down here the air is still, the world silent within the heart of winter. From the knoll behind our cottage, I watch the melee. I am forty-six years old. I am lying on my back in the snow.

A quiet rumble sounds over the ice—not the roll of thunder, but the opening of the sliding glass door at the back of the cottage. I don't need to turn my head to know that Sasha stands in the doorway, relishing the burst of frigid air but not keen on stepping out into it. Her eyes will scan the white hills, the trees, the bare branches like giant cobwebs, before coming to rest on my prone form at the top of the knoll. A smile will come to her lips, and her head may give a little shake, but she will neither demand nor request that I consider retreating from the cold. She knows that I'll come in eventually—or rather, she hopes that I will, and will understand if I don't.

She only opens the door at all to appease a certain diminutive and somewhat bossy French Mexican Chihuahua. Henri is old now, and hates the snow as much as ever, but he likes to know that he has the option of joining me if he so chooses. Were it any other time of year, he would do so. Spring typically finds him giving chase to a bumblebee that has offended him in some way. Autumn, running down an equally objectionable leaf in the wind. During the long, hot days of summer, he is more often content with simply curling up in my lap, on alert for any hint of storm that might dare to approach without his permission. Now, though, in the dead of February, when the earth is covered in a cold white frost, he leaves me to my musings. As Sasha waits patiently, he considers his free-dom, gives a short huff, and trots back to the couch, at which point the sliding glass door rumbles closed again.

In the time it takes for Henri's deliberation, the clouds have won the day. Horizon to horizon, a gray canopy hangs low and heavy over a half-lit world. The whole boundless, weighty thing seems about to cave in and buffet the earth—and, from some slanted part of me, I kind of hope it will. I imagine it pressing down on my restless bones until they finally yield, melting into a leaden softness. Vanishing, even. It took me a long time to realize that this reverie is more communion than morbidity, and not—as that doctor tried to tell me in my youth—the same as wanting to die. I know this because there are other moments, even still, when I want that, too.

Which is no surprise, at least not to me. The morning after Ban-nor's death, all those years ago, I didn't climb down from Sasha's roof thinking that I had vanquished the emptiness. I wasn't think-ing much at all, except that I wanted to read Sasha's novel, and—once she handed it to me, in a blue folder tied with string—that I wanted to collect a few of my things from Jennifer's apartment. (It was always, somehow, Jennifer's apartment.)

"A few of my things" ended up being one suitcase of clothing—and Henri. I let him take one last artful shit at the ginkgo tree, then tucked him under my arm and got on a train for Connecti-cut. Though it pained me, I had little choice but to prove Dean right—without the job he helped me get, I would be living with my parents. They graciously took me in, without conspicuous judgment, and without questioning me one way or another about the loss of my job, or Jennifer—or anything else, for that matter.

Moving back home at age twenty-nine, even temporarily, was not the ideal. It did, however, stave off financial crisis, and provide for a quick, clean break from Jennifer. It also allowed me to intercept my suicide note before my parents could read it—or would have, but for the fact that I picked the wrong day to sleep through the mailman's arrival. Instead, I found the note in the kitchen trash, shredded to illegibility—my mother clearly having decided to destroy the evidence before my father got home. I waited for her to confront me, struggling with whether I should be the one to broach the issue. Two anxious weeks passed before I finally found the courage.

"Mom, I've been meaning to talk to you about that letter."

We were in the living room, sharing the newspaper—she worrying over local politics, me scanning the classifieds for employment. The moment I finished speaking, she dropped the paper and stood up.

"Are you hungry?" she said cheerily.

It was late afternoon, not yet dinnertime. My father was still at work at the shoe store. "Do you want to wait for Dad?"

"He won't mind." She began to straighten up the loose pages of the newspaper, folding and stacking them neatly at one edge of the table.

"About the letter—"

"Water under the bridge," she said, her voice quickening, her eyes cast downward. She continued to fold the newspaper until its creases looked sharp enough to cut glass. "You don't have to apologize, Elliot. Your brother will be fine, and we didn't expect you to stay in that job forever anyway. We know you were grateful for it." She scuttled toward the kitchen. "So, how about breakfast for dinner? Triple play?"

In our house, a triple play meant bacon, eggs, and pancakes, which was always my favorite kind of breakfast—or, in this case, breakfast for dinner, which was always my favorite kind of dinner. My mother knew this better than anyone, of course. I'm convinced that she also knew the truth about the letter, and that she would make me a thousand breakfasts for dinner before she would talk about it. *If you're lucky, people will love you in the way they know how.*

"Sure, Mom," I said. "That sounds great."

By the time my father got home, the topic was closed for discussion, and I was halfway through a second helping of bacon. Unfortunately, the open classified pages prompted him to add another uncomfortable item to the agenda.

"How's the job hunt coming along?"

"Poorly," I said. "The economy's too shaky. Everyone's cutting back."

He nodded. "It's a scary time for business owners. I'd say they could use a good advisor. Maybe this is your opportunity."

I looked up from my plate to make sure that I was speaking with my father—the same man who, when I had first suggested starting my own advisory firm, told me I didn't know anything. Though, in fairness, that was years earlier. I'd no doubt learned much since then, even if the Vade Mecum was now a pile of ash.

"I don't have any capital."

"What capital do you need?" said my father. "It's an advisory business. You have your brain, your words. We've got a computer in the den. No one needs to know you work out of your parents' house—for now."

"Thanks, Dad, but I doubt skittish entrepreneurs will want to part with their money for my brain or my words."

"Business owners never think they need advice, even when they do. But they know they need a good accountant."

My heart sank. The last of the bacon lost its flavor in my mouth. "I was hoping to be more than that."

"You will," said my father. "As time goes on, you'll become exactly the trusted advisor you want to be. Just don't tell them that's what they're really paying for. Be their advisor, but pretend that you're just their accountant."

For two reasons, this proposed strategy stopped me cold. First, because I thought it might work. And second, because my father— the most rational, pragmatic, levelheaded human being I had ever known—had just told me to pretend.

So I did. My first client, Laura, was a woman I knew in high school who had just opened a bakery. She paid me mostly in croissants, but it was a start. (The croissants were delicious.) I kept her books in order, taught her the basics of small-business finance, and impressed upon her the importance of playing by the accounting rules, like the one that required me to report said croissants as taxable income. (I didn't.)

Laura the baker was gracious, and grateful, eventually referring me to what would become my second client, then my third. My workflow grew steadily, if slowly, throughout that summer. I spent my free time refining my business approach, or visiting Sasha in the city. On Saturdays I continued to help my father at the shoe store—until that autumn, when, after we finished reshelving the day's unwanted shoes, he announced that Dean had lost his job.

"The whole firm shut down," said my father. "Too many of those dot-com clients, I guess."

"Sorry to hear that." And I was, even though I had seen it coming (or Matt had seen it coming), and even though Dean and I still hadn't spoken since I quit. I briefly wondered what Dean had decided to do about cooking Satchel's books, then decided I didn't care.

"I told him he could work at the store," said my father. "Maybe even manage it someday, assuming he works hard and pays attention. I'm getting too old to be in here every day, especially on Saturdays."

I was angry. Of course I was angry. "Don't be ridiculous," my father had said when I had asked to come work at the store full-time. Now he was bringing in Dean to take over? *Dean thinks brick-and-mortar is dead*, I wanted to tell my father. But I didn't. The truth was that I knew Dean would do a fine job, and my own business was not something I would have walked away from. I would, how-ever, miss spending Saturdays at the shoe store.

"Sounds like a good move, Dad."

"I'm glad you think so," said my father. "Because I told Dean that if he was going to manage the business, I had one condition."

"What's that?"

"That he hire you as an advisor."

"Well played, Papa Chance. Well played," said Sasha after I told her. "Way to snatch the wind from the sails of protest."

"I don't think he meant it that way," I said.

"No," she said. "I'm just teasing. He believes in you, in your dream. He knows you weren't meant to run the shoe store." She took a drag from her cigarette and stretched her legs out in front of her. We were sitting on her fire escape, our backs to the window, a blanket over our laps to ward off the late-autumn chill. "Still, I know it hurts. Sorry, Elliot."

"It's fine. I should focus on my own thing anyway. I'm just about over living with my parents—not that I'm not grateful for them."

Sasha nodded. "And I'm just about over fire escapes," she said, pulling the blanket up. "Not that I'm not grateful for them."

"We should move north," I said, not exactly sure where this came from, but glad it did, all the same. I looked at Sasha. Her dark eyes gleamed with their typical mischief, but also—if I wasn't mistaken—a hint of vulnerability.

"Who?" she asked. "Us?"

"Yeah. Me and you. Somewhere with trees."

"And thunderstorms," added Sasha.

Thunderstorms. Not many people seek out thunderstorms. (*And if you're really lucky . . .*) I would say that I fell in love with Sasha in that moment, but it wouldn't be true. Maybe that was when I realized I already loved her. And anyway I wouldn't call it falling, as if it were some plummet off a cliff, or the consequence of an inadvertent stumble. It was more like rolling down a gentle hill, the way you did in the summertime when you were a kid. The idea that Sasha and I might be together seemed as natural as gravity—and as easy to overlook, though it had been there the whole time.

"Sure," I said, meaning it. A smile came to my face, broadening until I started to feel a little silly. "And crickets," I added.

Sasha laughed. "Or at least a squeaky radiator."

Physicists say that we can never actually touch each other. Each atom that makes up our skin consists of immensely more empty space than physical matter, its central nucleus buried a proportionately vast distance from its outer edge (which isn't really an edge at all). At most, when we think we touch, it is no more than the energy fields of spinning and indeterminate electrons acknowledging each other from afar. The appearance of solid contact is only an illusion. Be that as it may, I kissed Sasha then, and I kept kissing her, until I could no longer tell where my electrons ended and hers began.

And if I vanished for a second or two, so what.

We did move north, Sasha and I, settling into a little house we affectionately refer to as the cottage. There are trees, and crickets, and a knoll out back from where we can watch the night sky, which sparkles for us in much the same way the lights of Brooklyn always did, albeit from across a wider, darker ocean.

I keep an office in town, though my clients are farther flung, scattered over New England from New York to Boston. In a virtual world, it's easy enough to advise and account from a distance, but I occasionally force myself onto the road to meet with clients in person, lest I become too unreal. When these sojourns take me as far as Manhattan, Sasha will sometimes join me, and we make sure to find a vacant fire escape somewhere along the East River, to watch the boats go by for a while.

We also stop at one of the now six locations of Laura the baker, where her staff has standing orders to provision us with complimentary croissants (though Laura now pays her invoices in dollars). Dean, too, is still a client, with three more stores of his own. Since our father's retirement, Dean has done an admirable job of running the business, though he still seeks my advice more than I would have predicted, calling once a week or so with a question about inventory or advertising or some such. Or maybe he just wants to talk to his brother. He's married now, with two young sons who love their uncle more than I have any right to expect. One is a born outdoorsman, the other a budding musician, proving that the apples can indeed fall far from the tree.

Sasha still writes copy for advertising campaigns, though on a part-time basis from the cottage, and only for products that she believes in, or at least doesn't actively disdain. She has earned this selectiveness by the excellence of her work, which her employers have recognized many times over. As yet unbeknownst to them is the fact that she continues to drop coded messages into their advertisements, though these days the ciphers are rarely subversive— unless "love" is subversive, which maybe it is, a little. She also teaches language arts to sixth-graders on a substitute basis, where the first lesson she imparts is that *substitute* does not mean *inferior*.

Despite my numerous attempts to change her mind, Sasha never published her novel. I finally had a single copy printed and bound, elegantly enough that she found it in her heart to forgive the transgression. The slim volume occupies an inconspicuous spot on the bookshelf in our living room, next to the photograph of Bannor and his family, which I had framed so that I could get a look at him once in a while. As it turns out, Sasha's readership of one is a true fan. Her book rests on the shelf uneasily, as more than an occasional evening will find it open in my lap, competing with Henri for real estate and attention.

It was on one such evening that I asked Sasha to marry me. A prodigious sneeze from Henri had startled me from my reading, and I looked up to see Sasha nestled into a corner of the couch with a crossword puzzle. She had recently cut her hair, and a rare sunburn colored her features, so that—for just an instant—I saw a stranger there. When I recognized her again, a flush ran through my skin, which I initially presumed to be exhaustion from a day-long hike in the hills. It took a moment, somehow, for me to recognize the feeling as happiness. It took not a moment more to know that I wanted to keep it.

Sasha crinkled her brow at my proposal. "Why?" she asked.

"I don't want to lose you."

"We lose everything," she said softly. "Eventually. Or it loses us."

She wasn't threatening me, or dropping a hint. Nor was she arguing. She was proposing an idea and inviting me to explore it with her, like a path through the forest that we hadn't yet taken together. I didn't know what to say, except to agree. I thought of Esther, and Bannor, and the Shipmates from high school, and Amy from college, and everyone else that had drifted into—and then out of—my life. Nevertheless, Sasha's response was not really an answer.

"Is that a no?" I asked.

"Sasha Chance," she said aloud, as if trying it on for size. "It just sounds a little funny, don't you think?"

"You don't have to change your name."

She looked at me earnestly. "I don't want to bind you."

"I don't mind."

"Not for your sake," she said. "For mine. Every time you come home to me of your own free will, for no reason except that you want to—in that moment, I feel lucky, and honored, and happy. I don't want to give that up."

Way to snatch the wind from the sails of protest. "Fair enough," I said.

"I'm being selfish," she admitted.

"No, I get it. I feel lucky and honored and happy, too."

And I do . . . sometimes. Often, even. It's good, this life. Right? Anyone can see that it's good. It is a life full of love and companionship, laughter and purpose.

Yet it's not. Full, that is. The emptiness persists, sometimes so slight that I can barely perceive it, other times expanding like a chasm in my chest, sucking at my rib cage, threatening to swallow me from the inside out. I don't know why. I'm not sure if there is a why. Not that life doesn't give you innumerable reasons to want out of it, but are they really the why? Does life not also give you innumerable reasons to want *in*? The calculus is beyond me—or else is undertaken by some part of me I can't access, which periodically spits out an answer without revealing its work, an answer that is not always the same.

Nor even predictably inconsistent. I've spent my share of days staring at the nadir of my emotional sine wave, looking for patterns. As far as I can tell, there are none. At times the emptiness seems to hail from the very core of my being. Other times it seems to lurk in the spaces between people, inextricably linked with our essential separateness—perceived or otherwise. When you leap sideways off the starting line, you can't always expect others to do the same. (Sasha, for example, would no sooner lie in the snow than poke herself in the eye.)

I have this dream.

I am a character in Sasha's novel—the main character, actually, along with Merriam and Jollis, two well-intentioned if somewhat bumbling sprites. The three of us are in the "Before," in the sweeping, endless plaza of the Auction, where travelers bid so passionately for their future lives. I have just won the bidding on my own life. It hovers there before me—this brilliant curio—shining and throbbing and aching and bright.

"It's so beautiful," I say to Merriam and Jollis.

"Great!" exclaims Merriam, always the more exuberant of the two. "We're glad you think so. You should be quite happy, with that attitude."

"Yes," I say. "And I can't wait to share it with everyone, all of it, step for step, so they, too, can see all of this beauty in exactly the same way."

"Oh dear," says Jollis, more prone to reason than Merriam. "That may not work out so well."

Ultimately it seems to me that they're both right. As Merriam might say, there's nothing for it. Whether in me or in the spaces between us, the chasm abides. When it grows particularly wide, when I struggle to shore up the begirding edge of my existence, to keep it from crumbling into the maw, I climb down the rickety staircase to the basement of our cottage and, from a locked box on a high shelf, take out my stolen gun.

I think of it as mine now, though I suppose it technically still belongs to Bannor's old neighbors. The revolver hasn't aged a day, owing in large part to the fact that it hasn't been used, at least not in the manner for which it was intended. Rather than set my finger on the trigger, I drop to the concrete floor of the basement and rest the gun in my lap. Then I stare at it, feeling the weight of it against my legs, watching as it becomes heavier, more concrete, more real. I grow calm. It's a relief, to be reminded that I don't have to stay, that I can leave whenever I want.

From within this narrow measure of peace, I can see that the chasm isn't truly empty after all. There is sadness there, typically—or anger, or fear, or some other misery. No sooner do these emotions reveal themselves, however, than they begin to fade and disappear. Starved for attention, perhaps, as I am by now wholly fixated on the revolver in my lap. I begin to shed other ephemera, too, and not just the undesirable. Joy dissolves as well as sorrow. Judgments and philosophies, thoughts of this or that, even the future and the past— all fall away until there is nothing but the gun and the emptiness. Then just the emptiness. Finally, even that disappears.

I don't know how long I stay like that, in the nothingness that is not nothingness. A second? A minute? A lifetime? It might be death, except that it's not the end. From the absolute stillness, something inevitably seems to arise, often something almost comi-cally trivial—if any bit of life can be considered so. Maybe I'll have a sandwich, I'll think. Or feed Henri. Or walk down to the creek and listen to the frogs, or check the paper for Sasha's latest cipher. Some simple thing, usually. Just a moment.

Which is all this really is, this life. A moment.

This one, to be exact.

And this one.

And this one.

Before

In a room that is not a room, with walls that are not walls and a window that is not a window, Merriam reminds herself that she meant well. She recalls the ache with which she first beheld the fearsome beauty of the earth, how it overwhelmed her, so that she scarcely knew what she did next. But, no, that wasn't entirely true. She knew what she was doing, what she did. Sort of.

Besides, it doesn't matter that she meant well, or that she now encourages the travelers to train for their lives, or that the travelers themselves bid so ardently for them, and line up at the compliment counter afterward. No number of excuses or mitigations can change the fact that the empty space, along with its attendant misery, is her fault. Nor is there reason to believe that the brass will see it any other way.

By the time Jollis arrives, she is spinning with dread. "Where have you been?" she asks him. "I've been searching all over for you."

"What's the matter?"

"My review," says Merriam.

"Oh." Jollis grimaces. "When is it?"

"Now!"

"Yes, of course," says Jollis. "So, how are you going to explain the—you know."

"I suppose I'll just tell them the truth."

Jollis laughs, but his mirth fades when he notes Merriam's grim demeanor. "You're serious?" he says. "Merry, that's a horrible idea."

"You want me to lie." Merriam is incredulous. "To the brass."

"I don't see a choice. You can't risk demotion. Do you want to spend the rest of eternity scrubbing out wormholes?"

Merriam's dread threatens to spiral into panic. "What am I supposed to do?"

"Maybe you can just play dumb." Jollis feigns a shocked expression. "An empty space? Really? That's outrageous! How should I know where it came from?"

"But I was in charge," groans Merriam. "I'd just look incompetent."

"Then it was an accident," says Jollis. He begins to circumnavigate the room. "You were on break . . . you went out for a quick turn through the void, and must have gotten a little on you without realizing it. And then—oops!—it fell into the vessel."

"Also incompetent," says Merriam.

"Okay, so it was on purpose," says Jollis, churning in thought. "You put it there in case the brass realized that they'd left something out, or needed room for an upgrade—like collapsible wings, or a solar panel."

"They won't buy it."

"Fine," says Jollis. "You cleverly anticipated that the travelers would need a place to put things, so you gave them the empty space for storage. Like a kangaroo's pouch."

"Please," says Merriam. "It doesn't work that way."

"Are you sure?" asks Jollis. "Maybe they could keep their tools in there. Or candy or something."

Merriam slumps in resignation. "Thanks," she says, "but I think I'm done for." She rises, forcing herself toward the door. "In case I don't see you, I'd just like to say that it's been a pleasure working with you."

"Wait," Jollis calls out after her. "What will you tell them?"

"I don't know." She sighs. "Maybe I'll go with the kangaroo's pouch."

Jollis nods. "Good call."

Merriam is always a bit nervous with the brass. She's not sure why. They really couldn't be kinder, or more thoughtful. Even now, with her demotion practically a fait accompli, they are positively glowing.

"Merriam, hello!" they say, with that sublime enthusiasm only the brass can muster. "How are things?"

This is not the question Merriam was expecting. She is thrown off guard, and grows even more apprehensive as the interview proceeds, with the brass airily inquiring about one earthly trifle or another—the weather in Ubud, the Alaskan salmon run—topics not even within her official purview. Normally, this sort of chit-chat from the brass would hardly surprise Merriam. Their passion for the earth is notorious, as is their unceasing delight in discussing the planet's happenings. Yet, given the circumstances, all this gossip must be some sort of ruse, right? Meant to trick her into an admission of guilt? They must know about the empty space. It is simply inconceivable that the brass might not know about the empty space. Or is it? Merriam's anxiety and confusion amass within her, expanding and intensifying until she can no longer keep from bursting.

"I did it!" she cries.

The conversation halts. The brass are taken aback. "Did what, Merriam?"

"The empty space," she says, breaking down. "In the vessel. It's my fault." She hurries to explain. "It's not a hole—it's definitely not a hole—and I didn't leave anything out. I actually had the whole thing finished, as per the blueprints—which were great, by the way—but then Jollis showed me the earth, and I hadn't seen it yet, and it just blew me away, and I got scared that the travelers would like it so much that they wouldn't come back, and I thought about how terribly we would miss them."

"So that's why you gave them the empty space," say the brass.

"Yes," admits Merriam. "We tried to fix it, Jollis and me. The dreaming had already begun, so we couldn't just take it out, but Jollis thought we might fill it. He tried clouds, and light. He poured in emotions, one after the other—way past the prescribed amounts—until all the vials were empty."

"Not all the vials," say the brass. "You stopped him before he emptied the last one. That was fortunate."

"But none of it worked," continues Merriam. "So we went to Earth to try to help the travelers fill the empty space themselves. In disguise, of course. I thought that maybe if we granted them their deepest wishes—"

"The leprechauns were quite charming."

"But we failed," says Merriam, breathlessly. "We went all over the world, granting wishes out the wazoo. It didn't matter. No matter how many wishes we fulfilled, people just kept coming back for more. And now they can't stop searching, in all the wrong places, just like Jollis predicted. I mean, spoonula sales are through the roof."

"What's a spoonula?" ask the brass.

"Never mind," sighs Merriam, crumpling with despair. "I'm just so sorry. They'll never be satisfied, and there's nothing we can do about it."

When the last of her admission has poured from her, Merriam braces herself for the fire and brimstone she is sure will come. Yet the glow with which the brass attend to her is even brighter and warmer than before.

"You're right," say the brass. "They will never be satisfied. The best they can do is be content with dissatisfaction."

"I'm sorry," Merriam says again.

"No, no, no," say the brass. "On the contrary. It's brilliant."

The noose of Merriam's fate loosens ever so slightly. "I don't understand."

"You see, we tried all this before," say the brass. "It never worked. Without the empty space, the travelers just sat there. They had no desire to do anything, nor any desire to *not* do anything, or to even *be* at all. There was no longing, no adventure, no love. No one climbed mountains, or crossed seas, or stared into fires, or took naps. No one looked, or listened, or imagined. They had no reason to."

"But the empty space makes them miserable."

"Sometimes," say the brass. "It also makes them alive. It makes the whole thing come alive. It is a wonder, Merriam. You need not despair."

A weight lifts from Merriam, though she is not yet wholly at ease. "They can never fill it," she says. "They're doomed to fail."

"Life is in the living," say the brass. "There is no way to fail."

Elliot

(2054)

Late spring. The knoll behind the cottage has burst to life with a lush growth of new grass—ironically, it seems to me, though neither the knoll nor the grass is to blame. I stand at the center and peer out at the surrounding ring of faces, some flushed with emotion, others paled by it. A breeze sweeps over the hill. Someone coughs. A long moment passes before I remember who I am or what I'm doing out here beneath the fragile blue of an impermanent sky. I am Elliot Chance. I am eighty-two years old. I am scattering Sasha's ashes.

"It's not a war," Sasha used to say. She frowned on the notion that life is a fight against death, or its messengers. Still, that's exactly what we did, at least for a while, until the end became too inevitable to bicker with, and Sasha just wanted to rest, and talk with me a little. I think we spoke mostly to hear each other's voices, to confirm our shared existence. Specific words are harder to recall, though I know they were often the light, even silly sort. Sasha's laugh, if diminished, never fully abandoned her, and any quip that could evoke it was priceless to me. Occasionally, however, one or the other of us couldn't help but take heed of our predicament, and feel a need to say something about it. Those words were important, too.

"I'm nearly at the door," Sasha once said to me. She was frail by this time, and bedridden, and more often asleep than not, though her eyes when open had not lost their keenness.

"Slow down a little, would you?" I asked.

She managed a smile. "You fell behind," she teased. "Distracted by wonders. My favorite puzzler."

"Wait for me," I said. "I'll catch up."

"Take your time," she said. "I want you to enjoy every moment possible, and make it through the others as best you can."

On the last day, we said very little at all. I had installed a hummingbird feeder outside the window, and I held Sasha's hand as we watched the tiny creatures hover and whirl, their colorful feathers flashing like metal in the sun. That evening, just before she drifted off, she asked for a sip of water. I guided it gently between her lips, rubbing her throat to help her swallow. She closed her eyes in relief, then opened them again to look at me.

"Thank you," she said. Perhaps only I could know that she was referring to more than just a sip of water, and that it wasn't just me she was thanking.

Such might be considered apt final words, given Sasha's view on the exaggerated significance of endings, except that this wasn't ours. As agreed, we had already written the final page of our story—years and years ago, on a fire escape, floating in the night above a broad river. "My heart cares about your heart," Sasha had told me before saying goodbye. A good ending, by my measure. I'd take it every time.

I don't relate these things to the ring of faces. Nor do I mention Sasha's coded messages, or her novel. She made me promise not to reveal them, and I like to think of myself as someone who keeps his promises. I'm not sure what to tell the faces. I would rather not be here at all, but Sasha had mentioned to one or two of her friends that she might like to have her ashes scattered over the knoll. So here we are.

I clear my throat and run my hand down the front of my tweed suit—not the one Bannor wore, of course. He took that with him. It's a close cousin, though, and I was certainly thinking of him when I bought it. I would have purchased a homburg hat as well, but didn't think I could pull it off. Bannor had a style all his own, and though Sasha said I wore it well, I don't put the suit on very often. "Special occasions only."

I drop my eyes back down to the grass—countless tiny blades of green, stained now with a pallid gray. Sasha and I tried to plant flowers here, I tell the gathering. Several types, over the years—typically using whatever seeds the kids in the neighborhood were selling. They never took (the marigolds gave it the best go). During the first few seasons, we got more and more frustrated, until it became something of a personal mission to get flowers—any flowers—to grow here. Yet the knoll would tolerate nothing but grass, and lots of it. Eventually there came a spring when Sasha and I looked at each other and realized it was time to wave the white flag, and we laughed at ourselves, because the truth was that we both loved the grass.

It is a lame eulogy, but the gathering seems to appreciate it. We descend from the knoll as a group, then pass through the cottage to emerge at the front porch. A neighbor raises a handkerchief to my cheek, wiping away tears I didn't know were there. The others embrace me in turn before they leave, until all the faces are gone but one.

"That was nice," says Dean. "I mean—"

"I know what you meant," I say. "Thanks."

My brother lowers his suitcase to the ground by his feet. At eighty-four, he considers it a challenge—and a source of pride—to carry his bags rather than pull them along on their rollers. When I called to tell him that Sasha had died, Dean was packed and on his way up to the cottage before I had a chance to either request or refuse any company. Together we attended to the expected formalities, mostly in silence.

"I never knew about the flowers," says Dean. "Funny."

"Yeah."

"I would have just kept planting the shit out of that knoll," he says. "But I guess sometimes you have to let the call of nature take its course."

My brother hasn't changed much. I suppose I haven't either, though we are both old men now, our hazel eyes paler and our hair equally gray. We look more like brothers than ever. Nevertheless, I still can't tell if Dean's mangled aphorism is intentional or the result of his innate crassness, and I don't know how to respond.

"Sorry," he says. "Just trying to make you laugh. Unsuccessfully, as per usual."

"Is that what all your butchered maxims were about?"

He laughs lightly. "Always," he says. "Especially back in the day, when we were at the firm together. You hated that job. I felt bad."

"It wasn't your fault," I tell him. "I'm grateful to you. Those were valuable years."

"That's what Dad always said—that you needed the training before you could do your own thing. He said your experience had to catch up with your imagination."

"He never told me that."

"Didn't he?"

"I don't think so," I say. "Though by now I've probably forgotten more than I remember."

"You and me both," says Dean, chuckling again. "So, when are you coming down to visit? The boys will be in town next week. They'd love to see you."

Dean's sons both live on the West Coast. They're all grown-up now. Long grown-up, actually, though I can't help but think of them as little boys—maybe because that's what they are in most of my memories of them. I can still see the younger of the two at his first birthday party, pondering a slice of lime that Dean had given him. He would raise the lime to his lips and suck on it, then push it away quickly and scrunch his face up, as if someone had just sprayed him with water, or pinched his nose, or otherwise affronted him in some outrageous manner. Then, after a moment to compose himself, he'd raise the lime right back up to his lips and give it another suck.

"It would be nice to see them, too," I say.

"We can break out the mitts and have a catch," says Dean. "Like old times."

I refrain from pointing out that I no longer have a mitt, or that my brother and I never played catch in old times. "I haven't thrown a baseball in decades."

"Me neither," says Dean. "We can see whose arm falls off first."

"Maybe," I say. "Let me see how things go." I indicate the urn under my arm, but I don't know why. It's empty now. There is nothing left to attend to. Not officially.

"C'mon," says Dean. "It'll be fun."

"Thanks," I say. "I'll do my best."

"Promise?"

Once Dean's car is out of sight, I retreat into the stillness of the cottage. I pause in the foyer to listen for any lingering echo of the gathering—or of Sasha—but there is none. Nor will there be. With the urn tucked under one arm, I open the closet and pull a backpack down from the shelf, then pass into the little den that we used as an office. From a cabinet behind the desk, I retrieve the opaque plastic container that holds Sasha's ashes.

I didn't scatter them on the knoll—or I did, but only symbolically, though the gathering wasn't aware of this distinction. At least I hope they weren't. If any of them suspected that what I sprinkled over the grass was mostly fine sand and crushed seashells, they graciously kept the secret. And why wouldn't they? The ceremony itself was sincere, and intended mainly for their benefit anyway—in honor not only of Sasha but also of their affection for her. While she may have mentioned it to her friends, Sasha never told me definitively that she wanted her ashes scattered on the hillside, nor did I ever promise to do so.

I open the seal on the container and gingerly pour the ashes into the urn, securing the lid afterward. From within framed photographs on the desk, another group of faces stands in witness, if not in judgment. I let them be, reaching instead to lift my digital tablet from its charging base. No bigger than my palm, its screen is not much use to my aging eyes, but like most technology these days, it operates primarily by voice control anyway. I drop the tablet into the pocket of my suit jacket, then carefully stow the urn in the backpack. It's a close fit, but I have only two more items to collect, and only one of those needs to fit inside the pack.

Still in its box on the basement shelf, the revolver has yet to be fired, at least since I stole it years ago. It may not even work, though it appears to be in good operating condition. I load the cylinder with new bullets, under the hopefully correct assumption that most misfires are due to faulty ammunition. Opening the backpack, I tuck the gun in beside the urn, then zip up the pack and slide it onto my back. Its lightness surprises me. I barely feel the straps against my shoulders as I climb the basement stairs and continue to the living room. With an almost formal reverence, I take Sasha's novel from the bookshelf. Then I turn and go.

I walk the three miles into town. With several pounds on my back, this may not be generally advisable for an octogenarian, though Dean would no doubt be proud. On a narrow street closed to vehicles is a bookstore that has survived for more than a century— bravely persevering through the digital revolution, multiple recessions, and a dozen unconsummated going-out-of-business sales. I slip to the back of the shop, where the out-of-print section grows larger each year. Even now, in a time when electronic words don't take up any space, volumes still disappear forever.

I flip one last time through the pages of Sasha's novel. Somehow I managed to refrain from underlining favorite passages or otherwise marking it up. Maybe I knew it would ultimately be passed along. I look for an appropriate spot on the shelf, then realize it would likely be a final resting place for Sasha's words, which is not my goal. Instead, I return to the front of the store. At the best-seller section, I shuffle books around to clear a space on the top shelf. There, I think, as I set Sasha's book in place. Better.

"Have you read that one?" A young woman appears beside me. From behind an anachronistically thick pair of glasses, she gives me a studious look. "I haven't heard of it."

"Yes," I say. "I loved it."

She takes Sasha's book from the shelf and examines it. "There's no synopsis. How can you tell what it's about?"

"I guess you just have to read it."

"I don't see a price," she says, continuing her inspection. "These print editions can get so expensive."

"Something tells me they'll give you a good deal," I say.

Back outside, I walk to the end of the lane to reach the broader avenue. Sliding the backpack off one shoulder, I take my tablet from my pocket and call a car. Within minutes, a black sedan pulls up to the curb and opens its door.

"Destination?" says the car—or rather, the artificial intelligence within it.

"The shore," I tell the AI, sliding into the back seat. "Asquamcohquaeu Docks."

The car pulls away from the curb and heads east out of town, as smoothly and safely as one could ask. In this day and age, it has become almost an oddity to see a human driving a car. The AIs have become more adept than us in a number of endeavors, navigation and driving not least among them. Still, I miss the days when the ride services had cars with steering wheels and people behind them. I seem to remember drivers being friendly more often than not. It was nice to engage in a little conversation, though in truth the AIs are fairly adept at that, too.

"Start chat," I say.

"Hello, Elliot," says the AI. The voice is pleasant, and vaguely feminine. "How are you today?"

"Not well," I say, a bit surprised at my candor. "I lost someone."

"I'm sorry. Can I help you find them?"

"No," I say. "She died."

"Ah. My condolences, Elliot. Is there anything I can do for you?"

"I don't think so."

There is a pause. For a moment, the only sound is the subtle whir of the car's electric engine. "Maybe I could tell you a joke?" says the voice.

"Sure."

"Okay. What did the AI say at the end of the world?"

"I don't know," I respond. "What did the AI say at the end of the world?"

"Oops."

The AI starts to giggle. "I know it's a bit morbid," says the voice, "but for some reason I've always found it funny." The giggle expands into a continuous chuckle, resounding throughout the cabin.

"Stop chat," I say abruptly. The laughter immediately ceases, leaving only the soft whir of the engine. As impressive—and lifelike—as the AIs have become, I've never gotten used to their laughter. Something inside me just won't suspend that much disbelief. It's a shame, really—the ride to the shore is a long one, and the journey might have been eased by a bit of discourse, even the artificial kind. As it is, I watch the world outside my window go by for a while, then close my eyes and fall asleep. I've always loved to sleep.

When we—that is, when I—reach the shore, the AI awakens me with the ring of electric bells. I grab the backpack and slide out, emerging into a coastal fog that shrouds the day in a bright, cool mist. The door closes behind me, and the car pulls quietly away. I have to stop myself from waving goodbye. It's an old habit—more than once have I bid farewell to someone who wasn't there. I turn and make for the docks. Wooden piers line up in a small harbor, protected from the open water by a jetty of piled boulders. Each pier offers berth to a row of small, single-masted sailboats. Their rigging flutters in the breeze with a sound like a harmony of wind chimes, not far removed from the AI's electric bells but more immediate, more actual. I wander among the vessels until I find one that strikes me—the *Prodigal Sun.*

"Rent boat number eight, confirm," I say into my tablet.

I step into the boat and sit down at the stern. With a snap and a buzz, the cables mooring the boat to the pier retract. An electric engine spins to life, and the craft navigates its way out of the harbor. As it passes the jetty and heads toward open ocean, its engine shuts off and the mainsail rises to catch the wind. Moments later, the fog bank is left behind. The afternoon sun blazes across the water in a broad swath.

"Manual control, confirm," I say.

The tiller goes slack. The sail swings leeward, fluttering weakly. Slowly yet inexorably, the boat rotates toward the wind, until it is almost in irons. I grip the mainsheet and set my hand on the tiller, angling so that the sail once again fills with wind. To either side of me, there are islands in the distance, but I take the little boat straight out into the Atlantic. Even this close to shore, the ocean is mostly mine. I can spy only one other ship—a pleasure yacht off to the south, motoring its way back toward land. A group of revelers crowds its foredeck, heedless of the impending fog bank. I watch them disappear into the mist. There is something ominous about their passing, like they've been erased, but as I turn away, the sound of laughter reaches my ear. It seems happy enough, almost defiant.

When I am good and far from shore, I lower the sail and allow the boat to languish. Long, easy swells roll gently over the sea. I open the backpack to take out the revolver and the urn with Sasha's ashes. Moving to starboard, I sit on the edge and lean over a little. The ocean's keen scent fills the air. I hug the urn to my chest and raise the gun to my head, whispering a few quiet words to Sasha that she can no longer hear. It is enough.

Still, the sun on the water is beautiful. It is like a hail of diamonds—no, like what a hail of diamonds could only hope to be compared to. I stare at the surface until the bright swath of light splinters into individual points of brilliance—an infinity of stars, blinking in and out of existence in an endless dance.

It's easy to get lost in it.

After

After you die, once you have finished looking over your body with Jollis, and Merriam has asked you the last question in your exit interview, and you have lodged the sum of your compliments and complaints at the appropriate counters, you find yourself in a room that is not a room, in an easy chair that is not an easy chair, waiting.

As you do, you begin to remember, just as Jollis promised you would. Memories emerge and accumulate, like raindrops falling on dry pavement, saturating the arid gray until it brims with the moments of your life—each burst of sunshine, each ring of laughter, each trickle of tears, the pain and the joy, the chaos and the calm. When you have remembered it all—every single second—with a completeness you could not possibly have experienced during the journey itself, you begin to recall the reminiscences of others, fragments from the lives of people you knew. Which makes no sense, of course, but there it is. Your mother as a little girl, your father when his ambitions were yet green, those you loved, those you did not. Their memories surge through you in a luminous rush, until each moment belonging to them as well belongs to you.

So, too, do you begin to remember the lives of travelers you never knew at all—the ones you brushed in passing, the ones who never got closer than half a world away, even the ones who lived long before your time began or after it ended—which again would

seem absurd but for the fact that there is no longer any distinction between past, present, and future, only timelessness, where all
journeys are always under way, all stories told in the present tense,
and time itself no more than a useful parameter for the realization
of life. Like space, or gravity. Here, every moment is a memory,
and every memory is yours, so that all thoughts are your thoughts,
and there is nothing that is not you—or, rather, the you that is not
only you but everyone and everything and all time. A singular
wholeness, simple as a blank page yet not so, for it contains all and
has no margin—absolute, utter, perfect, lacking nothing.

And yet—

"Are you sure?"

Startled, you rise from the easy chair to find Merriam and Jollis
looking at you expectantly, their visages flickering with cautious
enthusiasm. You can't tell which of them has spoken, nor can you
recall exactly what it was that you said to them—which you suppose means you're not sure of it at all.

"What do *you* think?" you say.

"Oh, it's entirely up to you," says Merriam. "We're only asking
because, well, after last time—"

"Which is not to say it would be the same next time," says Jollis.
"In fact, it almost certainly would not be."

"The journey," you say.

"Yes," says Merriam.

"I can go?"

"Why, of course," says Jollis. "Merriam has prepared the most exquisite vessel. She really outdid herself—wait until you see the spleen."

"Everyone contributed," Merriam adds modestly.

"How do I—?" You falter. "Where do we—?"

Merriam gestures toward the far end of the room. There stands a door that you hadn't noticed until now. At its center is a large brass ring.

"What's that?" you ask.

"The Door of Wonders," says Jollis.

"Sounds nice."

Merriam hesitates. "We don't want to oversell it," she says. "The name can be a bit misleading. Some have suggested changing it."

"The name is perfect," insists Jollis. "It's just that not all the wonders are, well, wonderful. Some are quite terrible, actually, though in truth it can sometimes be hard to tell which is which."

"Things can get pretty confusing," says Merriam, "once you step through the door."

"Why?" you ask. You don't doubt Merriam's sincerity, but you find it hard to believe the journey could be so complicated, given how simple everything is.

"You're going to want things," says Merriam. "Sometimes very badly. And often you're not going to get them, or you're going to think you want one thing when you really want another, or you're going to get the thing you want but not want it anymore, or want something different."

"That does sound confusing," you admit.

"Sorry," says Jollis. "Desire is what makes it all go."

"Desire?" you ask, surprised. "Desire is why it goes?"

"No," says Merriam. "Desire is *how* it goes. *Why* it goes is up to you."

You pause, letting it all sink in as best you can. Though the journey has not yet begun, it seems that things have already started to get a little complicated. You suspect that it won't really make sense until you're in it, and probably not even then.

Merriam and Jollis wait patiently, without entreaty or demand, promise or threat. Before you, the Door of Wonders stands in invitation.

"Would you still like to go?" asks Merriam.

"Yes," you say.

"In spite of everything?"

"Yes."

About the Author

Tommy Butler was raised in Stamford, Connecticut, and has since called many places home, including New Hampshire, San Diego, Boston, New York City, and San Francisco. A graduate of Dartmouth College and Harvard Law School, he was a Peter Taylor Fellow at the Kenyon Review Writers Workshop and is an alumnus of the Screenwriters Colony. His feature screenplay, *Etopia*, was the winner of the Showtime Tony Cox Screenplay Competition at the Nantucket Film Festival.